APRENDO A LEER con las letras divertidas

AF876257

Pilar López Ávila M.ª Luisa Torcida

Bruño

LOS PERSONAJES:

LA **M MAGA**,
QUE CONVIERTE
GUISANTES
EN ELEFANTES.

LA **O OCULISTA**,
QUE TIENE
MUY BUENA VISTA.

LA **R GUITARRISTA,**
QUE ES TODA
UNA ARTISTA.

LA **A AVENTURERA,**
QUE SIEMPRE QUIERE
SER LA PRIMERA.

SÚPER S,
LA LETRA
QUE QUIERE SALVAR
EL PLANETA.

EL **SEÑOR SUCIO,**
QUE APESTA Y MOLESTA
A LAS LETRAS.

LA **PROFE ABEJA**,
QUE AYUDA
Y ACONSEJA.

ACOMPAÑA AL **COLE**
A TUS AMIGAS
LAS LETRAS DIVERTIDAS.

¡CON SUS AVENTURAS
APRENDERÁS A LEER ENSEGUIDA!

Valentín Beato, 21; 28037 Madrid
Dirección Editorial: Begoña Lozano
Edición: Cristina González
Diseño y bocetos: M.ª Luisa Torcida
Preimpresión: Equipo Bruño

ISBN: 978-84-696-4265-8
Depósito legal: M-4896-2024
Printed in Spain

PAPEL DE FIBRA CERTIFICADA

www.brunolibros.es

APRENDO A LEER
con las
letras divertidas

¿DÓNDE ESTÁ EL ORO DEL COFRE DEL TESORO?

Textos: Pilar López Ávila
Ilustraciones: M.ª Luisa Torcida

Bruño

HOY ES UN DÍA PARA JUGAR
EN LA ESCUELA
DE LAS LETRAS DIVERTIDAS.

¡LA PROFE ABEJA
VA A ANUNCIAR
UNA ACTIVIDAD CHULÍSIMA!

ESCONDERÉ UN COFRE DEL TESORO
CON MUCHAS MONEDAS DE ORO.

¡METERLO EN LA PAPELERA PARECE UNA GRAN IDEA!

LAS LETRAS ESTÁN MUY CONTENTAS
Y NO PARAN DE DAR VUELTAS.

BAILAN Y SALTAN DE ALEGRÍA.
¡QUÉ BIEN COMIENZA EL DÍA!

LA A AVENTURERA
QUIERE SER LA PRIMERA
Y SALE A LA CARRERA.

MIRA DETRÁS DE LAS PUERTAS,
¡PERO EL COFRE NO ENCUENTRA!

LA M MAGA, SENCILLAMENTE,
LO VUELVE TODO TRANSPARENTE.

LA PROFE ABEJA
LA REGAÑA:

LA O TIENE BUENA VISTA
Y ADEMÁS ES MUY LISTA.

¡ENCONTRARÉ ESE TESORO Y ME LLEVARÉ TODO EL ORO!

LA R GUITARRISTA
PREFIERE NO HACER NADA.

ME DA IGUAL
EL TESORO,
¡ME QUEDO
AQUÍ SENTADA!

LA S GIRA,
BUSCA Y SALTA
ENTRE LAS PLANTAS.

MIRA EN SU FIAMBRERA
Y BAJO LA ESCALERA.

¿DÓNDE ESTARÁ EL COFRE?

¡LAS LETRAS
NO LO ENCUENTRAN
Y ESTÁN SUPERMOLESTAS!

LA PROFE ABEJA LES PREGUNTA:

LAS LETRAS SE UNEN
PARA BUSCAR EL TESORO.

¡AY, NOOOOOOO!
¡EL SEÑOR SUCIO
SE HA ADELANTADO
Y EL COFRE
HA ENCONTRADO!

¡ES QUE SOY MUUUUY ESPABILADO!

MIENTRAS EL SEÑOR SUCIO
RÍE A CARCAJADAS,
LAS LETRAS
SE QUEDAN CHAFADAS.

¡NO HAY QUE CONSENTIRLO!
¡VAMOS A PERSEGUIRLO!

LAS LETRAS
NO ESPERAN,
Y UNA TRAS OTRA,
FORMAN
UNA ESCALERA.

PRIMERO VA LA A.
A CONTINUACIÓN, LA R.
DESPUÉS, LA O.
LUEGO, LA M.

¡Y LA S SUBE LA ESCALERA
DE UN SALTO
PARA ATRAPAR
AL MALVADO!

¡AY!
¡SE ME HA
ESCAPADO!

RÁPIDAMENTE, LA M LANZA
UN HECHIZO POTENTE.
PERO SE EQUIVOCA Y CONVIERTE
AL SEÑOR SUCIO EN...

... UN ELEFANTE GRANDE,

ENORME,

¡GIGANTE!

LA M LO ARREGLA CUANTO ANTES.

Y EL SEÑOR SUCIO
REAPARECE AL INSTANTE.

ENTRE TODAS
LO CAPTURAN.

¡SE TERMINÓ MI AVENTURA!

CUANDO AL FIN ABREN EL COFRE,
A LAS LETRAS SE LES QUEDA
CARA DE AGUACATE...

LAS MONEDAS DEL TESORO
NO SON DE ORO,
¡SINO DE CHOCOLATE!

Queridos papás y mamás:

Vuestro papel es fundamental a la hora de transmitir a vuestros hijos que leer es tanto o más divertido que jugar. Si conseguís que asocien la lectura con el disfrute, ¡no querrán parar de leer!

Animaos a interactuar con ellos, representad juntos las aventuras de las letras divertidas, dramatizad sus diálogos, adivinad qué va a pasar a continuación, comentad los dibujos...

Aprovechad la musicalidad de los textos rimados, destacad bien la entonación y marcad las pausas para ayudar a los niños a seguir la lectura sin perder la concentración.

Jugad a imitar el sonido de cada letra para que vuestros hijos aprendan a diferenciarlo de los del resto de letras del alfabeto.

Acompañadlos en las siguientes sugerencias de juegos (¡o inventaos otros parecidos!) para que la experiencia lectora sea más enriquecedora.

En definitiva, iniciad a vuestros niños en el maravilloso mundo de la lectura con ayuda de esta colección de historias breves y sencillas, todas en letras mayúsculas y protagonizadas por sus amigas las letras divertidas.

JUEGOS

1. Contesta estas preguntas sobre el libro que acabas de leer:

- ¿Dónde esconde la profe Abeja el cofre del tesoro?
- ¿Quién encuentra primero el cofre del tesoro?
- ¿En qué convierte la M maga al señor Sucio?

2. Con las cinco letras divertidas que aparecen en este libro se pueden formar muchas palabras distintas. Por ejemplo:

¡Prueba a formar otras palabras diferentes con las mismas letras!

JUEGOS

3. Termina estas rimas uniéndolas con el dibujo correspondiente:

La M maga
convierte un guisante
en un grandísimo…

No es lo mismo
un aguacate
que un bombón de…

La A aventurera
quiere ser la primera
y sube veloz la…

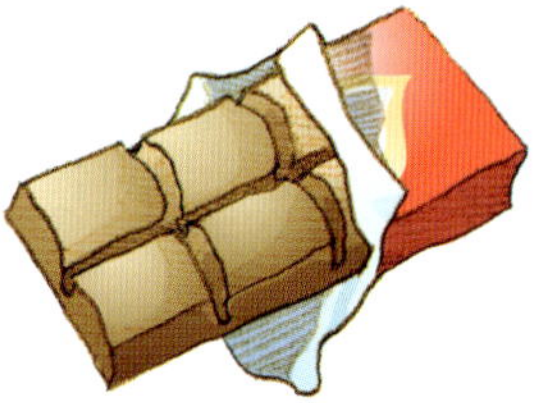

4. ¿Qué camino debe seguir la R guitarrista para llegar al cofre del tesoro?

TÍTULOS PUBLICADOS

To my wife, Steffi,
and to Jeremy Sarkin and Kai Ambos

Contents

CHAPTER I

Introduction

1 Introduction

The key to understanding how penalties are imposed for war crimes and crimes against humanity under the International Tribunal for the prosecution of persons responsible for serious violations of international humanitarian law committed in the territory of the former Yugoslavia (hereinafter ICTY), is the context in which the Tribunal was established.[1] This is because the ICTY is, in effect, the first international criminal tribunal to be established by the international community since the trials of Nuremberg and Tokyo.[2] Its establishment after over 50 years of dormancy has, therefore, meant that it has basically had to start from scratch in its quest to hold accountable those individuals who committed gross human rights violations in the course of the armed conflict in the former Yugoslavia.[3] As aptly expressed by *Wald*:

> '[t]he ICTY is a bold experiment... It is performing three functions: adjudicating international crimes, developing international humanitarian law, and memorializing important ... events of modern history. Except for Nuremberg and Tokyo and subsequent isolated war crimes prosecutions..., the Tribunal has very little case law to rely upon.'[4]

The sentencing of individuals for war crimes and crimes against humanity under the ICTY has to be viewed, therefore, from the above perspective. In other words, owing to the lack of action, there were very few international criminal rules on sentencing for war crimes and crimes against humanity available for the ICTY to rely upon.[5]

---

1 See Tomuschat, C. (1994), *International Criminal Prosecution: The Precedent of Nuremberg Confirmed*, 5 Criminal Law Forum, Nos. 2-3, p. 240, confirming that the context in which the ICTY was established needs to be taken into consideration when making an overall assessment of the tribunal. For a comprehensive overview of the legislative history and Statute of the Yugoslav Tribunal, See O'Brien, J.C. (1993), *The International Tribunal for Violations of International Humanitarian Law in the Former Yugoslavia*, 87 American Journal of International Law, p. 639; See SC Res. 827 (May 25, 1993), reprinted in 32 ILM p. 1203 (1993).

2 See Tomuschat, id., p. 238.

3 See Ferencz, B.B. (1999), *Getting Aggressive about Preventing Aggression*, The Brown Journal of World Affairs. Extracted from <http://www.iccnow.org/html/ferencz199907.html> (last visited June 2004).

4 See Wald, P.M. (2001), *The International Criminal Tribunal for the former Yugoslavia Comes of Age: Some Observations on Day-To-Day Dilemmas of an International Court*, 5 Washington University Journal of Law and Policy, p. 89. See also Ferencz, B., *From Nuremberg to Rome: A Personal Account*. In: Lattimer, M. & Sands, P. (2003), *Justice for Crimes against Humanity* (Hart Publishing). Extracted from <http: //www.benferencz.org/remarks2.htm> (last visited July 2004) (identifying the difficulties faced by the ICTY at the onset).

5 See *Prosecutor* v. *Kupreskic et al.*, Case No. IT-95-16, 14 January 2000, para. 740, (ICTY Trial Chamber).

In addition, a second factor that constitutes an impediment to the ICTY's ability to impose penalties for war crimes and crimes against humanity resulted from the scant attention given to this issue by the World War II Tribunals.[6] In this respect, the Trial Chamber of the ICTY in the *Kupreskic* case made the following relevant observation:

> 'Under Article 6 of the London Agreement of 8 August 1945 some acts could qualify both as war crimes and crimes against humanity: *e.g.*, mass murder or deportation of foreign civilians in occupied countries. True, that provision made it clear that some actions could only be characterised as crimes against humanity: for example, persecution on religious or political grounds of enemy civilians or persecution, on those same grounds, of civilians having the same nationality as the persecutor. By the same token, other actions could only qualify as war crimes: for example, wanton destruction of enemy property not justified by military necessity, pillage, use of prohibited weapons or execution of hostages. Nevertheless, as stated above, there was an area where the two categories overlapped. In addition, those instruments which provided for the various penalties consequent upon the various crimes did not distinguish between war crimes and crimes against humanity: they envisaged the same penalties (death sentence, imprisonment etc.) for both categories in the same terms. This holds true, for example, for Control Council Law No.10. It is therefore not surprising that the International Military Tribunal at Nuremberg (IMT) convicted many defendants both of war crimes and crimes against humanity for the same act. Similarly, the various military courts sitting at Nuremberg after World War II found many defendants guilty of both categories of crimes and sentenced them for both.'[7]

In light of the above, the following relevant questions therefore emerge. Why is it important for the ICTY to have a clear and coherent sentencing policy for war crimes and crimes against humanity? And if the World War II tribunals did not have sentencing policies yet still managed to sentence all convicted, are such policies even necessary? There is one answer to both questions and it lies in the different legal environments in which the ICTY and the World War II Tribunals were established.

Furthermore, the above opinion can be explained in the following way. In the case of the World War II Tribunals, it should be recalled that international human rights law was still in its infancy at the end of World War II.[8] Thus, at

---

6 See Danner, A.M. (2001), *Constructing a Hierarchy of Crimes in International Criminal Law,* 87 Virginia Law Review, p. 415. Extracted from <http://www.psci.unt.edu/~meernik/danner.htm> (last visited July 2004).

7 See *Kupreskic* case, *supra* note 5, paras. 674-675.

8 See Schabas, W.A. (1997), *Sentencing by International Tribunals: A Human Rights Approach,* 7 Duke Journal of Comparative and International, p. 461, at p. 514.

that time, there were no authoritative rules on the international plane governing the imposition of penalties for international crimes. The absence of authoritative rules, therefore, gave the World War II Tribunals a *carte blanche* to do as they pleased.[9] This meant that, first, they did not have to focus on the arduous task of distinguishing between the erstwhile newly invented concepts of war crimes and crimes against humanity, and, second, they could apply the provisions governing these crimes in an arbitrary fashion.[10]

However, a different legal atmosphere surrounds the establishment of the ICTY today.[11] The fact that the specialised rules on international human rights law, such as those contained in the 1948 Universal Declaration of Human Rights[12] and the 1966 International Covenant on Civil and Political Rights (ICCPR),[13] existed has meant that a carefree approach to the imposition of penalties for war crimes and crimes against humanity would no longer be tolerated.[14] Thus Article 15 of the ICCPR, for example, stipulates the following:

> '1. No one shall be held guilty of any criminal offence on account of any act or omission which did not constitute a criminal offence, under national or international law, at the time when it was committed. Nor shall a heavier penalty be imposed than the one that was applicable at the time when the criminal offence was committed. If, subsequent to the commission of the offence, provision is made by law for the imposition of the lighter penalty, the offender shall benefit thereby.
>
> 2. Nothing in this article shall prejudice the trial and punishment of any person for any act or omission which, at the time when it was committed, was criminal according to the general principles of law recognized by the community of nations.'[15]

---

9 See Olusanya, O. (2004), *Double Jeopardy Without Parameters: Re-characterization in International Criminal Law,* Antwerp; Oxford: Intersentia, p. 7.

10 See id; see also *Kupreskic, supra* note 5.

11 See Schabas, W.A. (1997), *Sentencing by International Tribunals: A Human Rights Approach,* explaining that unlike World War II tribunals, the establishment of the ICTY and ICTR draws upon international criminal law, international humanitarian law and international human rights law.

12 See Universal Declaration of Human Rights, adopted and proclaimed by General Assembly resolution 217 A (III) of December 1948.

13 See International Covenant on Civil and Political Rights, Adopted and opened for signature, ratification and accession by General Assembly resolution 2200A (XXI) of 16 December 1966, entry into force 23 March 1976.

14 See Olusanya, O. (2004), *Double Jeopardy Without Parameters: Re-characterization in International Criminal Law.*

15 See Article 15 ICCPR.

The above provision draws attention to two main sentencing obligations of the ICTY:

1. The prohibition on prosecution for offences, which were not crimes when committed.
2. Equality in sentencing.

In relation to the prohibition on retroactive prosecutions, this obligation was recognized by the ICTY in its judgment in the *Delalic et al.* case where it observed that:

> 'The principles *nullum crimen sine lege* and *nulla poena sine lege* are well recognised in the world's major criminal justice systems as being fundamental principles of criminality. Another such fundamental principle is the prohibition against *ex post facto* criminal laws with its derivative rule of non-retroactive application of criminal laws and criminal sanctions. Associated with these principles are the requirement of specificity and the prohibition of ambiguity in criminal legislation. These considerations are the solid pillars on which the principle of legality stands. Without the satisfaction of these principles no criminalisation process can be accomplished and recognised.'[16]

As noted above, apart from ensuring that crimes are not defined after the fact, the prohibition on retroactive prosecutions also imposes an obligation to define precisely by law all crimes within a court's jurisdiction. From the point of view of the ICTY, this means that a person may only be prosecuted and sentenced for offences such as war crimes and crimes against humanity where they are clearly defined. Prior to setting penalties for war crimes and crimes against humanity, the ICTY must first of all explain the different interests violated by both categories of international crimes and how the penalties it has chosen to impose reflect these interests.[17]

In addition, the prohibition on retroactive criminal law also bars the imposition of a heavier penalty than was prescribed in law at the time of the offence, although a court is obliged to apply retroactively a lighter penalty if it is subsequently provided for by law.[18] Translating this obligation into the context of the

---

[16] *Prosecutor* v. *Delalic et al.*, Case No. IT-96-21-T, 16 November 1998, (ICTY Trial Chamber), para. 402.

[17] The Trial Chamber in the *Kupreskic* case for instance attempted to observe this obligation vis-à-vis genocide and war crimes (*supra* note 5, paras 718- 719). See also See Carcano, A. (2002), *Sentencing and the Gravity of the Offence in International Criminal Law*, 51 International and Comparative Law Quarterly, p. 590, emphasizing the importance of specifying the different interests protected by offences when sentencing under domestic law.

[18] See Article 11 of the Universal Declaration and Article 15(1) of the ICCPR.

ICTY means that the Tribunal's sentencing policy must be consistent vis-à-vis war crimes and crimes against humanity.[19]

In terms of the obligation to ensure equal sentencing, this requirement stipulates that the punishments imposed upon conviction following a fair trial must be proportionate to the gravity of the crime and the circumstances of the offender.[20] This also means that a court may not impose a heavier penalty than the one that applied when the crime was committed.[21] In relation to the relevance of proportionality in sentencing in the context of the ICTY, *Meernik* and *King* made the following statement:

> 'Therefore, it is crucial that the sentences meted out be generally viewed as proportionate, fair, and understandable. If, at the end of the day, these punishments are perceived as inconsistent or biased and thus, inexplicable by the standards of the ICTY Statute and the Rules of Procedure and Evidence, the verdict on the ICTY will be flawed. While there will always be some criticism of these sentences for no court is perfect and some may never be satisfied, if the collective wisdom is that the punishments handed down were essentially fair and consistent, the ICTY can contribute to its other statutory aims—facilitating peace and reconciliation in the Balkans and promoting deterrence of international crimes.'[22]

It follows from the above that the ICTY's sentencing rules for war crimes and crimes against humanity need to reflect fairness, proportionality and clarity so as to ensure the legitimacy of the Tribunal, to facilitate peace and reconciliation in the Balkans and to promote deterrence of war crimes and crimes against humanity. Therefore, implementing a penalty scheme for both categories of international crimes under the ICTY based on an extrapolation of the penalty scheme of the World War II Tribunals would be detrimental to the rights of the accused, since this scheme was inconsistent, unclear and disproportional.

These preliminary conclusions, therefore, draw attention to the following additional questions:

1. In view of the lack-lustre state of pre-existing rules on war crimes and crimes against humanity, has the ICTY so far managed to substantively distinguish between both categories of international crimes?

---

19 See *Prosecutor* v. *Delalic et al.*, *supra* note 16, para. 756, recognizing that consistency of punishment is one of the fundamental elements in any rational and fair system of criminal justice.

20 See for example Report of the 8th UN Congress on the Prevention of Crime and Treatment of Offenders, UN Doc. A/Conf.144/28, rev.1 (91.IV.2), Res. 1(a), 5(c), 1990.

21 Article 11 of the Universal Declaration, Article 15(1) of the ICCPR, Article 9 of the American Convention, Article 7(1) of the European Convention, see also Article 7(2) of the African Charter.

22 See Meernik, J. & King, K. (2003), *The Sentencing Determinants of the International Criminal Tribunal for the Former Yugoslavia: An Empirical and Doctrinal Analysis,* 16 Leiden Journal of International Law, pp. 717-750.

2. In what way has this distinction, if any, been translated into penalties for both categories of international crimes?

The best way of answering the above questions is by tackling the second question first, and the answer to this question is that, in cases where an accused is held to have committed war crimes and crimes against humanity in relation to the same act, the ICTY has resorted to the imposition of a global sentence approach rather than an approach based on individual sentences.[23] The reliance on a global sentencing approach has in turn led to the following negative effects. First, it has contributed to what *Ashworth* terms a 'cafeteria system' of sentencing, which permits judges involved in sentencing persons convicted of war crimes and crimes against humanity to pick and choose, with little constraint, a rationale which seems appropriate at the time of the imposition of penalties.[24]

Second, and as a corollary, it has obscured the distinction between war crimes and crimes against humanity under the ICTY, since no explanation is given as to why a particular sentence has been imposed for a particular crime. This has been the case, for example, with national law offences. For those, we know that murder is a more serious offence than theft since it involves taking someone's life, whilst theft involves stealing someone's property. Murder, therefore, would attract a higher penalty than theft.[25] However, in the case of international crimes, the fact that they embrace broad clusters of identical offences, such as murder, rape and torture, means that it is difficult to explain in the course of an armed conflict what the difference is between murder as a crime against humanity and murder as a war crime.

The third and last significant effect of the single global sentence approach, vis-à-vis war crime and crime against humanity offences, is that it has led to a lack of transparency in the sentencing process for defendants under the ICTY.[26]

Furthermore, all of these effects have a bearing on the first question posed above; that is, in view of the lack lustre state of pre-existing rules on war crimes

[23] For evidence of the imposition of single sentences for multiple counts under the ICTY, see the following cases: *Prosecutor* v. *Kordic*, Case No. IT-95-14/2-T, 26 February 2001, para. 854 (ICTY Trial Chamber); *Prosecutor* v. *Kunarac*, Case No. IT-96-23-T, 22 February 2001, para. 855 (ICTY Trial Chamber); *Prosecutor* v. *Blaskic*, Case No. IT-95-14, 3 March 2000, para. 805 (ICTY Trial Chamber).

[24] See Ashworth, A. (1995), *Sentencing and Criminal Justice. Principles of Criminal Law*, 2nd ed., Oxford, p. 331.

[25] See Bing Bing Jia, N. (1999), *The Differing Concepts of War Crimes and Crimes against Humanity in International Criminal Law*. In: Guy-Goodwin-Gill and Stefan Talmon (eds.), *The Reality of International Law*, Oxford: Clarendon Press, p. 269, footnote 115, quoting *Andrew Ashworth*, Principles of Criminal Law, id., p. 35; See also *Prosecutor* v. *Kambanda*, Case No. ICTR 97-23-S, 4 September 1998, (ICTR Trial Chamber), para 12.

[26] See Danner, A.M. (2001), *Constructing a Hierarchy of Crimes in International Criminal Law*, footnote 341, drawing attention to the issue of transparency in sentencing.

and crimes against humanity, has the ICTY so far managed to distinguish between both categories of international crimes? Unfortunately, the ICTY has imposed global sentences for war crime and crime against humanity offences without any explanation for how such penalties have been calculated, and, therefore, this constitutes evidence of the failure of the ICTY to substantively distinguish between the two categories of international crimes.[27]

In addition, the above opinion is supported by the lack of consensus among ICTY judges on the issue of what separates crimes against humanity from war crimes. There are essentially two schools of thought on this issue. The first school of thought is that crimes against humanity and war crimes are of equal gravity and that any difference between them is merely jurisdictional and not substantive.[28] Supporters of this point of view argue that crimes against humanity were merely created in 1945, as a 'jurisdictional extension' of the prohibition against war crimes.[29] In other words, they were designed for the purpose of criminalizing conduct committed in situations where the nationality of victims and violators were the same, an action that was considered to be revolutionary at that time since it challenged the sacrosanct concept of state sovereignty.[30]

On the other hand, the second school of thought argues that crimes against humanity are a more serious category of international crimes than war crimes because, unlike war crimes, which in their view are often committed in a random and isolated fashion, crimes against humanity are normally perpetrated in a widespread and systematic fashion and therefore result in a comparatively greater loss of life.[31]

The issue of sentencing for war crimes and crimes against humanity cannot be divorced from the wider issue of the substantive law on both categories of crimes. In other words, until and unless a credible and uniform basis for distinguishing between crimes against humanity and war crimes substantively is proposed, it is impossible to talk about imposing penalties for both categories of crimes in a fair, proportional and understandable manner. It is this factor, the search for the ideal substantive framework for making a hierarchical distinction

---

27 See Danner, id., explaining how global sentences are a tool employed by the judges of the ICTY to avoid making distinctions between war crimes and crimes against humanity.

28 See Separate and Dissenting Opinion of Judge Li, *Prosecutor* v. *Erdemovic*, Case No. IT-96-22, 7 October 1997, para. 21 (ICTY Appeals Chamber), arguing that war crimes and crimes against humanity are of equal gravity.

29 See Bassiouni, M.C. (1992), *Crimes Against Humanity in International Criminal Law*, Dordrecht: Martinus Nijhoff, p. 182. He for example refers to the inclusion of crimes against humanity in the Nuremberg Charter as a 'jurisdictional extension' of the prohibition against war crimes.

30 See XIX Trial of the Major War Criminals Before the International Military Tribunal 471-72 (1948) (remarks by Sir Hartley Shawcross, British Chief Prosecutor).

31 See Separate and Dissenting opinion of Judge Cassese, *Prosecutor* v. *Tadic*, Case Nos. IT-94-1 and IT-94-1-A*bis*, 26 January 2000, p. 18 (ICTY Appeals Chamber).

between both categories of international crimes for the purpose of sentencing, that constitutes the primary impetus for this book.

Finally, having explained the justification for the analysis in this book, the next subsections summarises its other main aspects. These are:

- overall goals of the book
- overview of the book
- research methodology
- overview on current literature

1.1 Overall Goals

The goals of this book can be divided into two: specific and general goals. The specific goal of this book is to establish a sentencing tariff for war crimes and crimes against humanity under the ICTY. Under the proposed tariff, crime against humanity offences will be treated as the more serious category of offences and will, consequently, attract the more severe sentences. In addition, the relationship between cases involving war crimes and crimes against humanity and the sentencing outcomes for both categories of international crimes will be made to operate in a fairly consistent and predictable way.

This book therefore intends to be the first comprehensive scholarly work on the establishment of a sentencing tariff for war crime and crime against humanity offences in the field of international criminal law.[32] Furthermore, in relation to the general goals of this book, the forthcoming chapters should contribute toward the development of sentencing rules for war crimes and crimes against humanity in international criminal law by:

- stimulating a critical reflection on the sentencing practices of relevant international criminal law enforcement institutions vis-à-vis war crimes and crimes against humanity through an examination of their statutory and case law;
- analysing the development of war crimes and crimes against humanity today and the change of judicial attitudes towards these crimes; and
- increasing the awareness of the continuity of judicial practices, which are incompatible with internationally accepted standards of sentencing and prosecution of war criminals.

---

[32] See Olusanya, O. (2004), *Do Crimes against Humanity Deserve a Higher Sentence than War Crimes?* Vol. 4, International Criminal Law Review, pp. 430-473.

1.2 Literature Overview

The majority of scholarly works on the imposition of relative penalties for crimes against humanity and war crimes merely suggest why the former category of international crimes are more serious than the latter, without going on to explain how this difference in gravity can be translated into a sentencing tariff. Some of the relevant scholars here include: *Bassiouni*,[33] *Danner*,[34] *Carcano*,[35] *Frulli*,[36] *Bohlander*,[37] *Günter Heine & Hans Vest*[38] and *Meernik & King*.[39]

In regards to *Bassiouni*, his proposal for a distinction between crimes against humanity and war crimes in terms of gravity is based on an assessment of the severity of harm suffered by the international community, *i.e.*, the different interest principle.[40] His approach to *inter alia* distinguishing between crimes against humanity and war crimes takes the following set of factors into consideration:

---

33 See Bassiouni, M.C. *The Sources and Content of International Criminal Law: A Theoretical Framework.* In: Bassiouni, M.C. (ed.) (1999), *International Criminal Law*, 2nd ed., Vol. 1, Kluwer Law International. See also Ambos, K. and Wirth, S., *Sentencing, Cumulative Charging, Genocide and Crimes against Humanity.* In: Klip, A. and Sluiter, G. (eds.) (2000), *Annotated Leading Cases of International Criminal Tribunals*, Volume II, The International Criminal Tribunal for Rwanda 1994 -1999, Antwerp: Intersentia; Kress, C. (1998), *Penalties, Enforcement and Cooperation in the International Criminal Courts Statute* (Parts VII, IX, X), 6/4 European Journal of Crime, Criminal Law and Criminal Justice, pp. 442-46; Walther, S., *Cumulation of Offences.* In: Cassese, Gaeta and Jones (eds.) (2002), *The Rome Statute of the International Criminal Court*, Vol. 1, New York: Oxford University Press; Stuckenberg, C.F. *Multiplicity of Offences: Concursus Delictorum.* In: Fischer, H., Kress, C., & Lüder, R. (eds.) (2001), *International and National Prosecution of Crimes under International Law: Current Developments*, Berlin: Berlin Verlag Arno Spitz; Nemitz, J.C. *Sentencing in the Jurisprudence of the International Criminal Tribunals for the Former Yugoslavia and Rwanda.* In: Fischer, H., Kress, C., & Lüder, R., id; Pickard, D.B.(1997), *Proposed Sentencing Guidelines for the International Criminal Court*, 20 Loyola of Los Angeles International & Comparative Law Journal, p. 123; Sharp, Sr., W.G. (1999), *The International Criminal Tribunal for the Former Yugoslavia: Defining the Offenses*, 23 Maryland Journal of International Law and Trade, p. 15.

34 See Danner, A.M. (2001), *Constructing a Hierarchy of Crimes in International Criminal Law.*

35 See Carcano, A. (2002), *Sentencing and the Gravity of the Offence in International Criminal Law.*

36 See Frulli, M. (2001), *Are Crimes against Humanity More Serious than War Crimes?*, 12 European Journal of International Law, Issue 2.

37 See Bohlander, M. (2000), *Prosecutor* v. *Dusko Tadic: Waiting to Exhale*, 11 Criminal Law Forum.

38 See Heine, G. & Vest, H. *Murder/Wilful Killing*, pp. 175, 194, in Gabrielle Kirk McDonald & Olivia Swaak-Goldman, (eds.) (2000), *Substantive and Procedural Aspects of International Criminal Law*, The Hague: Kluwer Law International.

39 See Meernik, J. & King, K. (2003), *The Sentencing Determinants of the International Criminal Tribunal for the Former Yugoslavia: An Empirical and Doctrinal Analysis.*

40 See Bassiouni, M.C. (1999), *The Sources and Content of International Criminal Law: A Theoretical Framework*, p. 3, pp. 95-100.

a) 'the social interest sought to be protected;
b) the harm sought to be averted;
c) the intrinsic seriousness of the violation;
d) the dangerousness of the transgressor manifested by the commission of a given transgression;
e) the degree of general deterrence sought to be manifested;
f) the policy of criminalization; and
g) the policy choices reflected in the opportunity of criminal prosecution.'[41]

On the basis of these factors, *Bassiouni* grouped international crimes into three categories: international crimes, international delicts and international infractions. Genocide, crimes against humanity and war crimes are in the category of 'international crimes', with genocide as the most serious, followed by crimes against humanity, then war crimes.[42] However, in spite of this hierarchy, *Bassiouni* does not propose any method for transposing this hierarchy into a sentencing tariff.

In regards to the second of the above-listed individual, *Danner*, her proposal for a distinction between crimes against humanity and war crimes in terms of gravity seems to be based on two separate approaches: the widespread and systematic attacks v. isolated acts approach and the persecution-type v. murder-type approach.[43]

Furthermore, in terms of the former approach, the widespread and systematic attacks v. isolated acts approach, *Danner's* view is that crime against humanity offences deserve higher penalties in comparison with war crime offences, because they are committed in a widespread and systematic fashion, unlike war crimes which are perpetrated on a small scale and in an isolated manner and, therefore, inevitably result in greater loss of life.[44] However, the author herself recognized the weakness of this rationale, as evidenced by the following statement:

> 'Revisiting the hypothetical question posed at the beginning of this Part, this Article answers that defendant Q, convicted of a crime against humanity should, all else being equal, receive a longer sentence than defendant Z, convicted of a war crime. The "all else being equal" is an important caveat, and a variety of other factors could affect the sentence ultimately imposed. The enumerated act, for example, would also play an important role in establishing the penalty. If Z's conviction of a war crime involved the killing of hundreds of people, his sentence

[41] See id., pp. 97; See Olusanya, O. (2004), *Double Jeopardy Without Parameters: Re-characterization in International Criminal Law.*

[42] See id., pp. 97-98.

[43] See Danner, A.M. (2001), *Constructing a Hierarchy of Crimes in International Criminal Law.*

[44] See id.

> should be longer than Q's if Q were convicted of the torture of one person as a crime against humanity. Additionally, the Trial Chamber might consider other factors, such as the defendant's position in the military or political *hierarchy* or his cooperation with the Tribunal. This Article's proposal does not, therefore, result in a rigid sentencing grid, but instead provides a starting point from which the Tribunals should construct an appropriate sentence.'[45]

The above statement basically highlights the major drawback of the widespread and systematic attacks v. isolated acts approach as a practical basis for making a hierarchical distinction between war crimes and crimes against humanity for the purpose of sentencing. Thus, as admitted by *Danner*, a widespread and systematic attacks v. isolated acts approach is unhelpful in instances where different offences constitute the basis of comparison, *i.e.* 'the killing of hundreds of people' as a war crime vis-à-vis 'the torture of one person as a crime against humanity'. In addition, Judge Li, in the *Erdemovic* case, explained this limitation in a more precise way when he made the following statement:

> 'Of course, crimes against humanity have the characteristics of being committed systematically or on a large scale. However, war crimes can also be committed in such a manner. For instance, prisoners of war may be killed systematically or on a large scale, as they were habitually and atrociously executed by the Nazi regime in the Second World War.'[46]

The above statement suggests that the widespread and systematic attacks v. isolated acts approach is arbitrary, since these elements are equally manifested by war crimes and crimes against humanity. This in turn means that not only radical comparisons, such as 'the killing of hundreds of people' as a war crime vis-à-vis 'the torture of one person as a crime against humanity', affect its workability but also more basic ones, such as the murder of one person as a war crime vis-à-vis the same murder as a crime against humanity.

Nevertheless, the widespread and systematic attacks v. isolated acts approach has been endorsed by other scholars such as *Carcano*,[47] *Frulli*,[48] *Bohlander*,[49] *Günter Heine & Hans Vest*[50] and *Meernik & King*.[51]

---

45 See id.

46 See Separate and Dissenting Opinion of Judge Li, *Prosecutor* v. *Erdemovic, supra* note 28, para. 20.

47 See Carcano, A. (2002), *Sentencing and the Gravity of the Offence in International Criminal Law.*

48 See Frulli, M. (2001), *Are Crimes against Humanity More Serious than War Crimes?*

49 See Bohlander, M. (2000), *Prosecutor* v. *Dusko Tadic: Waiting to Exhale.*

50 See Heine, G & Vest, H. *Murder/Wilful Killing*, suggesting that the multiple commission of crimes required for crimes against humanity increases the gravity of the single crime as it increases the danger of the individual perpetrator's conduct.

51 See Meernik, J. & King, K. (2003), *The Sentencing Determinants of the International Criminal Tribunal for the Former Yugoslavia: An Empirical and Doctrinal Analysis.*

On the other hand, in relation to the persecution-type v. murder-type approach, the *modus operandi* of this approach was explained by *Danner* in the following way:

> 'With persecution, the link between international crimes and bias crimes moves from the structural to the explicit. As explained earlier, the heavier punishments associated with bias crimes derive from the conviction that these crimes inflict greater harm on a greater number of victims than other kinds of crimes. Increasing the punishment for crimes committed on the basis of the victim's group identity is particularly appropriate for the kinds of crimes litigated before the Tribunals. Many of the worst violations of human rights are committed on discriminatory grounds. The nature of the conflicts that precipitated the crimes heard by the Tribunals, conflicts which pitched Serbs against Croats and Muslims, and Hutus against Tutsis, supports this assertion. Crimes based on discriminatory animus are also more likely to be committed on a wider scale. Discrimination may serve as a prelude to other crimes: Dehumanizing parts of the population of a country through propaganda and other discriminatory actions facilitates the subsequent commission of greater crimes by other groups in that society. In addition, the perpetrator of a bias crime deserves greater punishment because his motivation offends important societal norms. Punishing discriminatory motive is particularly appropriate in an international forum. A commitment to equality constitutes one of the foundational principles of the United Nations. Punishing bias crimes more severely than other crimes expresses the international community's condemnation of such crimes, which have posed great danger to the lives of civilians throughout the twentieth century. International criminal proceedings may, in fact, have a particularly powerful role in the articulation of a universal human dignity. International crimes motivated by group bias challenge and degrade this ideal. For these reasons, defendant R, convicted of persecution as a crime against humanity, should generally receive a longer sentence than either defendant Q, convicted of a murder-type crime against humanity or defendant Z, convicted of a war crime.'[52]

The following inferences can be drawn from the above statement:

1. War crimes involve non-persecutory conduct;[53]
2. Crimes against humanity partly involve persecutory conduct;[54]
3. Offences under the persecution category of crimes against humanity should attract higher penalties than war crime offences, because they pose a greater danger to the lives of civilians.[55]

---

[52] See Danner, A.M. (2001), *Constructing a Hierarchy of Crimes in International Criminal Law.*

[53] See id.

[54] See id.

[55] See id.

However, the problem with *Danner's* attempt to rely on the persecution-type v. murder-type approach is that the approach only tries to explain one part of the puzzle of imposing relative penalties for war crimes and crimes against humanity, that is, the theoretical part. It, therefore, does not resolve the more important question of how sentencing ranges for war crimes and crimes against humanity can be calculated. It is perhaps owing to this limitation that the author herself made the following statement:

> 'This Article will neither discuss how long any individual sentence should be nor advocate a concrete sentencing tariff for particular international crimes. It also will not treat evaluations of culpability, responsibility, or other aggravating and mitigating factors at sentencing.'[56]

Finally, the last individual to have considered the issue of relative penalties for crimes against humanity and war crimes, albeit not listed above because he holds a different opinion from the others, is *Bing Bing Jia*. The author in his article, '*The Differing Concepts of War Crimes and Crimes Against Humanity*',[57] discounted relying on the widespread and systematic attacks v. isolated acts approach as a basis of distinguishing between crimes against humanity and war crimes when he stated that:

> '...the vast scale of such crimes was not deemed by the IMT as a conclusive criterion of their definition, nor was the fact of the crimes being systematic and organized. On the other hand, although the fact that the acts concerned were widespread is a necessary condition for establishing the existence of a crime against humanity, it can also characterize war crimes, even though war crimes need not always be widespread. Such a factor, therefore, should not be relied on in distinguishing two crimes if both may show it in certain situations.'[58]

In addition, after an extensive review of customary law on sentencing for war crimes and crimes against humanity, the author came to the conclusion that crimes against humanity and war crimes can only be separated jurisdictionally but not substantively. In other words, the former should be restricted to protecting the civilian population, whilst the latter should be confined to ensuring fair play between military forces.[59] However, the problem with this approach is that it focuses on the offences, which underlie war crimes and crimes against

56 See id.

57 See Bing Bing Jia, N., *The Differing Concepts of War Crimes and Crimes against Humanity in International Criminal Law.* In: Goodwin-Gill, G. and Talmon, S. (eds.) (1999), *The Reality of International Law.* Oxford: Clarendon Press.

58 See id., p. 253.

59 See id., p. 250 and p. 268.

humanity, *i.e.*, murder, theft, etc., rather than on the international crimes themselves. This in turn negatively impacts the sentencing aims of the ICTY, which are *inter alia* to ensure retribution and deterrence vis-à-vis crimes against humanity and war crimes.

1.3 Chapter Overview and Methodology

This book is divided into five chapters. The following involves a summary of these chapters.

1.3.1 Chapter 1: Introduction

This chapter is evident and introduces the subject of the book and its motivation.

1.3.2 Chapter 2: Historical Impediments to the Imposition of Relative Penalties for War Crimes and Crimes against Humanity and Methodology

This chapter examines the history of the imposition of penalties for war crimes and crimes against humanity in international criminal law. This examination is conducted in the context of World War II Tribunals, since they were the first institutions to recognize, prosecute and sentence both categories of international crimes.

In addition, Chapter 2 is based on two sets of assumptions. The first is that crimes against humanity were regarded by World War II Tribunals as a more serious category of international crimes than war crimes. And the second is that the source of the current divisions between ICTY judges over the issue of whether a hierarchical distinction can be made between both categories of international crimes, for the purpose of imposing penalties, can be traced back to the activities of the World War II Tribunals.

In order to adequately confront the issue of the imposition of penalties for war crimes and crimes against humanity today, the historical questions that constitute the focal point of Chapter 2 are:

- Were war crimes and crimes against humanity invented to protect different interests?
- If so, to what extent were these different interests reflected in terms of penalties?

In order to thoroughly address these issues, this chapter is divided into two parts. The first part will examine the question of why war crimes and crimes against humanity were invented by World War II Tribunals and make the following arguments: first, that both categories of international crimes were invented to protect different interests and, second, that on the basis of the different interests protected by both categories of international crimes, crimes against humanity were clearly more serious than war crimes. This is achieved by delving into the intentions of the framers of the relevant World War II Statutes, in so far as the codification of war crimes and crimes against humanity is concerned, and by comparing the concepts of war crimes and crimes against humanity as codified under the Statutes of World War II Tribunals. On the other hand, the second part of this chapter links the discussion in the first part on the different interests protected by war crimes and crimes against humanity to the examination of the factors that affected the ability of the World War II Tribunals to accurately translate these different interests into relative penalties for both categories of international crimes.

In relation to the goals of this chapter, they are the following:

- To develop a thorough understanding of the historical roots of sentencing for crimes against humanity and war crimes in international criminal law.
- To build a conceptual foundation for subsequent chapters.
- To describe the major aspects of the legal history of international criminal sentencing.

Finally, the main conclusions that emerge from this chapter are:

- War crimes and crimes against humanity, as codified under the statutes of the World War II Tribunals, clearly protected different interests.
- The different interests protected by both categories of international crimes could have been used as a basis for making a hierarchical distinction between them for the purpose of sentencing.
- It was the lackadaisical attitude of the WWII Tribunals, which constituted the main obstacle towards the imposition of relative penalties for war crimes and crimes against humanity.

1.3.3 Chapter 3: Impediments to the Imposition of Relative Penalties for War Crimes and Crimes against Humanity under the ICTY and Methodology

Chapter 3 of this book identifies and analyses the current impediments to the imposition of relative penalties for war crimes and crimes against humanity under the ICTY. This is achieved by linking the results of the analysis in Chapter 2 with the examination in the present chapter. In other words, the assumption here is that the jurisprudence of World War II Tribunals on the imposition of penalties for both categories of international crimes has sent mixed signals to the judges of the ICTY, and that these signals have led to the birth of three schools of thought. In addition, the main argument is that each of the schools of thought individually constitutes an impediment to the imposition of relative penalties for war crimes and crimes against humanity under the ICTY.

The aim of this chapter is, therefore, to thoroughly examine each of the schools of thought on the imposition of relative penalties for war crimes and crimes against humanity under the ICTY and to point out their limitations. This approach is ultimately instrumental in building a clear picture of what is currently wrong with the ICTY's system of sentencing for war crimes and crimes against humanity, and how an appropriate solution can be devised. The side goals of this chapter are the following:

- To analyse the development of the substantive law on war crimes and crimes against humanity under the ICTY.
- To draw attention to the continuity of judicial practices under the ICTY, which are incompatible with internationally accepted standards of sentencing and prosecution of war criminals.
- To utilise the activities of the ICTY as a basis for globalising the problem of sentencing for war crimes and crimes against humanity.
- To memorialise the atrocities committed in the former Yugoslavia.

Finally, the conclusion is based on the results of the analysis of the three schools of thought on the imposition of relative penalties for war crimes and crimes against humanity under the ICTY.

1.3.4 Chapters 4 and 5: Solution, Conclusion and Methodology

Chapter 4 devises a sentencing tariff for crimes against humanity and war crimes under the ICTY. The proposed tariff is derived from a combination of domestic law on bias crimes and the existing ICTY penalty framework. In addition, on the basis of the proposed approach, mandatory minimum and maximum penalties for war crimes and crimes against humanity offences under the ICTY are established. This will in turn enable the ICTY to set a minimum and maximum threshold beyond which it cannot fall nor rise for offences such as murder, rape, torture, etc., depending on whether they are committed as a war crime or as a crime against humanity. Furthermore, the advantages of the envisaged approach are the following:

1. It will establish a credible link between the substantive law on crimes against humanity and war crimes and the determination of penalties for both categories of international crimes.
2. As part of its efforts to develop sentencing ranges, it will take into consideration all other relevant variables for the sentencing calculus of crimes against humanity and war crimes such as the rank of the offender and the offender's response to the charges.
3. Owing to (1) and (2) above, it will help to resolve the following types of problematic situations:

(a) Situations where one defendant, on the basis of the same act, has been cumulatively convicted of and sentenced for both crimes against humanity and violations of the laws and customs of war.
(b) Situations where two different defendants have been convicted of the same offence, *albeit* under two different headings, *i.e.*, one, defendant A, convicted of murder as a crime against humanity and another, defendant B, convicted of wilful killing as a violation of the laws and customs of war.
(c) Situations where two different defendants have committed two different crimes, *e.g.*, torture as a crime against humanity vis-à-vis murder as a war crime.

Finally, the concluding chapter, Chapter 5, re-emphasises the value of this research. In other words, there is no published work that has proposed a credible system for calculating penalties for war crimes and crimes against humanity,[60] and this study will, therefore, be of interest to legal practitioners. It also highlights the value of the results obtained for the International Criminal Court and the fact that the findings of this book are also significant for improving the procedural and substantive rules of international criminal law.

60 See Olusanya, O. ,*Do Crimes against Humanity Deserve a Higher Sentence than War Crimes?*

CHAPTER 2

Historical Impediments to the Imposition of Relative Penalties for War Crimes and Crimes against Humanity

2.1 Introduction

On the 26th of January 2000, in the International Criminal Tribunal for the former Yugoslavia case of *Prosecutor* v. *Dusko Tadic*,[1] Judge *Shahabuddeen*, in his separate opinion, referred to the *Einsatzgruppen* case of World War II.[2] The defendants in that case were primarily convicted of war crimes and crimes against humanity for the same acts and sentenced to death by hanging.[3] Judge *Shahabuddeen's* aim was to rely on the precedent set in *Einsatzgruppen* to support his opinion that war crimes and crimes against humanity attract the same level of punishment.[4] The activities of the World War II Tribunals therefore marked the beginning of the imposition of penalties for war crimes and crimes against humanity in international criminal law, as they serve as the only historical precedent referred to by both the ICTY judges and academic scholars.[5]

The present chapter is based on two sets of assumption: The first is that crimes against humanity were regarded by World War II Tribunals as a more serious category of international crimes than war crimes. And the second is that the source of the current division between ICTY judges over the issue of whether a hierarchical distinction can be made between both categories of international crimes for the purpose of imposing penalties can be traced back to the activities of the World War II Tribunals.

In order to adequately confront the issue of the imposition of penalties for war crimes and crimes against humanity today, the historical questions that constitute the focal point at the early stage of this book are:

- Were war crimes and crimes against humanity invented to protect different interests?
- And, if so, to what extent were these different interests reflected in terms of penalties?

In order to thoroughly address these issues, this chapter is divided into two parts. The first part examines the question of why war crimes and crimes against humanity were invented by World War II Tribunals and makes the following arguments: first, that both categories of international crimes were

---

1 See Separate Opinion of Judge Shahabuddeen, *Prosecutor* v. *Tadic*, Case No. IT-94-1 and IT-94-1-A*bis*, 26 January 2000, (ICTY Appeals Chamber).

2 See Separate Opinion of Judge Shahabuddeen, *id.* pp. 43-44.

3 See specifically Trials of War Criminals before the Nuremberg Military Tribunals under Control Council Law No. 10, IV (Washington, DC, 1949), Vol. IV, pp. 48-49 (hereinafter: Trials of War Criminals).

4 See Separate Opinion of Judge Shahabuddeen, *supra* note 1, Chapter 2.

5 See Bing Bing Jia, N., *The Differing Concepts of War Crimes and Crimes against Humanity in International Criminal Law*; Carcano, A., *Sentencing and the Gravity of the Offence in International Criminal Law*; Danner, A.M., *Constructing a Hierarchy of Crimes in International Criminal Law.*

invented to protect different interests; second, that on the basis of the different interests protected by both categories of international crimes, crimes against humanity were clearly more serious than war crimes. This is achieved by delving into the intentions of the framers of the relevant World War II Statutes, in so far as the codification of war crimes and crimes against humanity is concerned, and by comparing the concepts of war crimes and crimes against humanity as codified under the Statutes of World War II Tribunals. On the other hand, the second part of this chapter, links the discussion in the first part on the different interests protected by war crimes and crimes against humanity to the analysis of the factors that affected the ability of World War II Tribunals to accurately translate these different interests into relative penalties for both categories of international crimes.

The goals of this chapter are:

- to develop a thorough understanding of the historical roots of sentencing for crimes against humanity and war crimes in international criminal law;
- to build a conceptual foundation for subsequent chapters;
- to describe the major aspects of the legal history of international criminal sentencing.

Finally, the main conclusions that emerge from the following sections are that:

- war crimes and crimes against humanity as codified under the statutes of the World War II Tribunals clearly protected different interests;
- the different interests protected by both categories of international crimes, could have been used as a basis for making a hierarchical distinction between them for the purpose of imposing penalties;
- it was the lackadaisical attitude of the WWII Tribunals, which constituted the main obstacle towards the imposition of relative penalties for war crimes and crimes against humanity.

2.2 World War II Tribunals

The Nuremberg Trials of 1945 – 1949, which were presided upon by the United States, France, the United Kingdom and the U.S.S.R., represented the first concrete international efforts to prosecute and punish individuals for international crimes.[6] Thus the black letter of Article 1 of the Nuremberg Charter (IMT) stipulated the following:

---

6 See Bassiouni, M.C., *The Journey to a Permanent International Criminal Court*. In: *International Criminal Court: Compilation of United Nations Documents and Draft ICC Statute Before the Diplomatic Conference.* Available at <http://www.npwj.net/cdrom/intro/intro.pdf> (last visited June 2004).

> 'In pursuance of the Agreement signed on the 8th day of August 1945 by the Government of the United States of America, the Provisional Government of the French Republic, the Government of the United Kingdom of Great Britain and Northern Ireland and the Government of the Union of Soviet Socialist Republics, there shall be established an International Military Tribunal (hereinafter called "the Tribunal") *for the just and prompt trial and punishment of the major war criminals of the European Axis.*'[7] [emphasis added]

In addition, in support of the goals of Article 1, was Article 6 of the Tribunal's Charter, which recognized the following categories of international crimes:

> '(a) CRIMES AGAINST PEACE: namely, planning, preparation, initiation or waging of a war of aggression, or a war in violation of international treaties, agreements or assurances, or participation in a common plan or conspiracy for the accomplishment of any of the foregoing;
>
> (b) WAR CRIMES: namely, violations of the laws or customs of war. Such violations shall include, but not be limited to, murder, ill-treatment or deportation to slave labor or for any other purpose of civilian population of or in occupied territory, murder or ill-treatment of prisoners of war or persons on the seas, killing of hostages, plunder of public or private property, wanton destruction of cities, towns or villages, or devastation not justified by military necessity;
>
> (c) CRIMES AGAINST HUMANITY: namely, murder, extermination, enslavement, deportation, and other inhumane acts committed against any civilian population, before or during the war; or persecutions on political, racial or religious grounds in execution of or in connection with any crime within the jurisdiction of the Tribunal, whether or not in violation of the domestic law of the country where perpetrated.'[8]

The purpose of the forthcoming sections is to focus on relevant aspects of war crimes and crimes against humanity as codified under Articles 6(b) and (c) respectively. The immediate issues, which are tackled in the next section, are whether both categories of international crimes were created to protect different interests, and if so, what exactly were these interests.

Finally, what justifies the analysis in the forthcoming sections is the fact that it is an important principle of sentencing that judges should give reasons for the

---

7 See Agreement for the Prosecution and Punishment of the Major War Criminals of the European Axis, 8 Aug. 1945, Annex, 59 Stat. 1544, 82 U.N.T.S. 279, reprinted in 39 American Journal of International Law 257 (Supp. 1945) [hereinafter Nuremberg Charter]; see also Paust, J.J., Bassiouni, M.C., Williams, S.A., Scharf, M., Gurule, J., Zagaris, B. (1996), *International Criminal Law,* 8th ed., Carolina Academic Press, pp. 291-293.

8 See id.

sentences they impose. This opinion is corroborated by *Fitzgerald* JA in *R* v. *JCE* in the following statement:

> 'A sentencing judge must explain his or her decision. That might require discussion of some other sentencing options with reasons why those options were not adopted. For example, that is implicit in s 5(1) and expressly provided for by s 5(2) of the Crimes (Sentencing Procedure) Act. However, it is obviously unnecessary for every possibility to be discussed in every case. For example, it is unnecessary to explain why community service is not an appropriate sentence for a murderer. Further, the ultimate decision, for example, whether a term of imprisonment should be eight years or nine years, frequently involves a subjective judgment, based on experience as well as information, which cannot be precisely and comprehensively articulated.'[9]

The above statement emphasizes the principle that a sentencing judge must give reasons for the penalties imposed. The reasons for this approach are that separation of the imposition of the penalties from the expression of the appropriate reasons not only creates a sense of injustice in the mind of all concerned with the sentencing process, but it also creates significant practical difficulties.[10] Similarly in *R* v. *Julie Anne Duffy, Sully* J said:

> 'I wish to add the following observations: the Remarks on Sentence, as I said during submissions, are unhelpful in their brevity. It is not expected that a sentencing judge and particularly a sentencing judge in the District Court, will write an essay in jurisprudence every time he or she comes to deliver remarks on sentence. But it is, I think, timely to say that the Court expects that primary sentencing judges will at least state, however briefly, the findings of fact upon which they are persuaded to proceed; and will then expose in relation to those facts as found a coherent process of reasoning which will sufficiently equip this Court to intervene if asked to do so, and if a cause for doing so is otherwise shown.'[11]

And third, in *R* v. *Thomson; R* v. *Houlton, Spigelman* CJ said:

---

9 See *R* v. *JCE* (2000) 120 A Crim Rp. 18 at p. 21.

10 See Kitto, F. (1992), *Why Write Judgments*, 66 Australian Law Journal, p. 787; Spigelman, (2000), *Seen to be Done: The Principle of Open Justice: Part 1*, 74 Australian Law Journal, p. 290, especially at pp. 294 and 295. Also see statement by Brennan J in *Jago* v. *District Court* (NSW) (1989) 168 CLR, p. 23 at p. 50. To similar effect are the observations of Sir John Barry (quoted with approval by McHugh J, Hayne J and Callinan J in *Pearce* v. *The Queen* (1998) 194 CLR, p. 610 at p. 622 [39]) concerning the criminal law. See also *Richmond Newspapers* v. *Virginia* 448 US 555 (1980) at pp. 571-572, per Burger CJ.

11 See *R* v. *Julie Anne Duffy* [1999] NSWCCA, p. 321.

'Sentencing judges are under an obligation to give reasons for their decisions. Remarks on sentence are no different in this respect from other judgments. This is a manifestation of the fundamental principle of the common law that justice must not only be done but must manifestly be seen to be done. The obligation of a court is to publish reasons for its decision, not merely to provide reasons to the parties....'[12]

2.2.1 The Different Interests Protected by War Crimes and Crimes against Humanity in 1945

The following subsections involve an inquiry into whether war crimes and crimes against humanity, as codified under the Nuremberg Charter, protected different interests and, if so, what these interests are. The idea is to link the results of this inquiry to the discussion in the second part of this chapter on the factors that affected the ability of World War II Tribunals to accurately translate these different interests into relative penalties for both categories of international crimes.

2.2.1.1 War Crimes

Article 6(b) of the IMT Charter defines war crimes in the following terms 'violations of the laws or customs of war. Such violations shall include, but not be limited to, murder, ill-treatment or deportation to slave labor or for any other purpose of civilian population of or in occupied territory, murder or ill-treatment of prisoners of war or persons on the seas, killing of hostages, plunder of public or private property, wanton destruction of cities, towns or villages, or devastation not justified by military necessity'.[13]

The use of the term 'laws or customs of war' in connection with the above-mentioned offences, suggests that the criminalizing of an offence as a war crime was dependent upon whether or not that offence complied with the laws or customs of war of that era, rather than on the illegality of that offence *per se*. In other words, offences such as murder, hostage taking and killing, reprisal attacks, etc., could not automatically be criminalised as war crimes unless they breached the laws or customs of war in existence at the time of the World War II trials.[14]

---

[12] See *R* v. *Thomson; R* v. *Houlton* (2000) 49 NSWLR 383, pp. 394-395; *Pettitt* v. *Dunkley* [1971] 1 NSWLR 376 at p. 382; *Housing Commission (NSW)* v. *Tatmar Pastoral Co Pty Ltd* [1983] 3 NSWLR 378 at pp. 385-386; *Public Service Board (NSW)* v. *Osmond* (1986) 159 CLR 656 at pp. 666-667; *Soulemezis* v. *Dudley (Holdings) Pty Ltd* [1987] 10 NSWLR 247 at p. 273, pp. 277-281.

[13] See Nuremberg Charter.

[14] See Raby (1968), *Bombardment of Land Targets*, p. 67, cited in Rosenblad, E. (1979), *International Humanitarian Law of Armed Conflict*, Geneva: Henri Dunant Institute, p. 141, explaining how attacks on civilian targets may be legitimised through meeting the requirements of military necessity and proportionality.

Furthermore, there are two main criteria for determining whether or not a particular act has breached the laws or customs of war. They are that:

1. The act must have been committed as part of a military objective.[15]
2. The act must comply with the principle of proportionality.[16]

The interplay between the above criteria vis-à-vis the criminalizing of an act as a war crime can, for instance, be demonstrated with the aid of the following finding by the Tribunal in the *hostage* case in relation to the legality of hostage taking and killing:

> 'An examination of the available evidence on the subject convinces us that hostages may be taken in order to guarantee the peaceful conduct of the population of occupied territories and, when certain conditions exist and the necessary preliminaries have been taken, they may, as a last resort, be shot... The occupant may properly insist upon compliance with regulations necessary to the security of the occupying forces and for the maintenance of law and order. In the accomplishment of this objective, the occupant may, only as a last resort, take and execute hostages.'[17]

The above statement points to the fact that, although hostage taking and execution were *prima facie* sanctioned under Article 6(b), they could nevertheless be considered as legal if they were implemented in a way that complied with the requirements of necessity and proportionality.[18]

However, this approach is not as simple as it sounds, because what is proportional or necessary is hard to determine. In respect to the difficulty of determining proportionality, *Fenrick*, for instance, made the following relevant statement:

> 'The main problem with the principle of proportionality is not whether or not it exists but what it means and how it is to be applied. It is relatively simple to state

---

15 See Rogers, A.P.V. (1996), *Law on the Battlefield*, Manchester; New York: Manchester University Press, pp. 27-46; Fenrick, W.J. (1997), *Attacking the Enemy Civilian as a Punishable Offense*, 7 Duke Journal of Comparative & International Law, p. 539. See Sandoz, Y., Swinarski, C., & Zimmerman, B. (eds.) (1987), *Commentary on the Additional Protocols of 8 June 1977 to the Geneva Conventions of 12 August 1949*, Geneva: Martinus Nijhoff Publishers, pp. 632-633.

16 See generally Gardam, J.G. (1993), *Proportionality and Force in International Law*, 87 American Journal of International Law, p. 391; see Article 51(5)(b), Article 57(2)(b), and Article 85(3) of Protocol Additional to the Geneva Conventions of 12 August 1949, and Relating to the Protection of Victims of International Armed Conflicts, Dec. 12, 1977, 1125 U.N.T.S. 3, 16 I.L.M. 1391 (1977) [hereinafter Protocol I].

17 See *US* v. *Wilhelm List, et al.* (Hostage Case) Trials of War Criminals, Vol. XI. Relevant facts extracted from <http://real-ale.wcl.american.edu/etp/MilitaryTribunals/NMT/HostageCase.html> (last visited June 2004).

18 See *infra* subsection 2.2.2.1.2.

that there must be an acceptable relation between the legitimate destructive effect and undesirable collateral effects. For example, bombing a refugee camp is obviously prohibited if its only military significance is that women in the camp are knitting socks for soldiers. Conversely, an air strike on an ammunition dump should not be prohibited merely because a farmer is plowing a field in the area. Unfortunately, most applications of the principle of proportionality are not quite so clear-cut. It is much easier to formulate the principle of proportionality in general terms than it is to apply it to a particular set of circumstances because the comparison is often between unlike quantities and values. How do you assess the value of innocent human lives as opposed to capturing a particular military objective?

The questions which remain unresolved once one decides to apply the principle of proportionality include the following:

1) What are the relative values to be assigned to the military advantage gained and the injury to non-combatants and or the damage to civilian objects?
2) What do you include or exclude in totalling your sums?
3) What is the standard of measurement in time or space? and
4) To what extent is a military commander obligated to expose his own forces to danger in order to limit civilian casualties or damage to civilian objects?

The answers to these questions are not simple. It may be necessary to resolve them on a case-by-case basis, and the answers may differ depending on the background and values of the decision maker. It is unlikely that a human rights lawyer and an experienced combat commander would assign the same relative values to military advantage and to injury to noncombatants. Further, it is unlikely that military commanders with different doctrinal backgrounds and differing degrees of combat experience or national military histories would always agree in close cases...."[19]

As is evident from the above, utilizing the principle of proportionality as a basis for determining what constitutes a war crime is not a straightforward exercise. In addition, this difficulty, as will be explained later on, also rules out the possibility of re-characterising war crime acts as crimes against humanity.[20]

Finally, it follows from the above clarification, that the purpose of Article 6(b) was to impose upon belligerents the obligation to behave in a fair manner in their choice of arms and targets, thereby sparing the enemy combatants

[19] See Fenrick, W.J. (1997), *Attacking the Enemy Civilian as a Punishable Offense*, pp. 545-546.

[20] See Wengler, W. (1964), *Völkerecht*, Berlin/Göttingen/Heidelberg: Springer Verlag, p. 1375, pointing out the danger of utilizing the principles of war as a basis for interpreting the concept of humanity; Szurek and Rona in *Débats', L'Article 31, ∫ 1 c, Du Statut de la Cour Pénale Internationale*. Revue Belge de Droit International 2000/2, p. 478, ruling out the possibility of utilizing the objective requirements of self defence (necessity and proportionality) vis-à-vis genocide and crimes against humanity; See Olusanya, O. (2004), *Double Jeopardy Without Parameters: Re-characterization in International Criminal Law.*

unnecessary suffering and protecting the population from the use of inhumane weapons.[21] This meant that certain acts, which would constitute crimes against humanity if perpetrated against civilians, were actually permissible in the context of military action.[22]

2.2.1.2 Crimes against Humanity

Article 6(c) of the IMT Charter[23] is viewed as recognizing two distinct categories of crimes against humanity: the murder type and the persecution type.[24] The former includes the basic offences of 'murder, extermination, enslavement, deportation, and other inhumane acts committed against any civilian population'; whilst the latter includes the same list of acts, *albeit* committed on political, racial or religious grounds. The crime of persecution therefore provides an additional basis for attributing criminal liability in relation to crime against humanity offences.[25]

---

[21] See Pictet, J. (1985), *Development and Principles of International Humanitarian Law*, Dordrecht/Geneva: Martinus Nijhoff and Henry Dunant Institute.

[22] See DeGuzman, M.M., *The Road from Rome: The Developing Law of Crimes against Humanity*, expressing a similar opinion. Extracted from <http://www.soc.umn.edu/~boyle/22.2deguzman.html> (last visited May 2004).

[23] See Nuremberg Charter.

[24] See United Nations War Crimes Commission (1948), *History of the United Nations War Crimes Commission and the Development of the Laws of War*, p. 194, making a similar distinction between the two types of crimes against humanity; See Fenrick, W.J. (1999), *Should Crimes Against Humanity Replace War Crimes?*, 37 Columbia Journal of Transnational Law, p. 767, p. 777, making the same distinction. See Danner, A.M. (2001), *Constructing a Hierarchy of Crimes in International Criminal Law*, writing: 'The ICTY and ICTR Statutes share similar definitions of crimes against humanity. The ICTY chapeau requires that the defendant have committed an enumerated act "in armed conflict" and "directed against any civilian population." The chapeau of the ICTR's provision mandates that the defendant have committed an enumerated act "as part of a widespread or systematic attack against any civilian population on national, political, ethnic, racial or religious grounds." The ICTY has read the language "civilian population" in Article 5 to include the ICTR Statute's requirement that the act form part of a widespread or systematic attack: "the acts of the accused must comprise part of a pattern of widespread or systematic crimes directed against a civilian population and . . . the accused must have known that his acts fit into such a pattern." "Widespread" means affecting multiple victims and "systematic" refers to "an attack carried out pursuant to a preconceived policy or plan." Article 5 of the ICTY Statute and Article 3 of the ICTR Statute contain a list of nine enumerated acts. The enumerated acts of crimes against humanity fall into two categories, "murder-type" and "persecution."'

[25] See id. writing: 'While the chapeau provision of war crimes has no particular mens rea, and the mens rea of the chapeau of crimes against humanity requires that the defendant knowingly associated himself with collective atrocity, the mens rea of persecution demands, in addition to the other elements of a crime against humanity, that the defendant have selected his victims based on their affiliation with a religious, political, or racial group. For this reason, persecution should generally be considered more serious, and punished with a longer sentence, than other crimes against humanity or war crimes.'

Crimes against humanity were created for the purpose of serving dual objectives: first, to criminalise non discriminatory acts when committed against civilians, both inside and outside the territory of Germany, second, to criminalise discriminatory acts when committed under the same circumstances. In reality, however, to the extent that crimes against humanity were applied primarily for the purpose of dealing with atrocities against the Jewish people and other victims targeted on the basis of their political beliefs, race and religion, greater emphasis seemed to have been placed on the persecution type of crimes against humanity than on the murder type. In fact, some authorities even go as far as to say that crimes against humanity were created only to deal with persecutory conduct. *Bing Bing Jia*, for example, made the following relevant statement:

> 'However, this hatred if proven may, it is admitted, provide a significant indicator to the distinct purpose of discrimination which is always behind the commission of crimes against humanity.'[26]

Similarly, the Trial Chamber of the ICTY in *Tadic* adopted the requirement of discriminatory intent for all crimes against humanity under the ICTY Statute.[27]

In light of the above, crimes against humanity as prosecuted by World War II Tribunals will be taken here to refer exclusively to its persecution category. This approach, therefore, necessitates a deeper analysis of the persecution category of crimes against humanity.

---

[26] See Bing Bing Jia, N., *The Differing Concepts of War Crimes and Crimes against Humanity in International Criminal Law*; see also, *e.g.*, Bassiouni, M.C. (1992), *Crimes against Humanity in International Criminal Law*, at pp. 251-53, listing a policy of discrimination as a prerequisite legal element of crimes against humanity; Bassiouni, M.C. (1994), *The Commission of Experts Established Pursuant to Security Council Resolution 780: Investigating Violations of International Humanitarian Law in the Former Yugoslavia*, 5 Criminal Law Forum, p. 279, pp. 322-23: 'In order to be convicted of crimes against humanity, one must have had the intent to engage in specific conduct against a given group. The acts must be done as part of a systematic policy of persecution against this group.' O'Brien, J.C. (1993), *The International Tribunal for Violations of International Humanitarian Law in the Former Yugoslavia*, pp. 639, 648, stating that crimes against humanity 'require proof that the act was committed because of the victim's affiliation with a group...'; Orentlicher, D.F. (1997), *Settling Accounts: The Duty to Prosecute Human Rights Violations of a Prior Regime*, 100 Yale Law Journal, at p. 2594, stating that the 'core principle' of the law of crimes against humanity is that 'atrocious acts committed on a mass scale against racial, religious, or political groups must be punished'; Interim Report of the Commission of Experts Established Pursuant to Security Council Resolution 780 (1992), U.N. SCOR, Annex I, p. 49, U.N. Doc. S/25274 (1993), concluding that a required element of crimes against humanity is that the acts be committed 'as part of an official policy based on discrimination against an identifiable group of persons'.

[27] See Opinion and Judgement, *Prosecutor* v. *Tadic*, Case No. IT-94-1-T, 7 May 1997, para. 655 (ICTY Trial Chamber).

Article 6(c) of the Nuremberg Charter, as well as similar provisions in other World War II Statutes such as Article II (c) of Control Council Law No. 10,[28] enabled the relevant tribunals to prosecute individuals for persecution as a crime against humanity offences only when committed on 'political, racial or religious grounds'. The use of the term 'grounds' has been interpreted to mean discriminatory intent. For example, the ICTR Statute defines crimes against humanity as acts that are 'part of a widespread or systematic attack against any civilian population *on national, political, ethnic, racial or religious grounds*'[29] and the ICTR has interpreted this phrase as requiring discriminatory intent.[30]

The association of the term 'grounds' with discriminatory intent, therefore, necessitates an explanation of the meaning of discriminatory intent. A discriminatory intent means that the perpetrator's purpose in attacking the victim would transcend the individual victim; the perpetrator would need to have a specific purpose for attacking the group to which the victim belongs.[31] In order to constitute a crime against humanity in 1945, a general intent to commit one of the enumerated acts combined with a general awareness of the probable consequences of such an act with respect to the immediate victim or victims would be insufficient. The definition of the crime required a particular state of mind or a specific intent with respect to the overall consequences of the prohibited act. In other words, expressed in more simplistic terms, a German soldier who killed a Jewish person must have committed his act whilst knowing that it would help to facilitate the extermination of Jewish people.

Furthermore, in terms of the distinction between crimes against humanity and war crimes in 1945, two cases where the Nuremberg Tribunal focused exclusively on crimes against humanity provide important clues.[32] They are the *Streicher* case[33] and the von *Schirach* case.[34] In relation to *Streicher*, he was convicted

---

[28] See Article II (c) of Control Council Law No. 10, 20 Dec. 1945, 3 Official Gazette Control Council for Germany 50 (1946), reprinted in Trials of War Criminals before the Nuernberg Military Tribunals Under Control Council Law No. 10 at xvi (1949) [hereinafter CCL No. 10].

[29] See Article 3 of the Statute of the International Criminal Tribunal for the Prosecution of Persons Responsible for Genocide and Other Serious Violations of International Humanitarian Law Committed in the Territory of Rwanda and Rwandan Citizens Responsible for Genocide and Other Such Violations Committed in the Territory of Neighbouring States Between 1 January 1994 and 31 December 1994, S.C. Res. 955, U.N. SCOR, 49th Sess., 3453d mtg., Annex, U.N. Doc. S/RES/955 (1994), reprinted in 33 I.L.M. 1598, 1602 (1994) [hereinafter ICTR Statute].

[30] See *Prosecutor* v. *Akayesu*, para. 584 (ICTR Trial Chamber). But see *Akayesu*, para. 466 (Appeals Chamber) where this requirement was interpreted jurisdictionally and no longer substantively.

[31] See DeGuzman, M.M., *The Road from Rome: The Developing Law of Crimes against Humanity.*

[32] See DeGuzman, id.

[33] See Trial of the Major War Criminals before the International Military Tribunal pp. 301-04 (1947) [hereinafter IMT Judgment].

[34] See id. at pp. 317-320.

of crimes against humanity for his roles as both the editor and publisher of 'Der Sturmer', an anti-Semitic weekly newspaper. Most of the evidence in the case was based on his speeches and articles, which were published between 1923 and 1945 and were designed to incite Germans to actively persecute the Jewish people to the point of annihilation. The following statement by the Tribunal serves as the *ratio*[35] of the case:

> 'Streicher's incitement to murder and extermination at the time when Jews in the East were being killed under the most horrible conditions clearly constitutes persecution on political and racial grounds in connection with war crimes as defined by the Charter, and constitutes a crime against humanity.'[36]

The conclusions that can be drawn from the above statement are the following:

1. Crimes against humanity, unlike war crimes, applied to persecutory conduct[37] and
2. Crimes against humanity required a particular state of mind or a specific intent with respect to the overall consequences of the prohibited act. Thus *Streicher's* actions were linked to the general atmosphere of hostility against Jewish people.

In terms of *von Schirach*, he was convicted of crimes against humanity for his roles as the Gauleiter of Vienna, Reichs Governor of Vienna, and Reichs Defence Commissioner for that territory. The basis of his conviction was his participation in the deportation of Jewish people from Vienna, after he had become Gauleiter of Vienna, and the fact that he knew that the best the Jewish people could hope for as a result of his actions was a miserable existence in the Ghettoes of the East.[38] This case, therefore, corroborates all of the findings made in respect to crimes against humanity above.[39]

---

35 See Bing Bing Jia, N., *The Differing Concepts of War Crimes and Crimes against Humanity in International Criminal Law, supra* note 57, Chapter 1, p. 259, identifying the *ratio* of the case.

36 See id.

37 See DeGuzman, M.M., *The Road from Rome: The Developing Law of Crimes against Humanity*, writing: 'The indictment accuses Streicher of publicly advocating the extermination of the Jewish race. Such incitement, while clearly not a war crime, did qualify as "persecutions on political and racial grounds." ....'. Also relevant, particularly to the issue of whether war crimes apply to discriminatory conduct today, is the following statement by the Appeals Chamber in *Vasiljevic*: 'A discriminatory state of mind is not an element of the crime of murder under Article 3 of the Statute and was not therefore taken into account in convicting the Appellant for the crime of murder.' (paras. 172-173).

38 See IMT Judgment, *supra* note 33, Chapter 2.

39 See IMT Judgment, see id., writing: 'Von Schirach was charged with participating in the deportation of Jews from Vienna. The Tribunal found that, because Vienna was occupied as part of a common plan of aggression, the crimes that Von Schirach committed in Vienna were connected to the war and therefore fell within the Tribunal's jurisdiction as crimes against humanity.'

Finally, what is clear from the above discussion on war crimes and crimes against humanity is that both categories of international crimes in 1945 clearly protected different interests. In other words, war crimes were created to deal with the conduct of combatants in times of war. The determination of culpability for war crimes, therefore, involved an assessment of whether or not acts committed by combatants in times of war were in line with the principles of proportionality, necessity, self defence and so on and so forth. In contrast, crimes against humanity were invented to deal with Hitler's persecution of Jewish people. In view of this difference, crimes against humanity were clearly the more serious category of international crimes.[40] The next sections consider the issue of why the different interests protected by both categories of international crimes did not lead to a policy of higher sentences for crimes against humanity vis-à-vis war crimes.

2.2.2 Factors Negating the Imposition of Relative Penalties for War Crimes and Crimes against Humanity Based on their Different Interests

The following sections identify and examine two main factors, which affected the imposition of relative penalties for war crimes and crimes against humanity. They are the following:

1. the lackadaisical attitude to the translation of the substantive law on War Crimes and Crimes against Humanity into penalties, and
2. the rudimentary state of international human rights law.

2.2.2.1 The Lackadaisical Attitude to the Translation of the Substantive Law on War Crimes and Crimes against Humanity into Penalties

This section demonstrates how the overly relaxed attitude of the World War II Tribunals in transposing the substantive law on war crimes and crimes against humanity into penalties affected the imposition of relative penalties for both categories of international crimes.[41] The cases that are considered

---

[40] See Carcano, A. (2002), *Sentencing and the Gravity of the Offence in International Criminal Law*, at p. 592. Writing in connection with the gravity of persecution as a crime against humanity vis-à-vis war crimes that: 'Another case where clarification on seriousness may be needed is that of persecution as a crime against humanity. This crime differs from other crimes against humanity in that conviction requires, inter alia, the presence of a discriminatory intent. Since the discriminatory element may be seen as making the crime more serious, one may argue that murder characterised as persecution and not as a war crime or as another kind of crime against humanity is per se a more serious offence.'

[41] See Wexler, L.S. (1994), *The Interpretation of the Nuremberg Principles by the French Court of Cassation: From Touvier to Barbie and Back Again*, 32 Colombia Journal of Transnational Law, p. 289, pp. 307-08. Writing: 'Although implicitly acknowledging that crimes against humanity were different than war

below are the *High Command* case,[42] *Hostage* case,[43] *Einstazgruppen* case[44] and the *RuSHA* case.[45]

2.2.2.1.1 High Command Case

The facts of this case were that the principal defendant, *Wilhelm von Leeb* and thirteen other individuals, who were former high-ranking officers in the German Army and Navy and officers holding high positions in the German High Command (OKW), were charged with crimes against peace, war crimes, crimes against humanity and conspiracy to commit such crimes.[46]

Furthermore, all of the fourteen defendants were acquitted on the count charging crimes against peace,[47] whilst the conspiracy count was dismissed by the Tribunal 'as tendering no issue not contained in the preceding counts'. As to counts two and three charging war crimes and crimes against humanity, two of the accused were acquitted, whereas eleven others were found guilty and sentenced to terms of imprisonment ranging from two years up to life imprisonment.[48] All of the war crimes and crimes against humanity charges against them were based on their involvement in implementing and executing the Comissar Order, the Barbarossa Jurisdiction Order, the Commando Order, the Night and Fog Decree, the Hostages and Reprisals Orders, murder and ill-treatment of prisoners of war and of the civilian population in the occupied territories and their use in prohibited work, discrimination against and persecution and execution of Jewish people and other sections of the population by the *Wehrmacht* in co-operation with the *Einstazgruppen* and *Sonderkommandos*

---

crimes, the Tribunal lumped the two together for the most part, leaving behind it a precedent whose scope and meaning were uncertain.' See also Lippman, M. (1997), *Crimes Against Humanity*, 17 Boston College Third World Law Journal, p. 201. Making the following relevant statement: 'In sum, the Nuremberg Tribunal failed to provide a principled distinction between war crimes and crimes against humanity. . . . [C]rimes against humanity thus were viewed as extending the scope of the humanitarian law of war rather than as an autonomous source of rights which accrued to individuals in periods of peace as well in [sic] war.'

42 See Trials of War Criminals *supra* note 3, Chapter 2, Vol. XI.

43 See id.

44 See id. Vol. IV.

45 See id. Vol. V.

46 See id. Vol. XI at pp. 695-96.

47 See id. at p. 491.

48 See id. XI at pp. 695-96; See generally Lippman, M. (1991), *Nuremberg and American Justice*, 5 Notre Dame Journal of Law Ethics and Public Policy, p. 951; Lippman, M. (1991), *Nuremberg: Forty Five Years Later*, 7 Connecticut Journal of International Law, p. 1; Lippman, M. (1992), *The Other Nuremberg: American Prosecutions of Nazi War Criminals in Occupied Germany*, 3 Indiana International and Comparative Law Review, p. 1; Lippman, M. (1993), *The Nazi Doctors Trial and the International Prohibition on Medical Involvement In Torture*, 15 Loyola of Los Angeles International and Comparative Law Journal, p. 395.

of the SD, SIPO and the Secret Field Police and plunder and spoliation and the enforcement of the slave labour programme of the *Reich*.[49]

In relation to the sentences imposed on the defendants, although *Wilhelm von Leeb*, who was the main defendant was given a relatively lower sentence of three years imprisonment on the basis of his war crime and crime against humanity convictions, a revisiting of his convictions suggests that he was in fact guilty of only war crimes and not of both war crimes and crimes against humanity as convicted. This opinion can be explained in the following way. First, count 2 of the indictment, which was titled as follows 'war crimes and crimes against humanity: crimes against enemy belligerents and prisoners of war', was exclusively a war crimes charge.[50] This opinion is based on a literal reading of Article II (c) of Control Council Law no. 10 on crimes against humanity, which is applicable to this case. This is because Article II (c) demonstrates that crimes against humanity were not applicable to attacks against enemy belligerents and prisoners of war, as evidenced by the following stipulation:

> 'Crimes against Humanity. Atrocities and offenses, including but not limited to murder, extermination, enslavement, deportation, imprisonment, torture, rape, or other inhumane acts committed against any civilian population, or persecutions on political, racial or religious grounds whether or not in violation of the domestic laws of the country where perpetrated.'[51]

The use of the term 'civilian population' above, suggests that the acts, which constituted crimes against humanity, must be directed against non-combatants. In addition, in support of the view that crimes against humanity applies exclusively to atrocities committed against civilians is the following statement by *DeGuzman*:

> 'The "civilian population" requirement has been interpreted to include two elements: 1) the constituent acts must be directed against noncombatants and 2) a large number of victims must be targeted. Crimes against members of the armed forces of warring states or of rival armed groups within a state constitute war crimes. The laws of war, which have developed over the centuries, provide detailed rules governing permissible military conduct. Certain acts, which would constitute crimes against humanity if perpetrated against civilians, are actually

---

49 See Law-Reports of Trials of War Criminals, The United Nations War Crimes Commission, Vol. XII, London, HMSO, 1949, para. 46.

50 For count 2 see *supra* note 3, Chapter 2 Vol. X. pp. 32-35. Extracted from <http://realale.wcl.american.edu/etp/MilitaryTribunals/NMT/HighCommandCase.html> (last visited August 2004).

51 See Article II (c) of CCL No. 10.

> permissible in the context of military action. The most obvious examples are the widespread or systematic killing or imprisonment of members of the opposing forces. The inclusion of the "civilian" element distinguishes crimes against humanity from such permissible military conduct.'[52]

As is evident from the above, the inclusion of the term 'civilian population' in the definition of crimes against humanity means that this category of crimes cannot be extended to attacks against enemy belligerents and prisoners of war.

Second, in terms of count 3, which was labelled as 'war crimes and crimes against humanity: crimes against civilians', and which dealt with the persecution of Jewish people and others, there was no evidence to suggest that the defendant was involved in this crime. In this respect, the following statements are relevant:

> 'For the reasons above stated we find this defendant guilty under Count III of the Indictment for criminal responsibility in connection with the transmittal and application of the Barbarossa Jurisdiction Order. Under Control Council Law No. 10 it is provided that superior orders do not constitute a defence but may be considered in mitigation of an offence. We believe that there is much to be said for the defendant von Leeb by way of mitigation. He was not a friend or follower of the Nazi Party or its ideology. He was a soldier and engaged in a stupendous campaign with responsibility for hundreds of thousands of soldiers, and a large indigenous population spread over a vast area. It is not without significance that no criminal order has been introduced in evidence which bears his signature or the stamp of his approval.'[53]

And:

> 'This Tribunal does not hold field commanders guilty for a failure to properly appraise the fine distinctions of International Law, nor for failure to execute court-martial jurisdiction which had been taken away from them, but it does consider them criminally responsible for the transmission of an order that could, and from its terms would, be illegally applied where they have transmitted such an order

---

52 See DeGuzman, M.M., *The Road from Rome: The Developing Law of Crimes against Humanity.* See also *Prosecutor* v. *Blaskic*, Case No. IT-95-14-A, 29 July 2004, para. 740, (ICTY Appeals Chamber), concluding: 'Read together, Article 50 of Additional protocol I and Article 4A of the Third Geneva Convention establish that members of the armed forces, and members of the militias or volunteer corps forming part of such armed forces, cannot claim civilian status. Neither can members of organized resistance groups, provided that they are commanded by a person responsible for his subordinates, that they have a fixed distinctive sign recognizable at a distance, that they carry arms openly, and that they conduct their operations in accordance with the laws and customs of war....'.

53 See <http://www.ess.uwe.ac.uk/WCC/ghctrial8.htm > (last visited July 2004).

without proper safeguards as to its application. For that failure on their part they must accept criminal responsibility.'[54]

The above statements suggest that, by rejecting any allegation that the defendant possessed a discriminatory intent at the time of the commission of the crimes attributed to him and instead pinning his culpability on his activities as a military officer, the standards used in criminalizing the conduct of the accused were based on the laws or customs of war rather than on crimes against humanity. In other words, they were based on the fact that his crimes were fundamentally military crimes committed as part of his efforts to ensure military victory for Germany.

Furthermore, a comparison of the sentence imposed on *von Leeb* with that of other defendants who were convicted of persecution as a crime against humanity, demonstrates that a nexus existed between the defendants' motives and their sentences. For instance, *von Kuechler,* who was additionally guilty of persecuting Jewish people, was given a higher sentence of 20 years imprisonment.[55] The following statement constitutes evidence of his guilt:

> 'The evidence showed that the accused von Kuechler had directed the enforcement of a decision to execute 230 insane and diseased women inmates of an asylum within his area of command to the SD...His attitude towards the Jewish question is shown by an order which he issued as early as July, 1940. In this order he stated among other things:
>
> "2. I am also stressing the necessity of ensuring that every soldier of the Army, particularly every officer, refrains from criticizing the ethnical struggle being carried out in the GENERAL GOUVERNEMENT, for instance the treatment of the Polish minorities, of the Jews and of church matters. The final ethnical solution of the ethnical struggle which has been raging on the Eastern border for centuries calls for one-time harsh measures."
>
> "Certain units and departments of the Party and the State have been charged with the carrying out of this ethnical struggle in the East.
>
> "The soldiers must, therefore, keep aloof from these concerns of other units and departments. This implies that they must not interfere with those concerns by criticism either."
>
> It is particularly urgent to initiate immediately the instruction concerning these problems of those soldiers who have been recently transferred from the West to the East ; otherwise, they might become acquainted with rumours and false information concerning the meaning and the purpose of that struggle.'[56]

---

[54] See id.

[55] See id.

[56] See <http://www.ess.uwe.ac.uk/WCC/ghctrial5.htm#(n)> (last visited July 2004).

This demonstrates that *von Kuechler* possessed the requisite intent for persecution as a crime against humanity and that this intent had an influence on his sentence.

Finally, another defendant in the case, *von Roques*, who was similarly convicted for his role in persecuting Jewish people,[57] was given a relatively high sentence of twenty years imprisonment The following statement constitutes evidence of his guilt:

> 'Many documents showed that ill-treatment and persecution of the civilian population took place within the accused von Roques' area of command. Other documents showed the establishment of ghettoes for the Jew; requirements that they should wear the Star of David ; the prohibition of Jewish rites; confiscation of Jewish ritual articles, terror killings of suspects and partisan sympathisers; so-called mopping-up operations and turning over of Jews and Communists to the SD ...These documents ...left no doubt that the accused von Roques actively supported and participated in the activities of the SD within his area of command.'[58]

This corroborates the opinion expressed in relation to *von Kuechler, i.e.*, that possession of the requisite intent for persecution as a crime against humanity had an influence on penalties.

2.2.2.1.2 Hostage Case

In the Hostage case, twelve defendants were accused of committing various offences in Yugoslavia, Albania and Greece. They included Field Marshal *Wilhelm List*, who had commanded the Twelfth Army, which was responsible for the invasion and conquest of Yugoslavia and Greece, until October 1941. His successor, Lt. General *Wilhelm Kuntze* was also a defendant. Also tried were General *Lothar Rendulic*, commander of the Second Panzer Army in Yugoslavia during 1943-44 and Lt. General *Hermann Fortsch*, Chief of Staff to *List*, *Kuntze* and von *Weichs*. Field Marshal Maximilian *von Weichs*, supreme commander of German forces in this region 1944-45, although arraigned, was separated from the case before its conclusion due to illness.[59]

The basic charge against all the defendants was responsibility for the unwarranted slaying of many thousands of Yugoslav and Greek civilians. Many were killed pursuant to an order, originally promulgated by *von Weichs*, directing the execution of one- hundred civilian 'hostages' for every German soldier killed by the partisans. On other occasions, all the inhabitants of particular villages, near which partisan action had occurred, were slaughtered and the villages burned.

---

57 See *supra* note 53, Chapter 2.

58 See *supra* note 56, Chapter 2.

59 See Trials of War Criminals, Vol. XI, p. 757.

Several of the defendants who had served on the Russian front were charged with killing uniformed prisoners of war pursuant to the notorious German 'Commissar Order'.[60]

Furthermore, the Tribunal convicted the defendants on the basis of four counts, which were the following:

1. Unlawful killing of innocent civilians as measures of reprisals;
2. Wanton destruction of villages and towns;
3. Issuing and distributing illegal orders that caused unlawful killing, and
4. Torture, deportation to slave labour and systematic terrorization of inhabitants of occupied territories.

Although all four of the above counts were dealt with under the joint heading of war crimes and crimes against humanity,[61] only one of them can arguably be described as a typical crime against humanity, *i.e.*, count 4, which involved torture, deportation to slave labour and systematic terrorization of inhabitants of occupied territories.[62] Counts one to three, on the other hand, were essentially war crime counts.

The above opinion can be clarified in the following way. First, in terms of counts 1 – 3, the following statements by the Tribunal conclusively prove that the offences recognized under these counts were war crimes and not jointly war crimes and crimes against humanity:

> 'there must be some connection between the population from whom the hostages are taken and the crime committed. If the act was committed ... without the knowledge or approval of the population or public authorities, and which, therefore, neither the authorities or the population could have prevented, the basis for the taking of hostages, or the shooting of hostages already taken, does not exist. ... The number of hostages shot must not exceed in severity the offenses the shooting is designed to deter. Unless the foregoing requirements [not all of which are included in the material quoted] are met, the shooting of hostages is in contravention of international law and is a war crime in itself.'[63]

And:

> 'Between 9/1939 and 5/1945, all of the defendants unlawfully, willfully, and knowingly committed war crimes and rimes against humanity, as defined in Article

60 See Taylor, T. (1949), *The Nuremberg War Crimes Trials. International Conciliation*, No. 450, p. 321.

61 See Trials of War Criminals, Vol. XI, p. 764.

62 See Bing Bing Jia, N. *The Differing Concepts of War Crimes and Crimes against Humanity in International Criminal Law*, p. 262, writing that 'the additional finding against Rendulic on count 4, ...described a typical crime against humanity....'.

63 See *supra* note 17, Chapter 2.

> II of Control Council Law No. 10, in that they were principals in, accessories to, ordered, abetted, took a consenting part in, were connected with plans and enterprises involving, and were members of organizations or groups connected with, the plundering and looting of public and private property, the wanton destruction of cities, towns and villages, frequently together with the murder of the inhabitants thereof, and the commission of other acts of devastation not justified by military necessity, in the occupied territories of Norway, Greece, Yugoslavia, and Albania, by troops of the German armed forces under the command and jurisdiction of responsible to, and acting pursuant to orders issued, executed, and distributed by, the defendants herein. The defendants ordered troops under their command and jurisdiction to burn, destroy, and level to the ground entire villages and towns, and, on numerous occasions, to execute the inhabitants of such villages and towns. Such arbitrary, inhumane, and disproportionately harsh measures of reprisal dislocated hundreds of families, made thousands of peaceful non combatants homeless and destitute, and brought untold suffering, humiliation, misery, and death to vast numbers of innocent civilians.'[64]

The above statements highlight the fact that what the Tribunal was in fact criminalizing was not the commission of the atrocities *per se*, but the fact that the offences, as committed, did not comply with the laws and customs of war.[65] The use of words such as 'the number of hostages shot must not exceed in severity the offenses the shooting is designed to deter', 'other acts of devastation not justified by military necessity', and 'such arbitrary, inhumane, and disproportionately harsh measures of reprisal' constitute evidence of this opinion.

In addition, in respect to the above view-point, it should be recalled that the principles of military necessity and proportionality do not serve as a basis for attributing criminal responsibility for crimes against humanity, because under this category of international crimes, attacks against a civilian population are prohibited in all circumstances. This in effect means that counts 1 – 3 were not crimes against humanity as additionally criminalised by the Tribunal.

On the other hand, in relation to count 4, evidence that this count constituted crimes against humanity, and not both war crimes and crimes against humanity, is provided by the following statement:

> 'Between 9/1939 and 5/1945, all of the defendants unlawfully, willfully, and knowingly committed war crime and crimes against humanity, as defined in Article II of Control Council Law No. 10, in that they were principals in, accessories

[64] See id.

[65] See Bing Bing Jia, N., *The Differing Concepts of War Crimes and Crimes against Humanity in International Criminal Law*, p. 262, writing in relation to count 1 that 'General Dehner was convicted on count 1 and given a sentence of seven years' imprisonment, on the strength of mitigating factors, such as his attempt to apply correctly the rules of warfare in the face of superior, illegal orders.'

> to, ordered, abetted, took a consenting part in, were connected with plans and enterprises involving, and were members of organizations or groups connected with, the murder, torture, and systematic terrorization, imprisonment in concentration camps, arbitrary forced labor on fortifications and entrenchments to be used by the enemy, and deportation to slave labor, of the civilian populations of Greece, Yugoslavia, and Albania, by troops of the German Armed Forces under the command and jurisdiction of, responsible to, and acting pursuant to orders issued, executed, and distributed by, the defendants herein. Great numbers of citizens – "democrats, nationalists, Jews, and gypsies" – were arbitrarily seized and thrown into concentration camps where they were systematically beaten, tortured, ill-treated, and murdered, while other masses of the civilian population were forcibly conscripted for labor in the Reich and the occupied territories, transported in trains without adequate heat or sanitary conditions, and here, separated from family and friends, were made to labor long hours under inhumane conditions.'[66]

From the point of view of the distinction between both categories of international crimes, what is interesting about the above statement is the language that was not employed. Thus the fact that the language of military necessity and proportionality is missing from the above statement provides proof that this was essentially a crimes against humanity count. Also significant here was the category of victims *i.e.* 'democrats, nationalists, Jews, and gypsies'; all of these categories matched the political, religious and racial grounds requirement of crimes against humanity.

Finally, in light of the above clarification, it is possible to discern a pattern of higher penalties for crimes against humanity vis-à-vis war crimes. This opinion can be illustrated by comparing the penalties for General *Rendulic*, General *Felmy* and General *Dehner.* This is because General *Rendulic* was convicted on counts 1, 3 and 4 and sentenced to 20 years imprisonment, whilst Generals *Felmy*, who was convicted on counts 1 and 2, was sentenced to 15 years imprisonment, and General *Dhener*, who was convicted on count 1, was given a sentence of seven years imprisonment. It follows that the additional finding of crimes against humanity against General *Rendulic* in count four, which was *ipso facto* crimes against humanity and not simultaneously crimes against humanity and war crimes, clearly led to a much heavier sentence than the convictions of the other defendants.[67]

---

[66] See *supra* note 17, Chapter 2.

[67] In terms of the issue of whether or not the additional conviction of crimes against humanity in this case, led to a higher penalty, the following statement by Bing Bing Jia, N. appears to be contradictory: 'General Rendulic was convicted on counts 1, 3, and 4 and sentenced to 20 years imprisonment. General Felmy was convicted on counts 1 and 2 and sentenced to 15 years' imprisonment. General Dehner was convicted on count 1 and given a sentence of seven years' imprisonment, ... The additional finding against Rendulic on count 4, which described a typical crime against humanity, did not lead to a much heavier sentence'; *The Differing Concepts of War Crimes and Crimes against Humanity in International Criminal Law*, p. 262.

2.2.2.1.3 Einsatzgruppen Case

The facts of this case were based on the activities of the *Einsatzgruppen*, which was a unit of the SS whose general task was to insure the political security of the conquered territories in Russia, and, as part of this function, its members were directed to exterminate all Jewish people, Gypsies, government officials, communist party leaders and other so-called undesirable elements in their assigned territories. With the support of the army leaders, this program was faithfully carried out and resulted in the murder of at least a million Jews and other human beings during the first two years of the Russian campaign.[68]

Although the twenty-four defendants in this case were principally convicted and sentenced of war crimes and crimes against humanity for their various actions (the third count of membership in a criminal organization was merely a formality), a revisiting of the judgment, in the case, reveals a number of errors. This opinion can be demonstrated, for example, with the aid of the following statement by the Tribunal, which demonstrates that the offences committed by the defendants were crimes against humanity and not both war crimes and crimes against humanity:

> 'In short, the crimes of the Einsatzgruppen were not, fundamentally, military crimes at all. They were not committed in order to make military victory possible. On the contrary, military victory was sought in order to put the victors in a position where these crimes could be committed. These crimes were a war objective, not a military means.'[69]

The Tribunal seems to have drawn a line between war crimes and crimes against humanity, in so far as the motives of the defendants in this case were concerned. In other words, the fact that their crimes were not committed to ensure military victory but were instead committed to facilitate the policy of persecuting individuals belonging to targeted groups meant that they were essentially crimes against humanity and not war crimes. The error here, therefore, stems from the Tribunal's failure to translate this distinction into relative penalties for war crimes and crimes against humanity.

In addition, a second statement by the Tribunal, which had it been properly handled, would have provided clear evidence that crimes against humanity were more serious than war crimes and therefore should have attracted heavier sentences, is in the following:

> 'But will any defendant dare to suggest to us that the execution of the Jews in Russia would have stopped if Russian military resistance had collapsed? On the

[68] See Trials of War Criminals, Vol. IV, pp. 411-587. See also Carcano, A. (2002), *Sentencing and the Gravity of the Offence in International Criminal Law*, at p. 592, stating the facts of the case.

[69] See id. p. 382.

> contrary, the evidence is compelling that a German victory would have enormously widened the scope of operations of the Einsatzgruppen and the holocaust would have been even more staggering.'[70]

This can be used to support the opinion that crimes against humanity were more serious than war crimes and this opinion can be clarified in the following way. As is evident from the above, and in light of Article II(c) of CCL 10, which governs this case, war crimes can only be committed in times of war, whilst crimes against humanity can be perpetrated both in times of war and peace.

War crimes, owing to their limited jurisdiction, would result in a lower loss of life than crimes against humanity, which can be committed both in times of war and peace. Thus if country X, which is engaged in an armed conflict with country Y, commits atrocities against the people of country Y, this would be both a war crime and a crime against humanity (*e.g.*, variable I). However, where country X succeeds in defeating country Y thereby signalling the end of the conflict but nevertheless continues to perpetrate atrocities against the defenceless people of country Y, then this would constitute crimes against humanity only (*e.g.*, variable H). The difference in terms of gravity between war crimes and crimes against humanity would thus be the following: war crimes – I (crimes committed in times of war); whilst crimes against humanity – I (crimes committed in times of war) + H (crimes committed in times of peace). Clearly, based on the results of the above calculations, crimes against humanity would lead to higher casualty figures and, therefore, attract a heavier sentence.

Another way of demonstrating how judgmental errors affected the distinction between war crimes and crimes against humanity is by focusing on the rejection of the defence of superior orders vis-à-vis the offences committed by the accused. In this respect, the following statement is relevant:

> 'Having noted these admissions which, revealing as they are, serve merely to confirm what is abundantly clear from the documentary proof, we may turn to the third general proposition which a number of the defendants have urged on the Tribunal. That is the defense of superior orders. A third group of defendants admit that Einsatz units under their command did carry out mass executions of Jews, gypsies, and political officials, but seek to escape the burden of guilt by pleading that they carried out these executions under the compulsion of superior orders. To this group belong Ohlendorf, Naumann, Blume, Braune, and Ott. It should be noted at the very outset that the putting forward of this plea of superior orders cuts the ground from under the defenses which we have just been considering. If, as Ohlendorf and these other defendants tell us, Hitler did order the Einsatz units to execute all Jews and political officials, and if, in obedience to Hitler's order, such executions were carried, then there is less than nothing left of defenses such as lack of knowledge, or that the victims of the executions were all partisans. And

[70] See id.

> in fact, the documents make it clear beyond the slightest doubt where the truth lies – the order for the mass executions of Jews and political officials was given, and it was carried out, and there remains for consideration only the question whether the fact that these defendants acted pursuant to an order shall be held to better their position before this Tribunal in any way.'[71]

To the extent that the above statement rejects the defence of superior orders vis-à-vis acts of persecution against the Jewish people and others, it could have been employed as a basis for making a hierarchical distinction between war crimes and crimes against humanity in terms of gravity.

In support of the above opinion are the following sources. The first is Article 33 of the Rome Statute of the International Criminal Court, which utilizes the defence of superior orders to distinguish between war crimes and crimes against humanity and which stipulates the following:

> **'Article 33**
> Superior orders and prescription of law
> 1. The fact that a crime within the jurisdiction of the Court has been committed by a person pursuant to an order of a Government or of a superior, whether military or civilian, shall not relieve that person of criminal responsibility unless:
> a) The person was under a legal obligation to obey orders of the Government or the superior in question;
> b) The person did not know that the order was unlawful; and
> c) The order was not manifestly unlawful.
> 2. For the purposes of this article, orders to commit genocide or crimes against humanity are manifestly unlawful.'[72]

Article 33 allows the defence of superior orders in the case of war crimes, which are not manifestly unlawful, but rejects it in the case of crimes against humanity.[73]

---

[71] See id. pp. 375-376.

[72] See Article 33 of the Rome Statute of the International Criminal Court, Opened for Signature 17 July 1998, U.N. Diplomatic Conf. of Plenipotentiaries on the Establishment of an Int'l Crim. Ct., U.N. Doc. A/CONF.183/9 (1998) *reprinted in* 37 I.L.M. 999 (1998) [hereinafter ICC Statute].

[73] See Gaeta, P. (1999), *The Defence of Superior Orders: The Statute of the International Criminal Court versus Customary International Law,* 10 European Journal of International Law, p. 172, writing the following in connection with the implications of Article 33 of the Rome Statute vis-à-vis war crimes and crimes against humanity: 'To put it differently, the plea of superior orders is never a defence to a charge of genocide and crimes against humanity since it is a priori established that orders to commit these crimes are always manifestly unlawful. In contrast, superior orders may be successfully used as a complete defence in those situations where the charge is one of war crimes. Indeed, Article 33 allows for the possibility that orders to commit war crimes, as opposed to genocide and crimes against humanity, are not manifestly unlawful. If the requirements (a) and (b) are met, then whenever an order is not manifestly illegal, it can be urged as a complete defence'.

The second source is the following statement by *Frulli* on Article 33 of the Rome Statute, which suggests that by rejecting the defence of superior orders vis-à-vis crimes against humanity but upholding it in the case of war crimes, the defence of superior orders can be employed as a basis for making a hierarchical distinction between war crimes and crimes against humanity in terms of gravity:

> 'What is interesting here is the second paragraph [*i.e.* Article 33(2)], establishing that superior orders can never be accepted as a defence for the charges of genocide and crimes against humanity, whereas they can be considered as a valid ground to exclude responsibility in the case of war crimes...the fact that the rule of absolute liability for international crimes has been embodied in the ICC Statute only for genocide and crimes against humanity tips the scale in favour of a higher degree of gravity, in the common perception, of these two categories of crimes as compared to war crimes.[74]

Finally, in light of the above, it is possible to establish a pattern of higher penalties for crimes against humanity vis-à-vis war crimes in the context of the case. This can be demonstrated by a comparison of the sentences imposed on two of the defendants – *Strauch* and *Schulz*. The former received a sentence of death by hanging, whilst the latter was sentenced to ten years imprisonment. Both were convicted of war crimes and crimes against humanity. In relation to *Schulz*, the Tribunal made the following statements, which are indicative of the factors which it took into consideration whilst sentencing the accused:

> 'The fact that Schulz still regarded himself as commander of Einsatzkommando 5, even though he knew he intended to be absent while on the trip to Berlin, is established by the fact that on the actual date of his departure, 24 August, he ordered the Kommando to move on from Berdichev to Skvira, 100 kilometers east of Berdichev, which removal actually took place on 26 August. Schulz' explanation for this removal is a laudable one, if true. He says that he wanted to avoid that his Kommando should come in contact with Higher SS and Police Leader Jeckeln who was set on execution of all Jews, including women and children....'[75]

And:

> 'In this regard the Tribunal is forced to the conclusion that Schulz did not respond to the obligations imposed upon him not only by the international law but the concept of law itself, of which, as a long police official, he could not be ignorant. *In*

[74] See Frulli, M. (2001), *Are Crimes against Humanity More Serious than War Crimes?*

[75] See Trials of War Criminals, Vol. IV, p. 520.

> *spite of this, however, it can be said in his behalf that, confronted with an intolerable situation, he did attempt to do something about it.*'[76] [emphasis added]

To the extent that the above statements link the defendant's action, in trying to protect Jewish people, with the relatively low sentence imposed upon him, they indicate that the absence of a discriminatory intent, which is a prerequisite for the persecution category of crimes against humanity, was treated as a mitigating factor.

In terms of *Strauch*, the Tribunal made the following statement, which is indicative of the factors that it took into consideration whilst sentencing the accused:

> 'By his own words Strauch was an unrelenting and merciless oppressor of the Jews and displayed considerable indignation when anyone sought to defend them. In a letter dated 25 July 1943, he related a plan whereby 5,000 Jews of the Minsk Ghetto were to be "resettled". The Jews, however, learned that the resettlement meant execution and Strauch bitterly attacked those responsible for this "treachery". He said, "We had no choice but to herd the Jews together by force." On 20 July 1943 he wrote a letter narrating how he had subjected 70 Jews to special treatment and expressing his resentment because complaint had arisen from the fact that he had had the gold fillings removed from the mouths of these Jews before they were killed... He admitted that, to his own knowledge, a Jew had to be killed just because he was a Jew.'[77]

To the extent that the above statement links the action of the defendant in seeking to oppress Jewish people with the relatively high sentence imposed upon him, it indicates that the presence of a discriminatory intent, which is a prerequisite for the persecution category of crimes against humanity, was treated as an aggravating factor.

2.2.2.1.4 RuSHA Case

The defendants in this case were leading officials of *RuSHA* or of three other offices or agencies of the SS. These four agencies, all branches of the Supreme Command of the SS, were the 'Staff Main Office of the Reich Commissioner for the Strengthening of Germanism' (*Stabshauptamt des Reichskommissars für die Festigung des deutschen Volkstums*, abbreviated RKFDV), 'Office for Repatriation of Ethnic Germans' (*Volksdeutsche Mittelstelle*, abbreviated VoMi), a subdivision of the RKFDV, the 'Race and Settlement Main Office' (RuSHA), and the '*Lebensborn*', which was both a private association (*Verein*) and a department of

---

76 See id. p. 521.

77 See id. pp. 564-565.

the Personal Staff of Heinrich Himmler and was used during the war for the selection for Germanization of 'racially valuable children' of foreign nationals.[78]

Furthermore, the defendants were charged with war crimes and crimes against humanity for atrocities committed in their functions as officials of the four agencies mentioned above. However, the following statement by the Tribunal provide evidence of the confusion of these charges:

'The indictment in this case is framed in three counts. The first and second counts charge the commission of crimes against humanity and war crimes, respectively. Count one alleges, in substance, that between September 1939 and April 1945, all of the defendants

> 'were principals in, accessories to, ordered, abetted, took a consenting part in, were connected with plans and enterprises involving, and were members of organizations or groups connected with atrocities and offenses, including but not limited to murder, extermination, enslavement, deportation, imprisonment, torture, persecutions on political, racial, and religious grounds, and other inhumane and criminal acts against civilian populations, including German civilians and nationals of other countries, and against prisoners of war.'

Count one further alleges that these:

> 'Acts, conduct, plans and enterprises were carried out as part of a systematic program of genocide, aimed at the destruction of foreign nations and ethnic groups, in part by elimination and suppression of national characteristics. The object of this program was to strengthen the German nation and the so-called 'Aryan' race at the expense of such other nations and groups by imposing Nazi and German characteristics upon individuals selected therefrom and by the extermination of 'undesirable' racial elements. This program was carried out in part by
> a) Kidnaping children.
> b) Abortions.
> c) Taking away infants of Eastern workers.
> d) Punishment for sexual intercourse with Germans.
> e) Preventing marriages and hampering reproduction of enemy nationals.
> f) Evacuating enemy populations from their native lands by force.
> g) Forced Germanization of enemy nationals.
> h) Plunder.
> i) Slave labor.
> j) Persecution of Jews.'

[78] See Trials of War Criminals, Vol. V, p. 599.

Count two, which charges the defendants with war crimes, alleges that all the defendants between September 1939 and April 1945:

> 'Were principals in, accessories to, ordered, abetted, took a consenting part in, were connected with plans and enterprises involving, and were members of organizations or groups connected with atrocities and offenses against persons and property constituting violations of the laws or customs of war, including but not limited to plunder of public property, murder, extermination, enslavement, deportation, imprisonment, torture, and ill treatment of and other inhumane acts against thousands of persons. These crimes embraced, but were not limited to "the ten specifications made in count one," and were committed against prisoners of war and civilian populations of countries and territories under the belligerent occupation of, or otherwise controlled by, Germany.'[79]

A comparison of counts 1 and 2, on crimes against humanity and war crimes respectively, demonstrates that the defendants were convicted and sentenced primarily for war crimes and crimes against humanity for many features of the Nazi 'racial' program. However, to the extent that the Tribunal treated these acts as both war crimes and crimes against humanity, the judgment in this case failed to recognize the substantive differences between war crimes and crimes against humanity as emphasized in the other cases above.

Finally, what is also interesting about the case was the unusually harsh penalties imposed upon the defendants. This opinion is evident in the following dissenting opinion of Judge *O'Connell* vis-à-vis the penalties imposed on *Greifelt, Creutz, Lorenz, Brueckner, Hofmann* and *Hildebrandt*:

> 'It is my reasoned judgment, based upon nineteen years of judicial service, related in large measure to imposition of prison sentences, that in respect to each of the above-named defendants, the sentence imposed is too extreme in fixed duration of time when consideration is given to the character and scope of the duties each performed... As applicable to the defendants Greifelt, Creutz, Lorenz, Brueckner, Hofmann, and Hildebrandt, the sentences which I believe should be decreed and in respect to which I record my judgment, are as follows:
> 1) The defendant, Greifelt, twenty (20) years,
> 2) The defendant, Creutz, ten (10) years,
> 3) The defendant, Lorenz, fifteen (15) years,
> 4) The defendant, Brueckner, ten (10) years,
> 5) The defendant, Hofmann, fifteen (15) years,
> 6) The defendant, Hildebrandt, fifteen (15) years,....'[80]

---

[79] See id. pp. 88-89.

[80] See id. pp. 168-169.

A linking of the unusually harsh penalties of the defendants to the argument that they were in fact guilty of only crimes against humanity and not of both war crimes and crimes against humanity adds weights to the opinion that crimes against humanity attracted higher penalties than war crimes.

2.2.2.2 The Rudimentary State of International Human Rights Law

The fact that international human rights law was still in its infancy at the time of the Nuremberg Trials in August 1945 can also be considered as an additional factor, which affected the ability of World War II Tribunals to accurately translate the different interests protected by war crimes and crimes against humanity into relative penalties for both categories of international crimes.[81]

Although the Universal Declaration of Human Rights (UDHR), which was adopted in 1948 and was therefore relevant to the World War trials, had provisions applicable to sentencing,[82] the fact that there is no legal obligation for a nation to enact laws based on the UDHR, meant that its provisions had no legally binding effect and therefore that the World War II tribunals did not have to adhere to them.[83] Thus Article 10 of the UDHR, which is one of its relevant provisions on sentencing since it stipulates that '[e]veryone is entitled in full equality to a fair and public hearing by an independent and impartial tribunal, in the determination of his rights and obligations and of any criminal charge against him',[84] was not legally binding. Had it been, it would have perhaps encouraged those Tribunals to specify the reasons for the sentences they imposed for war crimes and crimes against humanity, thereby ultimately ensuring a more accurate reflection of the different interests protected by them from the view-point of the imposition of relative penalties.

---

[81] See Schabas, W.A. (1997), *Sentencing by International Tribunals: A Human Rights Approach.* On the history of human rights protection at the international level see Robertson, A.H. (1972), *Human Rights in the World,* Manchester: Manchester University Press (observing that human rights protection at the international level began in the nineteenth century).

[82] See for example Article 11 of the Universal Declaration.

[83] Although it is not a legally binding document per se, since it was adopted by a resolution of the General Assembly, the principles contained there in are now considered to legally binding on States either as customary international law, general principles of law, or as fundamental principles of humanity. In its dictum in the case concerning the hostages in Tehran, the International Court of Justice clearly invoked "the fundamental principles enunciated in the ... Declaration" as being legally binding on Iran. See *United States Diplomatic and Consular Staff in Tehran (United States of America* v. *Iran)*, Judgment, ICJ Reports 1980, p. 42, para. 91.

[84] See Article 10 of the Universal Declaration.

Furthermore, it is also interesting to note the adoption of legally binding international human rights law treaties, after the World War II trials, specifying internationally recognized standards regarding the rights of the accused, such as the European Convention on Human Rights (1950) (ECHR)[85] and the International Covenant on Civil and Political Rights (1966) (ICCPR).[86] This sequence of events also meant that there were no incentives for those Tribunals to ensure a more accurate reflection of the different interests protected by war crimes and crimes against humanity from the perspective of the imposition of relative penalties.

Finally, although these treaties were adopted after the World War II trials, they will nevertheless be discussed here for illustrative purposes. It follows that one provision, which is common to both treaties and which is relevant in terms of sentencing, is the prohibition on double jeopardy. This prohibition is recognized under Article 14(7) of the ICCPR and Article 4 of Protocol 7 to the ECHR.[87] One of its main aims is to prevent a person from being tried or punished more than once for the same crime. Thus, Article 14(7) of the ICCPR stipulates the following:

> 'No one shall be liable to be tried or punished again for an offence for which he has already been finally convicted or acquitted in accordance with the law and penal procedure of each country.'[88]

Equally Article 4 of Protocol 7 to the European Convention states that:

> '1. No one shall be liable to be tried or punished again in criminal proceedings under the jurisdiction of the same State for an offence for which he has already been finally acquitted or convicted in accordance with the law and penal procedure of the State.
>
> 2. The provisions of the preceding paragraph shall not prevent the re-opening of the case in accordance with the law and penal procedure of the State concerned, if there is evidence of new or newly discovered facts, or if there has been a fundamental defect in the previous proceedings, which could affect the outcome of the case.
>
> 3. No derogation from this Article shall be made under Article 15 of the Convention.'[89]

---

85 See European Convention on Human Rights (1950) (ECHR).

86 See ICCPR.

87 See Article 14(7) of the ICCPR and Article 4 of Protocol 7 to the ECHR.

88 See id.

89 See id.

The juxtaposition of crimes against humanity and war crimes at the sentencing stage may, in retrospect, have violated the principle of double jeopardy.[90]

2.3 Conclusion

The main conclusions that can be drawn from the above examination are the following. First, war crimes and crimes against humanity, as codified under the statutes of the World War II Tribunals, clearly protected different interests. Second, the different interests protected by both categories of international crimes could have been used as a basis for making a hierarchical distinction between them for the purpose of sentencing. And, third, it was the lackadaisical attitude of the WWII Tribunals, which constituted the main obstacle towards the imposition of relative penalties for war crimes and crimes against humanity. It follows that the criminalizing of acts of persecution against Jewish people as war crimes had no legal basis. In fact, such an approach, although it did not, could have led to the ridiculous situation where atrocities against Jewish people could have been legalized if they met with the war crime principles of necessity and proportionality. Similarly, the branding of atrocities against military personnel as crimes against humanity made no sense, because the relevant statutory provisions on crimes against humanity limited this category of crimes to civilian victims so as to separate them from war crimes. Finally, in light of the above analysis, there is no doubt that had the World War II Tribunals adopted a more stricter approach to the matching of the atrocities committed with the relevant international crimes, a clear pattern of higher penalties for crimes against humanity vis-à-vis war crimes would have emerged.

90 See generally Olusanya, O. (2004), *Double Jeopardy Without Parameters: Re-characterization in International Criminal Law.*

CHAPTER 3

Impediments to the Imposition of Relative Penalties for War Crimes and Crimes against Humanity under the ICTY

3.1 Introduction

After a half-century of inaction following the World II trials,[1] a great deal of progress is currently being made in relation to the development of the law on war crimes and crimes against humanity. Much of the credit has been given to the ICTY owing to its statutory and case law on both categories of international crimes.[2] In addition, complementing the ICTY's role in clarifying the law on war crimes and crimes against humanity are other notable institutions such as the *ad hoc* tribunal for Rwanda,[3] the International Criminal Court,[4] 'hybrid' or 'internationalised' processes such as the Special Court for Sierra Leone[5] and national criminal justice systems.[6]

This section argues that, in spite of the mushrooming of international criminal law enforcement institutions and the relatively advanced state of the law on war crimes and crimes against humanity, the jurisprudence of the World War II Tribunals still constitutes the backbone of international criminal law today and therefore still has an impact upon it, whether positive or negative.

In relation to the imposition of relative penalties for war crimes and crimes against humanity under the ICTY, the assumption is that the overly relaxed attitude of the World War II Tribunals to this issue, as demonstrated by the previous chapter, has had a negative effect on this process today. In other words, the jurisprudence of World War II Tribunals on the imposition of penalties for both categories of international crimes has sent mixed signals to the judges of the ICTY, and these signals have led to the birth of three schools of thought which are the following: the same interest approach, the widespread and systematic attacks v. isolated acts approach and the persecution-type v. murder-type approach.

Furthermore, this chapter thoroughly examines each of the schools of thought on the imposition of relative penalties for war crimes and crimes against humanity under the ICTY and points out their limitations. This approach will ultimately be instrumental in building a clear picture of what is currently wrong with the ICTY's system of sentencing for war crimes and

---

1 See Ferencz, B.B. (1999), *Getting Aggressive about Preventing Aggression,* The Brown Journal of World Affairs.

2 This is partly because of the fact that unlike the ICTR, most of the defendants under the ICTY have been prosecuted for war crimes and crimes against humanity.

3 For Rwanda, see the Statute of the International Criminal Tribunal for Rwanda.

4 See Rome Statute of the International Criminal Court.

5 See S.C. Res. 1315 (2000), 14 August 2000.

6 See *Regina* v. *Bartle and the Commissioner of Police for the Metropolis and Others* Ex Parte *Pinochet*; *Regina* v. *Evans and Another and the Commissioner of Police for the Metropolis and Others* Ex Parte *Pinochet* (On Appeal from a Divisional Court of the Queen's Bench Division) on 24 March 1999.

crimes against humanity and how an appropriate solution can be devised. Whilst the side goals of this chapter are the following:

- to analyse the development of the substantive law on war crimes and crimes against humanity under the ICTY;
- to draw attention to the continuity of judicial practices under the ICTY, which are incompatible with internationally accepted standards of sentencing and prosecution of war criminals;
- to utilise the activities of the ICTY as a basis for globalising the problem of sentencing for war crimes and crimes against humanity; and
- to memorialise the atrocities committed in the former Yugoslavia.

Finally, the conclusion is based on the results of the analysis of the three schools of thought on the imposition of relative penalties for war crimes and crimes against humanity under the ICTY.

3.2 The International Criminal Tribunal for the Former Yugoslavia (ICTY)

A prerequisite for understanding the significance of the issue of penalties for war crimes and crimes against humanity under the ICTY is the purpose for which the Tribunal was established.[7] In this respect, it should be recalled that the ICTY was set up to achieve the following goals:[8]

1. to do justice;[9]
2. to deter further crimes;[10] and
3. to contribute to the restoration[11] and maintenance of peace.[12]

---

7 See Tomuschat, C. (1994), *International Criminal Prosecution: The Precedent of Nuremberg Confirmed*, CLF Vol.5.

8 See Scharf M.P. (2000), *The Tools for Enforcing International Criminal Justice in the New Millennium: Lessons from the Yugoslavia Tribunal*, 49 DePaul Law Review, p. 925.

9 See generally Hirsch, A. von (1976), *Doing Justice: The Choice of Punishments: Report of the Committee for the Study of Incarceration*, New York: Hill and Wang.

10 See id.

11 For literature on restorative justice See Aukerman, M.J. (2002), *Extraordinary Evil, Ordinary Crime: A Framework for Understanding Transitional Justice*, 15 Harvard Human Rights Journal, p. 39, at pp. 77-78.

12 See Statement of UN Under-Secretary for Legal Affairs Carl-Aug. Fleischhauer, cited in Bruin, G. de (1993), *Yugoslavia: War Crimes Tribunal Inaugurated in The Hague*, Inter Press Service, 17 November 1993, available at 1993 WL 2532943. See also Sharp, W.G. (1999), *The International Criminal Tribunal for the Former Yugoslavia: Defining Offenses*, 23 Maryland Journal of International Law and Trade, p. 15, at pp. 20-26; Morris, V. and Scharf, M.P. (1995), *An Insiders Guide to the International Criminal Tribunal for the Former Yugoslavia*, Vols. I and II, New York: Transnational Publishers.

It is therefore within the background of the tripartite objectives of the ICTY that the following subsections examine the issue of sentencing for crimes against humanity and war crimes. In other words, justice, deterrence of future atrocities and restoration and maintenance of peace can only be achieved where there is a credible method of imposing penalties for war crimes and crimes against humanity. One way of illustrating the above opinion is through the concept of deterrence. Deterrence is based on the premise that it is possible to prevent atrocities by making it clear to the offender and others that they will be appropriately punished if they behave in like fashion.[13] It is, therefore, essential for the purpose of deterring future atrocities that war crimes and crimes against humanity attract appropriate levels of punishment, otherwise a wrong signal may be given to those who might be tempted to organise or commit them.[14] A similar position was, for example, held albeit in relation to domestic offences, in the Australian case of *DPP (Cth)* v. *El Koran,* which involved the importation of a trafficable quantity of heroin by an elderly man from Lebanon, who was funded and instructed by an apparently unknown person; the Court of Criminal Appeal in that case, made the following relevant statement:

> '[The trial judge] observed in this case that it was most unlikely that this elderly, frail and sick man would ever be tempted to offend again. But that leaves another audience to be addressed.... It is those in Lebanon, or elsewhere outside Australia, who might be tempted to organise or commit this type of offence. To them it is necessary to send the message of general deterrence. To the extent that his Honour felt unable to consider that matter, when he should have, the exercise of his sentencing discretion miscarried.'[15]

Finally, prior to delving into the issue of the imposition of penalties for war crimes and crimes against humanity under the ICTY, the next section examines the substantive law on both categories of crimes in the context of the Statute of the Tribunal. This approach is due to the fact that it is impossible to discuss the imposition of penalties for war crimes and crimes against humanity in the context of the ICTY without a prior knowledge of these crimes, as codified under its Statute.

---

13 See Fletcher, G.P. (1978), *Rethinking Criminal Law,* Boston: Little, Brown, p. 414.

14 See Danner, A.M. (2001), *Constructing a Hierarchy of Crimes in International Criminal Law,* note 111.

15 See *DPP (Cth)* v. *El Karhani* (1990) 21 NSWLR 370 at p. 378 per Kirby P, Campbell and Newman JJ. For criticism of deterrence see Zimring, E. and Hawkins, G. (1973), *Deterrence: The Legal Threat in Crime Control,* Chicago: University of Chicago Press, at pp. 189-190.

3.2.1 War Crimes and Crimes against Humanity as Codified under the Statute of the ICTY

This section identifies the main similarities and differences between war crimes and crimes against humanity under the ICTY Statute. This will in turn facilitate an understanding of the various sentencing approaches of the ICTY vis-à-vis both categories of international crimes in subsequent sections.

In terms of similarities, the main similarities between war crimes and crimes against humanity as codified under the ICTY Statute are the following. First, crimes against humanity and war crimes contain an identical list of offences such as murder, rape, deportation and imprisonment. This opinion is evident in the following statement by the ICTY in the *Kupreskic* case:

> 'Unlike provisions of national criminal codes or, in common-law countries, rules of criminal law crystallised in the relevant case-law or found in statutory enactments, each Article of the Statute does not confine itself to indicating a single category of well-defined acts such as murder, voluntary or involuntary manslaughter, theft, etc. Instead the Articles embrace broad clusters of offences sharing certain *general* legal ingredients... In addition, under the Statute of the International Tribunal, some provisions have such a broad scope that they may overlap...For instance, murder, torture or rape of enemy civilians normally constitute war crimes; however, if these acts are part of a widespread or systematic practice, they may also be defined as crimes against humanity. Plainly, Articles 3 and 5 have a different scope, which, however, may sometimes coincide or overlap.'[16]

The above statement recognizes the extent of overlap between war crimes and crimes against humanity offences under the ICTY Statute. This overlap, as is demonstrated in subsection 3.2.2.1 of the present chapter, has had an influence on the imposition of penalties for both categories of international crimes.

A second similarity is the fact that the ICTY Statute criminalizes offences as crimes against humanity only when they are 'committed in armed conflict, whether international or internal in character.'[17] This nexus to an armed

---

[16] See *Kupreskic* case, *supra* note 5, Chapter 1, paras. 697-698.

[17] See Cassese, A.(2003), *International Criminal Law*, New York: Oxford University Press, p. 216, note 3. Writing: 'In *Jelisic* (Appeal) the ICTY Appeals Chamber discussed the relations between murder as a war crime and as a crime against humanity as well as between cruel treatment as a war crime and 'inhumane acts' as a crime against humanity. It held that each of the relevant provisions of the ICTY Statute required an element not demanded by the other (war crimes under Article 3 of the ICTY Statute, requires 'a close link between the acts of the accused and the armed conflict'; according to the Court, this element was not required by Article 5 of the Statute, on crimes against humanity; in contrast, Article 5, on crimes against humanity, requires 'proof that the act occurred as part of a widespread or

conflict, as will be demonstrated in the present chapter, has had a general impact on the imposition of penalties for both categories of international crimes.

A third similarity is that under the ICTY Statute, unlike for example the ICTR Statute, crimes against humanity do not expressly have to be committed as part of a widespread or systematic attack against any civilian population.[18] They, therefore, appear to be applicable to all sorts of situations of attack, *i.e.*, isolated, widespread, systematic or random attacks, just as is the case with war crimes.[19] The lack of an expressed inclusion of the widespread or systematic elements under Article 5 of the ICTY Statute on crimes against humanity, as will be demonstrated in subsection 3.2.2.3, has had a significant effect on the imposition of penalties for both categories of international crimes.

Finally, in terms of differences, perhaps the only undisputed difference between crimes against humanity and war crimes under the ICTY Statute is the fact that crimes against humanity are codified as composing of two categories – the 'murder-type' and the 'persecution-type.'[20] The acts included under both the former and the latter category are essentially the same and consist of murder, extermination, enslavement, deportation, imprisonment, torture, rape and 'other inhumane acts'. What however distinguishes the 'persecution-type' from the 'murder-type' of crimes against humanity is that the underlying offences of murder, extermination, enslavement, deportation, imprisonment, torture or rape must be committed on political, racial, or religious grounds, *i.e.*, with a persecutory intent.[21] This dichotomization of crimes against humanity,

---

systematic attack against a civilian population, an element not required by Article 3...'. A Trial Chamber upheld this view in *Kvocka and others ...It is submitted, with respect, that this interpretation of the ICTY Statute is wrong, for under both provisions a close link with an internal or international armed conflict is required.'* [emphasis added] See also Olusanya, O. (2004), *Double Jeopardy Without Parameters: Re-characterization in International Criminal Law*, pp. 105-110.

18 See Cassese, A. *Crimes against Humanity*. In: Cassese, A. *et al.* (2002), *Rome Statute of the International Criminal Court: Commentary*, New York: Oxford University Press, Vol. 1 p. 353. Writing: 'Although no express reference is made in the ICTY Statute to such a requirement, the case law of the both the ICTY and ICTR has nevertheless specified that in order to comprise crimes against humanity, the acts in question must form part of widespread or systematic criminal conduct'. See however Olusanya id., pp. 111-114.

19 See Olusanya id., pp. 111-114.

20 See Danner, A.M. (2001), *Constructing a Hierarchy of Crimes in International Criminal Law*. See also United Nations War Crimes Commission (1948), *History of the United Nations War Crimes Commission and the Development of the Laws of War*; see Fenrick, W.J. (1999), *Should Crimes Against Humanity Replace War Crimes?*

21 See Danner, id; Kupreskic, *supra* note 5, Chapter 1, para. 607. Stating: 'Although the *actus reus* of persecution may be identical to other crimes against humanity, what distinguishes the crime of persecution is that it is committed on discriminatory grounds. The Trial Chamber therefore accepts the submission of the Prosecution that "[p]ersecution, which can be used to charge the conduct of ethnic cleansing on discriminatory grounds is a serious crime in and of itself and describes conduct worthy of censure above and apart from non-discriminatory killings envisioned by Article 5".'

as will be explained in subsection 3.2.2.5, has had an important effect on the imposition of penalties for both categories of international crimes.

3.2.2 The Sentencing Approaches of the ICTY to War Crimes and Crimes against Humanity

The following subsections identify and examine three schools of thought on the imposition of penalties for war crimes and crimes against humanity under the ICTY. They are the following: the same interest approach, the widespread and systematic attacks v. isolated acts approach and the persecution-type v. murder-type approach.

3.2.2.1 The Same Interest Approach

The same interest approach is based on the assumption that offences such as murder, torture and rape under national law are equal to their international criminal law counterparts.[22] This approach draws strength from jurisprudence of the World War II Tribunals, Article 24 of the ICTY Statute[23] and Rule 101[24] of its rules of procedure. However, since Chapter 2 has already covered the jurisprudence of the World War II Tribunals, only the latter sources will be examined here.

It follows that Article 24 stipulates:

> **'Penalties**
> 1. The penalty imposed by the Trial Chamber shall be limited to imprisonment. In determining the terms of imprisonment, the Trial Chambers shall have recourse to the general practice regarding prison sentences in the courts of the former Yugoslavia.
> 2. In imposing the sentences, the Trial Chambers should take into account such factors as the gravity of the offence and the individual circumstances of the convicted person.
> 3. In addition to imprisonment, the Trial Chambers may order the return of any property and proceeds acquired by criminal conduct, including by means of duress, to their rightful owners.'[25]

[22] See Ambos, K. and Wirth, S. (2002), *The Current Law of Crimes Against Humanity, An Analysis of UNTAET Regulation 15/2000*, 13 Criminal Law Forum No. 1, 2002, p. 47. Equating murder under national law with murder under International Criminal Law, by stating: 'Within the international law of murder (and generally in international criminal law) developed by the *ad hoc* Tribunals, murder has been classified according to the common law conception of a crime based on a core criteria of *actus reus* and *mens rea*.'

[23] See Article 24 ICTY Statute.

[24] See Rule 101 Rules of Procedure of the ICTY.

[25] See Article 24 ICTY Statute.

The above provision has been interpreted as opening the way for extending sentences to offences such as murder, rape, torture, etc., under the law of the former Yugoslavia to murder, rape, torture, etc, under the ICTY's subject matter jurisdiction.[26]

The latter provision, *i.e.* Rule 101 states:

> **'Penalties**
> (A) A convicted person may be sentenced to imprisonment for a term up to and including the remainder of the convicted person's life.
> (B) In determining the sentence, the Trial Chamber shall take into account the factors mentioned in Article 24, paragraph 2, of the Statute, as well as such factors as:
> (i) any aggravating circumstances;
> (ii) any mitigating circumstances including the substantial cooperation with the Prosecutor by the convicted person before or after conviction;
> (iii) the general practice regarding prison sentences in the courts of the former Yugoslavia;
> (iv) the extent to which any penalty imposed by a court of any State on the convicted person for the same act has already been served, as referred to in Article 10, paragraph 3, of the Statute.
> (C) Credit shall be given to the convicted person for the period, if any, during which the convicted person was detained in custody pending surrender to the Tribunal or pending trial or appeal.'[27]

To the extent that section (B) of the above provision refers to Article 24, it equally appears to suggest that offences such as murder, rape, torture, etc., under the law of the former Yugoslavia should be awarded the same sentences as murder, rape, torture, etc., under the ICTY's subject matter jurisdiction.

---

[26] See Separate Opinion of Judge Robinson, *Prosecutor* v. *Tadic*, Case No. IT-94-1, 11 November 1999, (ICTY Appeals Chamber). Also available at <http://www.un.org/icty/tadic/trialc2/judgement/tad-tsojrob991111e.htm> (last visited June 2004). Writing: 'Article 24, paragraph 2, merely mandates the Trial Chamber to take into account the gravity of the offence as a factor in determining sentence. However, the point is that nowhere does the Statute, either in express or implied terms, grade the four categories of crimes that fall within the Tribunal's jurisdiction according to their gravity. For sentencing purposes, the relevant comparison is not between the four categories of crimes on the basis of their classification or nomenclature; rather, the comparison should be between the specific acts that constitute the specific crimes....'

[27] See Rule 101 Rules of Procedure of the ICTY.

Finally, the next subsections examine the same interest approach in greater detail in connection with both ICTY cases and the statutory laws of countries, which have embraced this approach. The ICTY cases which will be examined include the *Krnojelac* case,[28] the *Tadic* case,[29] the *Erdemovic* case,[30] the *Vasiljevic* case,[31] the *Mladen Naletilic* and *Vinko Martinovic* cases[32] and the *Blaskic* case,[33] whilst the countries which will be analysed are New Zealand, Canada, the United Kingdom, Australia, Finland and Holland.[34]

3.2.2.1.1 Prosecutor v. *Erdemovic (Separate and Dissenting Opinion of Judge Li)*

The facts of this case evolved out of the breach of an agreement between the United Nations and Serbian forces operating in the Republic of Bosnia and Herzegovina[35] and can be summarized in the following way. On the 16th of April 1993, the Security Council of the United Nations, acting pursuant to Chapter VII of its Charter, adopted Resolution 819 in which it demanded that all parties to the conflict in the Republic of Bosnia and Herzegovina treat Srebrenica and its surroundings as a 'safe area', which was to be free from any armed attack or any other hostile act.[36] The Serbs, however, ignored this demand and perpetrated attacks against Muslims in the Srebrenica enclave.[37]

These attacks led to the fall of the Srebrenica enclave and triggered the flight of thousands of Muslim civilians towards various locations. Some sought refuge in the United Nations base at Potocari, whilst others fled across the woods towards Tuzla, an area under the control of the Bosnian government. In response, the Serb police and army sought to capture the escapees and to execute them. The accused *Drazen Erdemovic* was one of the soldiers involved in these executions.[38]

In relation to his role in these executions, the accused was convicted initially for crimes against humanity and sentenced to ten years imprisonment. However, on appeal, his conviction was changed to that of war crimes and his sentence was commuted to five years imprisonment.[39] This commutation led to

---

[28] See *Prosecutor* v. *Milroad Krnojelac*, Case No: IT-97-25, 15 March 2002, (ICTY Trial Chamber).

[29] See Separate Opinion of Judge Robinson, *supra* note 26, Chapter 3.

[30] See Separate and Dissenting Opinion of Judge Li, *Prosecutor* v. *Erdemovic, supra* note 28, Chapter 1.

[31] See *Prosecutor* v. *Vasiljevic*, Case No. IT-98-32, 29 November 2002, (ICTY Trial Chamber).

[32] See *Prosecutor* v. *Mladen Naletilic et al.*, Case No. IT-98-34-T, 31 March 2003, (ICTY Trial Chamber).

[33] See *Prosecutor* v. *Blaskic*, Case No. IT-95-14-A, 29 July 2004, (ICTY Appeals Chamber).

[34] See *infra*.

[35] For the facts of the case see generally *Prosecutor* v. *Erdemovic*, 29 November 1996, (ICTY Trial Chamber).

[36] See id.

[37] See id.

[38] See id.

[39] Compare sentences imposed in judgment of 29 November 1996 *id.* with *Prosecutor* v. *Erdemovic*, 5 March 1998, (ICTY Trial Chamber).

intense debates, which later spread like wildfire towards other ICTY cases.[40] The central issue of the debates was essentially whether crimes against humanity are a more serious category of international crimes than war crimes and, therefore, owing to this factor, whether they should receive a higher sentence than the latter category of international crimes.

The present section is concerned with the opinion of Judge *Li* on the issue of higher penalties for crimes against humanity vis-à-vis war crimes. This is because Judge *Li,* in his separate and dissenting opinion in the *Erdemovic* case, endorsed the same interest approach, when he made the following statement:

> 'With respect to these arguments, I submit, in the first place, that the gravity of a criminal act, and consequently the seriousness of its punishment, are determined by the intrinsic nature of the act itself and not by its classification under one category or another. Take the present case: the Appellant killed seventy to one hundred innocent Muslim civilians. Whether his criminal act is classified under crimes against humanity or war crimes, the harm done to individuals and society is exactly the same, neither an iota more nor less.'[41]

The above statement demonstrates that the same interest approach primarily relies on the elements of the underlying offences of crimes against humanity and war crimes, rather than on the actual crimes themselves. Thus it does not matter whether murder, rape, or torture is labelled as crimes against humanity or as war crimes; what matters is the fact that murder, rape, or torture has been committed.[42]

However, the main weakness of this approach is that it obscures distinctions between the respective criminal intentions and motives for war crime and crime against humanity offences.[43] This opinion is, for example, evident in the following statement by *Bing Bing Jia,* which draws attention to the crimes *ipso facto* committed in the former Yugoslavia:

> 'Because the dividing line between the warring parties in the territory of Bosnia and Herzegovina was ethnicity, particularly after the formal withdrawal of the Yugoslav Army in May 1992, the conflict was so permeated with ethnic differences

40 The rationale of Judge Li in the *Erdemovic* case was cited by Judge Robinson, *infra, inter alia* utilised by Judge Shahabuddeen *infra* and denounced by Judge Cassese, *infra.*

41 See Separate and Dissenting Opinion of Judge Li, *supra* note 28, Chapter 1, para. 19.

42 See Ambos and Wirth, *The Current Law of Crimes Against Humanity, An Analysis of UNTAET Regulation 15/2000, supra* note 22, Chapter 3.

43 See Ambos and Wirth, id. pp. 49-50, writing: 'The use of the same formula for the requirement of *mens rea* in *Kupreskic* and *Celibici* is striking and demonstrates the willingness of the ICTY at least to treat murder and wilful killing as the same offence, whether they are crimes against humanity or war crimes.'

and hatred that all offences thus committed might be considered as crimes against humanity. Could we really convincingly argue that some parts of the opposing military forces or local populations might not be aware of the ethnic nature of the armed conflict, and that, if charged with breaching international humanitarian law, their intent would only be that required for war crimes?'[44]

As is evident from the above statement, if in fact crimes against humanity were actually what were committed in the former Yugoslavia, calling these acts war crimes and claiming that war crimes are equal to crimes against humanity for penalty purposes, as was done by Judge *Li*, is incorrect. In other words, if the source of Judge *Li's* conclusion that war crimes are of equal gravity to crimes against humanity is his confusion of the substantive law on war crimes with that of crimes against humanity, it is difficult to support his claim.

3.2.2.1.2 Prosecutor v. *Tadic (Separate Opinion of Judge Robinson)*

The *Tadic* case involved the commission of crimes in the Prijedor region of Bosnia-Herzegovina between the 25th of May 1992 and early August of the same year. The facts of the case are based on events that took place at a camp at Omarska, where large numbers of Bosnian Muslims and Croats were detained by Serb forces.[45] The charges and convictions dealt with accusations of rape, unlawful killing, torture and cruel treatment. In respect to each of the alleged incidents, the indictment charged the defendant for crimes against humanity and war crimes on the basis of the same set of acts.[46] The case generated a number of divergent opinions on the issue of whether crimes against humanity are a more serious category of international crimes than war crimes, both procedurally and from the point of view of the imposition of relative penalties.[47] This section is concerned with the separate opinion of Judge *Robinson* on relative penalties.

Judge *Robinson*, in his separate opinion in the *Tadic* case, essentially embraced Judge *Li's* approach in *Erdemovic*.[48] This viewpoint is based on the following statements made by him:

'Judge Li identifies eight reasons why crimes against humanity are not more serious than war crimes: ...I find all these reasons persuasive....'[49]

---

44 See Bing Bing Jia, N. (1999), *The Differing Concepts of War Crimes and Crimes against Humanity in International Criminal Law*.

45 For the facts of the case see generally *Tadic* opinion and judgment, *supra* note 27, Chapter 2.

46 See id.

47 See *infra*.

48 See Separate and Dissenting Opinion of Judge Li, *supra* note 28, Chapter 1.

49 See Separate Opinion of Judge Robinson, *supra* note 26, Chapter 3.

And:

> 'The best way of determining whether the history of crimes against humanity supports the contention that they constitute more serious offences than war crimes is by examining the penalties imposed in respect of these crimes by the tribunals established immediately after the Second World War. Such a survey shows that the tribunals did not treat crimes against humanity as being graver offences than war crimes. For example, in the *Milch Case*, defendant Milch was convicted on both charges of war crimes and crimes against humanity for the same acts, and sentenced to life imprisonment.'[50]

Finally, as is evident from the above statements, particularly the second one, Judge *Robinson's* justification for endorsing the same interest approach vis-à-vis the issue of penalties for crimes against humanity and war crimes is based primarily on historical precedents. In other words, because he assumed that the World War II Tribunals imposed identical penalties for offences such as murder, torture and rape, whether they were committed as a crime against humanity or as a war crime, he believed that the same rationale should be applied in the context of the ICTY. However, the problem with this approach is that because the Word War II precedents in general failed to make any clear distinctions between crimes against humanity and war crimes particularly in terms of penalties, they lack credibility as precedents for equal penalties for both categories of crimes.[51]

3.2.2.1.3 Prosecutor v. *Tadic (Separate Opinion of Judge Shahabuddeen)*

The *Tadic* case,[52] as stated above, led to a number of opinions on the issue of relative penalties for crimes against humanity and war crimes. The following section is concerned with that of Judge *Shahabuddeen.*

Judge *Shahabuddeen,* in his separate opinion in the case, toed the line of Judge *Robinson.* This opinion is evident in two statements made by him. The first is as follows:

> 'In a separate opinion which Judge Robinson appended to the sentencing judgment..., he expressed the view that there is no basis for "the conclusion that, as a matter of principle, crimes against humanity are more serious violations of international humanitarian law than war crimes..." Judge Robinson noted that a

50 See id.

51 See generally Chapter 2; see DeGuzman, M.M., *The Road from Rome: The Developing Law of Crimes against Humanity*, writing: 'The Nuremberg proceedings contained remarkably little discussion of the legal foundations of the newly codified crimes against humanity. In fact, throughout the IMT Judgment, the Tribunal conflated crimes against humanity and war crimes.'

52 See *Tadic* Appeals Chamber Judgement, Separate Opinion of Judge Shahabuddeen, *supra* note 1, Chapter 2.

recent survey showed that the tribunals established immediately after the Second World War did not treat crimes against humanity as being graver offences than war crimes. I support that view....'[53]

The above statement demonstrates that Judge *Shahabuddeen* shared Judge *Robinson's* opinion that crime against humanity offences are of equal gravity to war crime offences. Whilst, the second statement by Judge *Shahabuddeen* is the following:

> 'This conclusion seems consistent with the cases decided after World War II. *Milch* is an example. There, convictions were made in respect of crimes against humanity and war crimes. The acts were the same, the holding of the United States Military Tribunal at Nuremberg being "that the same unlawful acts of violence which constituted war crimes under Count One of the Indictment also constitute crimes against humanity as alleged in Count Three of the Indictment". A common sentence of life imprisonment was imposed in respect of the convictions on those two counts. A common sentence of imprisonment was likewise imposed in the cases of *Creutz, Huebner, Lorenz, Bruekner, Hildebrandt* and *Schwalm*, in *United States* v. *Greifelt and Others*. In *Einsatzgruppen, supra*, there was a common death sentence.'[54]

As is evident from the above, Judge *Shahabuddeen*, like Judge *Robinson*, similarly based his argument on the precedent laid down by the World War II Tribunals. Therefore to the extent that Judge *Shahabuddeen* relied on the jurisprudence of the World War II Tribunals, the same criticisms made in relation to Judge *Robinson* equally apply here.

In addition, the following statement by *Danner*, which was incidentally directed at Judge *Shahabuddeen's* approach to the imposition of penalties for war crimes and crimes against humanity, serves as an additional criticism:

> 'Judge Shahabuddeen's argument suffers from several weaknesses. First, the current chapeau elements for a crime against humanity were not present in the London Charter, which stated only that the enumerated acts must be committed against "any civilian population" and "in execution of or in connection with any crime within the jurisdiction of the Tribunal." In light of this latter phrase, the Nuremberg Tribunal found that the pre-1939 persecution of the Jews, arguably the reason for the inclusion of the concept of a crime against humanity in the London Charter in the first place, was not a crime under the London Charter. The IMT's cramped treatment of crimes against humanity has been widely criticized

53 See id., pp. 35-36.

54 See id., p. 46.

and, today, is anachronistic. The jurisdictional origin of crimes against humanity therefore should not be used to limit a full consideration of all of the category's elements under contemporary international humanitarian law. More importantly, Judge Shahabuddeen fails to credit the normative change surrounding the concept of crimes against humanity that has developed since Nuremberg. The change in the chapeau elements of the crime that has occurred since 1946 concretely illustrates this evolution, as does the crime's delinkage from armed conflict under customary law. The increasing importance of the norms underlying crimes against humanity reflects the changing nature of armed conflict. Civilians have become the casualties of contemporary armed conflicts in numbers unimaginable in earlier decades. The norms underlying crimes against humanity elevate the protection of civilians above all other values, including military necessity. Most importantly, the category now extends beyond the limitations of armed conflicts and protects citizens against their government in times of "peace" as well as those of declared strife. This extension of the doctrine has occurred post-Nuremberg and reflects an erosion of state sovereignty and a corresponding elevation of fundamental principles of human rights.'[55]

Finally, the above statement basically criticizes the jurisprudence of World War II Tribunals on crimes against humanity as outdated and, therefore, unreliable for drawing conclusions about their relative gravity vis-à-vis war crimes today.

3.2.2.1.4 Prosecutor v. *Krnojelac*

The accused in this case was charged and convicted of crimes against humanity and war crimes in relation to acts of imprisonment and beatings, committed against Muslim and other non-Serb civilian detainees, in his position as a commander of the Foca Kazneno-Popravni Dom between April 1992 to August 1993.[56]

Furthermore, in relation to the above offences, he was handed down a single sentence of seven-and-a-half years imprisonment for war crimes and crimes against humanity. The rationale for this approach is evident in the following statement made by the Trial Chamber:

'The punishment which could have been imposed on the Accused in the former Yugoslavia at the relevant time is dealt with in Article 142(1) ("War crimes against the civilian population") of the SFRY Criminal Code. It gives effect to the provisions of Geneva Convention IV and the two Additional Protocols, which are incorporated into the jurisdiction of the Tribunal by Article 2 of the Statute. There appears to be no provision of the SFRY Criminal Code giving specific effect to the

---

55 See Danner, A.M. (2001), *Constructing a Hierarchy of Crimes in International Criminal Law.*

56 See *Prosecutor* v. *Milroad Krnojelac, supra* note 28, Chapter 3, para. 1497-1499.

> crimes against humanity enumerated in Article 5 of the Statute, although genocide (a specific category of crimes against humanity) is dealt with in Article 141 of the SFRY Criminal Code. In line with recent Appeals Chamber Judgments, the Trial Chamber has not considered that crimes against humanity should in principle attract a higher sentence than war crimes.'[57]

The above statement demonstrates that the Trial Chamber relied on the same interest approach as a basis for imposing penalties for the accused war crime and crime against humanity offences. In other words, since there was no separate provision on crimes against humanity under the SFRY Criminal Code, it basically extended the existing provision on war crimes to crimes against humanity, thereby treating both categories of international crimes as if they serve the same interests.

However, the main weakness of the above approach is that it obscures the distinctions between the respective criminal intentions and motives for war crime and crime against humanity offences.[58] In this respect, it should be recalled that a perpetrator of a war crime might not necessarily share the intention of someone who commits a crime against humanity. This opinion can be illustrated by comparing war crimes with crimes against humanity. The concept of war crimes as developed over the centuries, provide detailed rules governing permissible military conduct.[59] As a result, certain acts, which would constitute crimes against humanity if perpetrated against civilians, are actually permissible in the context of military action. For example, the displacement of civilians from their homes by an enemy army may not necessarily be a war crime, since it can be argued that the displacement is being carried out for the protection of the civilians.[60]

Furthermore, it may not be a war crime for the air force of one country to bomb an enemy's television station because of the propaganda in the broadcasts. Under the Geneva Convention, this is not a war crime.[61] Just about all aspects of a state's infrastructure – roads, bridges, power stations, and factories – become legitimate targets if they are put to military use. Article 56(2)(c) of Protocol I permits attacks against power plants or generating stations supplying

---

[57] See id., para. 1525.

[58] See Ambos and Wirth, *supra* note 22, Chapter 3.

[59] See, *e.g.*, Geneva Convention (I) for the Amelioration of the Condition of the Wounded and Sick in Armed Forces in the Field (Geneva I), adopted 12 Aug. 1949, 6 U.S.T. 3114, 75 U.N.T.S 31, (entered into force 21 Oct. 1950) (entered into force for U.S. 2 Feb. 1956); Geneva Convention (III) Relative to the Treatment of Prisoners of War (Geneva III), adopted 12 Aug. 1949, 6 U.S.T. 3316, 75 U.N.T.S. 135 (entered into force 21 Oct. 1950) (entered into force for U.S. 2 Feb. 1956).

[60] See Kafala, T (2001), *What is a War Crime?* Available at <http://news.bbc.co.uk/2/hi/europe/1420133.stm> (last Visited April 2003).

[61] See id.

mainly civilians with power, as these will not be restricted to serve only civilian purposes.[62] The same seems to apply to attacks on dams or dikes (or nuclear power stations) where Article 56(3) of Protocol I is only seen to prohibit attacks that might breach these dams or dikes and cause the release of their stored water (or cause the release of nuclear radiation from a nuclear power station). Other types of attacks are not constrained by Article 56.[63]

In addition, armed attacks only become war crimes if they violate the principle of proportionality, *i.e.*, if the extent of collateral damage to civilians and civilian interests resulting from the attack would be excessive compared to the military advantage gained from the attack.[64] However, the principle by its nature requires subjective reasoning and is therefore easily subject to abuse.[65] One writer has even come to the general conclusion that through meeting the requirements of military necessity and proportionality, the damage or loss of life will always be incidental and lawful.[66]

In view of the above, it is clear that applying the same interest approach to war crimes and crimes against humanity will result in a misrepresentation of the facts, since there is a difference between being charged and convicted for war crimes, which sometimes involve negligence conduct; and being charged and convicted for crimes against humanity which involve intentional conduct.[67]

---

62 See Aldrich, G.H. (1991), *Prospects for United States Ratification of Additional Protocol I to the 1949 Geneva Conventions*, 85 American Journal of International Law, at p. 13.

63 See id.

64 See Chapter 2.

65 See id.

66 See Raby (1968), *Bombardment of Land Targets*, *supra* note 14, Chapter 2.

67 See Sarooshi, D., *Command Responsibility and the Blaskic Case*. In: Evans, M.D. (ed.) (2001), *Decisions of International Tribunals*, International and Comparative Law Quarterly, p. 456. Identifying negligence as a *mens rea* for war crimes by writing in connection with the *Blaskic* case that: 'Having established that the conflict was international in nature, the Chamber then went on to find the remaining precondition for Article 2 to apply... Accordingly, the Chamber considered that the six counts of grave breaches which refer to the following five sub-headings of Article 2 of the Statute were of application *in casu*: wilful killing, inhuman treatment, wilfully causing great suffering or serious injury to body or health, extensive destruction of property, and the taking of civilians as hostages. The general *mens rea* required for commission of any of these offences include "both guilty intent and recklessness which may be likened to serious criminal negligence".' See Saul, B. (2000), *The International Crime of Genocide in Australian Law*, 22 Sydney Law Review, p. 567. Ruling out the possibility of negligence as a basis for proving discriminatory intent in connection with the crime of genocide which is similar to persecution as a crime against humanity, by stating: 'Despite such flexible interpretation, the need for a "pattern of purposeful action" clearly excludes the concept of "negligent genocide". As evidence of the Senate Committee suggested, mere negligence, inaction or carelessness is not sufficient to ground a charge of genocide.' See also Olusanya, O. (2004), *Double Jeopardy Without Parameters: Re-characterization in International Criminal Law*, p. 171.

Apart from obscuring the distinction between the respective criminal intentions and motives for war crime and crime against humanity offences, a second negative effect of the same interest approach, as evidenced by this case, is that it resulted in the imposition of a global sentence of seven-and-a-half years imprisonment in respect of the accused cumulative convictions for war crimes and crimes against humanity.[68] This is because the selection of a global sentence, rather than individual sentences for each count of conviction, further exacerbates the problem of distinguishing between the harms associated with each of the two categories of crimes. A similar opinion was also expressed by *Danner* who wrote:

> 'The ICTY Trial Chambers have begun to adopt the ICTR's practice of pronouncing a single sentence that covers all counts on which the defendant was convicted. The Rules of both Tribunals were recently amended to allow explicitly for this practice. While the imposition of a global sentence, rather than individual sentences for each count of conviction, is no doubt easier for the Tribunals' judges to implement, this practice represents a misstep in the quest to develop more coherent sentencing practices. A global sentence obscures the distinction between different crimes – whether the differences lie in the enumerated acts or in the chapeaux – and it allows the Trial Chamber to avoid making specific decisions about the harm resulting from individual acts. Global sentencing results in a lack of transparency in the sentencing process for the defendants, the Appeals Chamber, and for society at large. Unless the crime of which the defendant is convicted involves a continuing course of conduct, as would be the case in a conviction of persecution, for example, the better practice is for the Trial Chambers to impose individual sentences for each count of conviction. As the Trial Chamber can order the sentences to be served concurrently, this practice does not necessarily result in a longer prison term for the defendant.'[69]

Finally, as is evident from the above, the imposition of a global sentence for war crimes and crimes against humanity leads to a number of additional problems. This includes lack of transparency in the sentencing process as well as inconsistent sentences.

3.2.2.1.5 Prosecutor v. *Vasiljevic*

The trial in the *Vasiljevic* case[70] arose out of events, which took place in 1992, in the town of Visegrad, close to the border with the Republic of Serbia.[71]

---

68 See *supra* note 28, Chapter 3, para. 536.

69 See Danner, A.M. (2001), *Constructing a Hierarchy of Crimes in International Criminal Law.*

70 See *Prosecutor* v. *Vasiljevic, supra* note 31, Chapter 3.

71 See id. para. 5.

The trial was concerned principally with two incidents that occurred in Visegrad during the month of June 1992.[72] The first, which took place on the 7th of June 1992, involved the following set of facts. *Milan Lukic*, and a number of other men, led seven Bosnian Muslim men to the bank of the Drina River, where they forced the Muslim men to line up on the bank of the river, facing it. Despite pleas by the Muslims for their lives, they were shot from behind. When it appeared that someone was still alive, the men lying in the water were shot at again, at close range. Five of the Muslim men were killed, but the other two men escaped by pretending to be dead as they lay in the water. This has been referred to as the Drina River incident.[73]

In addition, the facts of the second incident, which took place on the 14th of June 1992,[74] are that about seventy Bosnian Muslim women, children and elderly men were directed to enter a house in Pionirska Street in the Mahala neighbourhood of the Visegrad municipality. An inflammable substance had been spread in the house beforehand. When the group had been forced inside the house, it was set on fire with an incendiary device. Most of the group died in the fire; some escaped before the fire, and others were successful in escaping during the fire. This has been referred to as the Pionirska Street incident.[75]

The accused, *Mitar Vasiljevic*, was charged separately with a number of international offences in relation to each of the two incidents. It was alleged that he acted in concert with others to commit murder (both as a crime against humanity and as a violation of the laws or customs of war), inhumane acts (as a crime against humanity) and violence to life and person (as a violation of the laws or customs of war). In relation to the Pionirska Street incident, the accused was also charged with extermination in concert with others (as a crime against humanity).[76]

Furthermore, the accused was given a single sentence of twenty years imprisonment for his war crimes and crime against humanity convictions based on the same interest approach. This opinion is evident in the following statement:

> 'The Trial Chamber imposes a single sentence of imprisonment reflecting the totality of the criminal conduct of the Accused, and in accordance with Articles 23(1) and 24(1) of the Statute and with Rules 101(A) and 87(C). The fact that the Accused was convicted cumulatively in relation to the same facts has been taken into account when determining the appropriate sentence, to ensure that he was not punished twice for the same act. The sentence which reflects the totality

---

[72] See id.

[73] See id.

[74] See id.

[75] See id.

[76] See id., para. 266.

of the Accused's criminal conduct and his overall culpability is imprisonment for 20 years. This section of the Judgment explains the considerations which led the Trial Chamber to impose that sentence. As a preliminary matter, Article 24(1) of the Statute provides, *inter alia*, that in determining the term of imprisonment the Trial Chamber "shall have recourse to the general practice regarding prison sentences in the courts of the former Yugoslavia". Although the Trial Chamber is not bound to follow the sentencing practice of the former Yugoslavia, recourse must be made to that sentencing practice as an aid in determining the sentence to be imposed. What is required must go beyond merely reciting the relevant criminal code provisions of the former Yugoslavia; the general sentencing practice of the former Yugoslavia must be considered. The punishment which could have been imposed on the Accused in the former Yugoslavia at the relevant time is dealt with in Article 142(1) ("War crimes against the civilian population") of the SFRY Criminal Code. It gives effect to the provisions of Geneva Convention IV and the two Additional Protocols, which are incorporated into the jurisdiction of the Tribunal by Article 2 of the Statute. There appears to be no provision of the SFRY Criminal Code giving specific effect to the crimes against humanity enumerated in Article 5 of the Statute, although genocide (a specific category of crimes against humanity) is dealt with in Article 141 of the SFRY Criminal Code. In line with recent Appeals Chamber Judgments, the Trial Chamber has not considered that crimes against humanity should in principle attract a higher sentence than war crimes.'[77]

Finally, to the extent that the above statement merely adopts the same line of reasoning in the *Krnojelac* case, the criticism expressed in relation to *Krnojelac* is also applicable here.

3.2.2.1.6 Prosecutor v. *Naletilic and Martinovic Judgement*

The indictment in this case concerned events alleged to have occurred between April 1993 and January 1994, in the course of a conflict between the Army of Bosnia and Herzegovina and the Croat Defence Council, in the South-western part of Bosnia and Herzegovina.[78]

The accused persons, *Mladen Naletilic* and *Vinko Martinovic*, were charged with multiple counts of crimes against humanity and war crimes based on the same sets of acts committed in their positions as commanders of the Convicts' Battalion and of the Vinko Skrobo ATG, respectively.[79] In addition, evidence of the reliance on the same interest approach can be demonstrated with the aid of the following statement made in relation to *Martinovic's* single sentence of

77 See id., para. 266

78 See *Prosecutor* v. *Mladen Naletilic et al., supra* note 32, Chapter 3.

79 See id.

eighteen years of imprisonment for his war crime and crime against humanity convictions:

> 'The Chamber has found Vinko Martinovic guilty of the most heinous crimes, which include murder. The gravity of these offences is of primary consideration in determining a sentence that reflects the criminal conduct of the accused.'[80]

Finally, the focus on the underlying offence of crimes against humanity and war crimes, *i.e.* murder, rather than on the actual crimes themselves, suggests that the same interest approach was relied upon in this case.

3.2.2.1.7 Prosecutor v. *Blaskic (Appeals Chamber)*

The relevant facts of the case are that the accused General *Blaskic* was convicted of persecution as a crime against humanity and war crimes for his role in orchestrating the attacks against Muslims in the municipalities of Vitez and Busovaca.[81] These attacks *inter alia* involved the plundering and burning of houses and stables, the killing of civilians regardless of age or gender, the slaughter of livestock and the destruction or damage of mosques. In addition, some civilians were arrested and transferred to detention centres where the living conditions were appalling and were forced to dig trenches.[82]

In relation to the above atrocities, the Trial Chamber cumulatively convicted the accused of war crimes and crimes against humanity and gave him a single sentence of forty-five years imprisonment.[83] This section is concerned with the following statements, which were recently made by the Appeals Chamber and which constitute evidence of a reliance on the same interest approach:

> 'In this case, the Appellant has been found guilty of particular instances of ordering what amounted to cruel and inhuman treatment of persons who were not participating in the hostilities and of failing to punish such conduct on the part of others. The crimes of which the Appellant has been convicted are serious violations of international humanitarian law, directed almost exclusively against Bosnian Muslims. *Their arbitrary detention in pitiful conditions, and in a climate of fear, combined with their employment for forced labour or as human shields, establishes the gravity of the offences in this case.* In particular the abuse of the sizeable number of 247 human beings as human shields – in doing so – endangering their lives in *abstracto* has to be seen as a serious aggravating factor.'[84] [emphasis added]

---

80 See id., para. 758.

81 For the relevant facts of this case see *Prosecutor* v. *Blaskic*, Case no. IT-95-14, 3 March 2000, (ICTY Trial Chamber).

82 See id.

83 See id.

84 See *Blaskic*, Appeals Chamber Judgement, *supra* note 33, Chapter 3, paras. 684-685.

And:

> 'The Appeals Chamber considers that the *mens rea* of crimes against humanity is satisfied when the accused has the requisite intent to commit the underlying offence(s) with which he is charged....'[85]

Finally, the above statements demonstrate that the primary focus of the Appeals Chamber, in so far as the issue of sentencing was concerned, was on the underlying offences of crimes against humanity and war crimes, *i.e.*, arbitrary detention, forced labour, use as human shields, rather than on the actual crimes themselves.

3.2.2.1.8 The United Kingdom

Under UK law, the International Criminal Court Act 2001, which applies to England and Wales and to Northern Ireland, gives UK courts universal jurisdiction *inter alia* over war crimes and crimes against humanity.[86]

Furthermore, in terms of penalties for war crimes and crimes against humanity, the relevant section of the Act, is section 53 which stipulates the following:

> 'The following provisions apply in relation to-
> a) offences under section 51 (genocide, crimes against humanity and war crimes),
> b)offences under section 52 (conduct ancillary to genocide, etc. committed outside jurisdiction) , and
> c) offences ancillary to an offence within paragraph (a) or (b) above. [...]
> 5) A person convicted of-
> a) an offence involving murder, or
> b) an offence ancillary to an offence involving murder, shall be dealt with as for an offence of murder or, as the case may be, the corresponding ancillary offence in relation to murder.
> In this subsection "murder" means the killing of a person in such circumstances as would, if committed in England or Wales, constitute murder.
> 6) In any other case a person convicted of an offence is liable to imprisonment for a term not exceeding 30 years.'[87]

---

85 See id., para. 124.

86 See International Criminal Court Act 2001. See Gilbert, J.A., *Legislation and Ratification: The UK's Approach to the Implementation of the Rome Statute.* In: Matthias Neuner (ed.) (2003), *National Legislation Incorporating International Crimes: Approaches of Civil and Common Law Countries*, Berlin: Berliner Wissenschafts Verlag, p. 55.

87 See section 53, id.

Evidence of the same interest approach is demonstrated by the fact that section 53(5) and (6) seem to suggest that murder or any other offences common to crimes against humanity and war crimes will attract the same level of penalties. This opinion is also shared by *Gilbert* who wrote:

> 'The domestic offence of murder in the case of an adult offender attracts a mandatory life sentence and the Act replicates this in the case of a killing in the context of the ICC offences, which would constitute murder in our law.'[88]

Finally, to the extent that UK law appears to recognize the same interest approach vis-à-vis the penalties for war crime and crime against humanity offences, the criticism expressed above, that this approach has the negative effect of obscuring the distinctions between the respective criminal intentions and motives for war crime and crime against humanity offences, also applies here.

3.2.2.1.9 Finland

Finland's law on crimes against humanity and war crimes is regulated primarily by its penal code, which has *inter alia* recognized both categories of international crimes, since 1995.[89] This opinion is evident in the following statement by *Nuutila*:

> 'In Finland the principle of legality and the requirement of transparency of criminal legislation have especially today a very strong standing. Amending existing sections in the Penal Code was not especially difficult, as the Finnish courts have already been exercising universal jurisdiction over crimes against humanity, war crimes and genocide since 1995. Therefore, the changes in the Finnish Penal Code concerned offences against the administration of the ICC. War crimes, crimes against humanity and genocide, were already in the Penal Code- defined even wider than in the Rome Statute.' [90]

---

88 See Gilbert, J.A. (2003), *Legislation and Ratification: The UK's Approach to the Implementation of the Rome Statute*, p. 60.

89 See Finnish Penal Code, Chapter II, War crimes and offences against Humanity (578/1995).

90 See Nuutila, A.M. (2003), *Implementing the Rome Statute: A pragmatic Approach from a Small Jurisdiction, supra* note 86, Chapter 3, p. 87. For literature on the implementation of international crimes under Finnish law, see Nuotio, K. (1999), *Transforming International Law and Obligations into Finnish Criminal Legislation – Dragon's Eggs and Criminal Law Irritants*, Vol. X Finnish Yearbook of International Law; Hannikainen, L. (1992), *Implementation of International Humanitarian Law in Finnish Law.* In: Hannikainen, L., Hanski, R., and Rosas, A., *Implementing Humanitarian Law Applicable in Armed Conflict: The Case of Finland*, Dordrecht: Martinus Nijhoff Publishers, 1992, at p. 120. Träskman, P.O. (1989), *Finland: National Report: Part II: Legal Problems Emerging from the Implementation of International Crimes in Domestic Criminal Law*, 60 Revue International de Droit Pénal, cited in Nuutila id.

Furthermore, one noticeable, relevant difference between the Finnish Penal Code and the Rome Statute is the use of the term 'violation of human rights in a state of emergency' instead of crimes against humanity. In spite of this difference in terminology, the prevailing opinion is that the term 'violation of human rights in a state of emergency' should be understood as referring to crimes against humanity. Thus *Nuutila* made the following relevant statement:

> 'The domestic definition of *violation of human rights in a state of emergency* is in some cases broader than the definition of "crimes against humanity" in the Rome Statute. On the other hand, the difference is only technical....'[91]

In light of the above, the relevant provisions governing crimes against humanity and war crimes under Finnish law are the following:

> **'Section 4. Violation of human rights in a state of emergency (578/1995)**
> 1. A person who violates or fails to comply with the rules on the protection of the wounded, the sick or the distressed, the treatment of prisoners of war and the protection of the civilian population, which according to international agreements binding on Finland or the established rules of public international law are to be followed during war, armed conflict or occupation, shall be sentenced for *violation of human rights in a state of emergency* to imprisonment for at least four months and at most six years.
>
> **Section 1. War crime (578/1995)**
> 1. A person who in an act of war
> 1) uses a prohibited means of warfare or weapon;
> 2) abuses an international symbol designated for the protection of the wounded or the sick; or
> 3) otherwise violates the provisions of an international agreement on warfare binding on Finland or the generally acknowledged and established rules and customs of war under public international law shall be sentenced for a *war crime* to imprisonment for at least four months and at most six years.'[92]

Evidence of reliance on the same interest approach is demonstrated both by the extent of overlap between the offences recognized under war crimes and crimes against humanity and by the fact that the same penalties are imposed for both categories of international crimes.

Finally, because Finnish law on sentencing for war crimes and crimes against humanity is similar to the UK's, the same criticism expressed in connection with the latter also affects the former.

---

[91] See Nuutila, id., p. 101.

[92] See Finnish Penal Code, *supra* note 89, Chapter 3.

3.2.2.1.10 Holland

The Dutch draft for an International Crimes Act (ICA) constitutes the latest legislation for the criminalization of war crimes and crimes against humanity under Dutch law.[93] The aims of the ICA are primarily the following: first, to bring together the 'core' international crimes in one separate law. In this respect, it should be recalled that, prior to the formulation of the ICA, specific laws already existed for war crimes, genocide and torture, but none addressed the criminalization of crimes against humanity. Second, to codify the status of international criminal law as it now stands and third, to apply existing provisions of the Dutch Penal Code for the purpose of clarifying the substantive law on international crimes.[94]

Furthermore, all of the above aims, when read together with the following relevant provisions on sentencing under Dutch law, demonstrate proof of a reliance on the same interest approach:

> **'Section 4**
>
> 1. Anyone who commits one of the following acts shall be guilty of a crime against humanity and liable to life imprisonment or a term of imprisonment not exceeding thirty years or a sixth category fine, if such acts are committed as part of a widespread or systematic attack directed against any civilian population, with knowledge of the attack:....
>
> **Section 5**
>
> 1. Anyone who commits, in the case of an international armed conflict, one of the grave breaches of the Geneva Conventions, namely the following acts if committed against persons protected by said Conventions...
>
> shall be liable to life imprisonment or a term of imprisonment not exceeding thirty years or a sixth category fine.'[95]

As is clear from sections 4 and 5 above, the same penalties are imposed for war crimes and crimes against humanity. This approach is not surprising given that the ICA applies existing provisions of the Dutch Penal Code for the purpose of clarifying the substantive law on international crimes. Furthermore, criticizing the approach of using so-called domestic equivalents to conceptualise international crimes is the following statement by *Gilbert*, which was made in the context of the UK:

---

93 See Bevers, H., Roording, J., and Swaak-Golman, O. (2003), *The Dutch International Crimes Act (Bill)*, p. 179.

94 See id., pp. 182-183.

95 See Sections 4 and 5 of the unofficial translation of the International Crimes Act, *supra* note 86, Chapter 3, CD-ROM attachment.

> 'An alternative opinion, which we considered but rejected, was to provide a more familiar framework of law, using existing UK offences where they corresponded to ICC ones, supplemented by newly created domestic offences where there were no existing UK analogues. The risk with UK analogues was that they might not wholly succeed in giving full effect to the Statute... The use of domestic analogues seemed likely to work reasonably well in the case of offences constituting crimes against humanity, since the basic defences available to a defendant in a case of, say murder or rape, would intrinsically be the same as those available to someone in a context devoid of any general attack on a civilian population. In both cases the accused would be treated as subject to normal civilian standards of behaviour. *However, treating a crime against humanity without reference to the circumstances which made it an international crime, and in exactly the same way as if it happened in an English market town over a week-end, would arguably have diminished its gravity. The real difficulties in that approach lay with war crimes offences. If we were to prosecute them in a way which reflected their gravity, we could not simply equate, say pillage with the domestic offence of theft. It would have been necessary to prove the theft was a serious violation of the law and customs applicable to international armed conflict. In doing that, however, it would also have been necessary to provide scope for proper defence (for instance, using the same offence, that the appropriation had been justified by military necessity).*'[96][emphasis added]

Finally, the above statement basically points out the negative effects of the same interest approach. In other words, it obscures the distinctions between the respective criminal intentions and motives for war crime and crime against humanity offences.

3.2.2.1.11 Canada

Under Canadian law, the Crimes Against Humanity and War Crimes Act of 2000,[97] which was enacted with a view to implementing the Statute,[98] gives Canadian courts universal jurisdiction *inter alia* over war crimes and crimes against humanity.[99]

---

96 See Gilbert, J.A. (2003), *Legislation and Ratification: The UK's Approach to the Implementation of the Rome Statute*, pp. 57-58.

97 See Wedgwood, R. (2000), *Augusto Pinochet and International Law*, 46 McGill Law Journal, p. 252 (discussing the Canadian Crimes against Humanity and War Crimes Act of 2000).

98 For general literature on the Act see Schabas, W.A. (2003), *Canadian Implementing Legislation for the Rome Statute: Jurisdiction and Defences*, pp. 35-43. See also Robinson, D. (2003), *Implementing International Crimes in National Law: The Canadian Approach*, pp. 45-54.

99 See Bill C-19, 2nd Sess., 36th Parl., pp. 48-49 Elizabeth II, 1999-2000, assented to 29 June 2000 (obtainable from: < http://www.parl.gc.ca/>) (Last visited June 2004). Previously, Section 318 of the Criminal Code, R.S.C. 1985, C-46, provided that genocide was a crime; News Release (December 10, 1999). *Canada Introduces New Act to Implement International Criminal Court.* Available at <http: //www.icc.gc.ca> (last visited June 2004); see also Green, L.C. (1988), *Canadian Law, War Crimes and Crimes against Humanity*, British Year Book of International Law, pp. 217-235.

Furthermore, in relation to penalties for war crimes and crimes against humanity, the relevant provisions here are sections 4(1) and (2) which stipulate the following:

> '(1) Every person is guilty of an indictable offence who commits
> a) genocide;
> b) a crime against humanity; or
> c) a war crime ...
>
> 2) Every person who commits an offence under subsection (1)...
> a) shall be sentenced to imprisonment for life, if an intentional killing forms the basis of the offence; and
> b) is liable to imprisonment for life, in any other case.'[100]

Reliance on the same interest approach is evidenced by the fact that section 4(2) *inter alia* imposes the same sentences for crimes against humanity and war crimes offences. Finally, to the extent that the Canadian law on sentencing for crime against humanity and war crime offences essentially mirrors the UK approach, the same criticism expressed in connection with the latter also affects the former.

3.2.2.1.12 Australia

Australian law on crimes against humanity and war crimes is regulated by two separate provisions.[101] The first is the International Criminal Court Act of 2002, which essentially gives Australian courts the authority to prosecute persons *inter alia* responsible for war crimes and crimes against humanity.[102] This opinion is evident in the explanatory sub-title for the Act which reads: 'An Act to Facilitate Compliance by Australia with Obligations Under the Rome Statute of the International Criminal Court, and for Related Purposes'.[103] Whilst the second provision, which is the International Criminal Court (Consequential

100 See Section 4, id.

101 See McCormack, T.L.H. (2003), *Australia's Legislation for the Implementation of the Rome Statute*, p. 66, recognizing that Australia's implementing legislation is contained in two separate Acts of Parliament; for other relevant literature see Doherty, K.L. & McCormack, T.L.H. (1999), *Complementarity as a Catalyst for Comprehensive Domestic Penal Legislation*, 5 University of California, Davis Journal of International Law and Policy, p. 147, at pp. 156-161; Balkin, R. (1997), *International Law and Domestic Law*. In: Blay, S. Piotrowicz, R. and Tsamenyi, M. (eds.), *Public International Law: An Australian Perspective*, Oxford: Oxford University Press, pp. 119-45.

102 The text of the International Criminal Court Act 2002 is available at <http//scaleplus.law.gov.au/html/comact/11/6513/pdf/0412002.pdf> (last visited July 2004).

103 See id.

Amendment) Act 2002, deals with both the substantive law of the individual international crimes and penalties.[104]

Furthermore, the following chart represents a compilation of the penalties attached to some of the offences common to crimes against humanity and war crimes under Australian law, as recognized by the International Criminal Court (Consequential Amendment) Act 2002:[105]

Underlying offences	*War crime (grave breach) penalties*	*Crime against Humanity penalties*
Murder/extermination/wilful killing	Life imprisonment	Life imprisonment
Torture/inhuman treatment/ rape	25 years imprisonment	25 years imprisonment
Deportation	17 years imprisonment	17 years imprisonment
Imprisonment/unlawful confinement	17 years imprisonment	17 years imprisonment
Wilfully causing great suffering/enslavement	25 years imprisonment	25 years imprisonment

Finally, evidence of reliance on the same interest approach is demonstrated by the fact that the same penalties are imposed for offences common to war crimes and crimes against humanity. Because Australian law on sentencing for crimes against humanity and war crimes is essentially identical to the UK's, the same criticism expressed in connection with the latter also affects the former.

3.2.2.1.13 New Zealand

In order to facilitate the application of the crime against humanity and war crime provisions of the Rome Statute, under New Zealand's law, implementing legislation in the form of the International Crimes and International Criminal Court Act was passed in 2000.[106] The New Zealand's International Crimes and International Criminal Court Act 2000 (ICC Act), therefore, *inter alia* created the new crimes of crimes against humanity and war crimes for the purpose of punishing them under New Zealand's law.[107]

---

[104] The text of the International Criminal Court (Consequential Amendments) Act 2002 is available at <http://scaleplus.law.gov.au/html/comact/11/6514/pdf/0422002.pdf> (last visited July 2004).

[105] See id.

[106] See International Crimes and International Criminal Court Act 2000. On the background to the ratification of the Act, see generally Hay, J. (2003), *Implementing the Rome Statute: A Pragmatic Approach from a Small Jurisdiction*, at p. 16.

[107] On the issues involved in creating the new crimes of crimes against humanity and war crimes, etc. See id. pp. 16-24.

Furthermore, in terms of the relevant penalties for war crimes and crimes against humanity, the ICC Act provides for a two-tier penalty: mandatory life imprisonment if the offence involves murder and a maximum penalty of life imprisonment in other cases.[108] This opinion is evident in the following relevant sections of the Act:

'Part 2

International crimes and offences against administration of justice ...
10 Crimes against humanity
1) Every person is liable on conviction on indictment to the penalty specified in subsection (3) who, in New Zealand or else where, commits a crime against humanity.
2) For the purposes of this section, a crime against humanity is an act specified in article 7 of the Statute.
3) The penalty for a crime against humanity is, ---
a) if the offence involves the wilful killing of a person, the same as the penalty for murder:
b) in any other case, imprisonment for life or a lesser term.

11 War crimes

1) Every person is liable on conviction on indictment to the penalty specified in subsection (3) who, in New Zealand or else where, commits a war crime.
2) For the purposes of this section, a war crime is an act specified in---
a) article 8(2)(a) of the Statute (which relates to grave breaches of the First, Second, Third, and Fourth Geneva Conventions); or
b) article 8(2)(b) of the Statute (which relates to other serious violations of the laws and customs applicable in international armed conflict); or
c) article 8(2)(c) of the Statute (which relates to armed conflict not of an international character involving serious violations of article 3 common to the 4 Geneva Conventions of 12 August 1949); or
d) article 8(2)(e) of the Statute (which relates to other serious violations of the laws and customs applicable in armed conflicts not of an international character).
3) The penalty for a war crime is, ...
a) if the offence involves the wilful killing of a person, the same as the penalty for murder:
b) in any other case, imprisonment for life or a lesser term.'[109]

---

[108] See id. p. 22.

[109] See Part 2 International Crimes and International Criminal Court Act 2000, id.

The utilization of the same interest approach is evident in the adoption of identical penalties for war crime and crime against humanity offences. Finally, the reliance on this approach, therefore, means that the criticism earlier expressed in connection with the UK equally affects New Zealand.

3.2.2.2 Limitations of the Same Interest Approach

3.2.2.2.1 Failure to Ensure Proportionality

The idea of proportionality as an important aspect of sentencing in the context of the ICTY was recognized in the *Blaskic* case, as evidenced by the following statement:

> 'However, the principle of proportionality, a general principle of criminal law, and Article 24(2) of the Statute call on the Trial Chamber to bear in mind the seriousness of the offence and could consequently constitute the legal basis for a scale of sentences.'[110]

In addition, proportionality is equally a central principle in the sentencing of offenders at common law.[111] The principle as developed in common law jurisprudence operates in two ways: first, to restrain excessive, arbitrary and capricious punishment by requiring that punishment must not exceed the gravity of the offence.[112] And, second, to ensure that a minimum level of punishment

---

110 See *Blaskic*, Trial Chamber, *supra* note 81, Chapter 3, para. 796. See also Meernik, J. & King, K. (2003), *The Sentencing Determinants of the International Criminal Tribunal for the Former Yugoslavia: An Empirical and Doctrinal Analysis*, p. 723, writing: 'Of the remaining three theories, retribution favors penalties appropriate to the criminal acts, and it has been considered at least as important as deterrence in some cases. Retribution is not "a desire for revenge", but an expression of "outrage of the international community at these crimes," and the community's unwillingness to tolerate such behavior. Society is justified in taking action, and the "severity of a sentence should be proportional to the seriousness of the criminal conduct."' See Morris, V. and Scharf, M.P. (1995), *An Insiders Guide to the International Criminal Tribunal for the Former Yugoslavia*, p. 275, stating: 'International law does not provide a standard for determining the appropriate penalty to be imposed for a crime under international law, other than the general principle of proportionality.' See Aukerman, M.J. (2002), *Extraordinary Evil, Ordinary Crime: A Framework for Understanding Transitional Justice*, 15 Harvard Human Rights Journal, p. 39, at p. 54.

111 See Dolinko, D. (1999), *The Future of Punishment*, 46 University of California, Los Angeles. School of Law Review, p. 1719, p. 1720, emphasizing that retributivism is the leading philosophical justification for punishment in the United States. For literature on proportionality as a sentencing model in national practice throughout the world see Kelk, C. *et al.*, *Sentencing Practice, Policy, and Discretion*. In: Fennell, P. *et al.* (eds.) (1995), *Criminal Justice in Europe*, Oxford: New York: Clarendon Press; Oxford University Press, p. 319, p. 323.

112 See especially Fox, R.G. (1994), *The Meaning of Proportionality in Sentencing*, 19 Melbourne University Law Review, p. 489.

is imposed upon the offender, in that a sentence which fails to give sufficient weight to the objective seriousness of the offence (and is therefore manifestly inadequate) will be quashed.[113]

In assuming that offences such as murder, torture and rape, when committed under national law, are equal to similar offences when committed as a crime against humanity or as a war crime, and therefore that the same penalties apply; the same interest approach fails to adequately ensure the second type of proportionality mentioned above. This opinion is based on two factors: first, the fact that even under national law, offences such as murder are often committed with different motives and that each of these motives attracts a different level of penalty.[114] And, second and as a corollary, the fact that in mistakenly assuming that national offences such as murder, torture and rape are one dimensional, sight is lost of the opportunity to link the multiple dimensions of each of these offences to the substantive law on war crimes and crimes against humanity.

Furthermore, in relation to the first factor above, *i.e.*, the opinion that there are different degrees of murder, which attract different levels of penalties under common law, evidence for this is supported by the following statement of Lord *Hailsham of St Marylebone* in *R* v. *Howe*:

> 'Murder, as every practitioner of the law knows, though often described as one of the utmost heinousness, is not in fact necessarily so, but consists in a whole bundle of offences of vastly differing degrees of culpability, ranging from brutal, cynical and repeated offences like the so-called Moors murders to the almost venial, if objectively immoral, "mercy killing" of a beloved partner.'[115]

Equally, in a House of Lords debate in April 1991, Lord *Richard* QC, expressed the same opinion when he stated that:

> 'The argument in favour of change is based upon one simple proposition – that murders vary greatly. They vary from those that are planned and calculated, or are for material gain or from political motives, to those that are committed under severe pressure and in emotional circumstances of great stress, including many domestic murders. As many Members who practise in the courts know, there are many cases in which the killing could hardly be said to be intentional. The intention may have been to cause grievous bodily harm to the individual, but perhaps to the regret of the person causing that harm the individual died.'[116]

---

[113] See id.

[114] See *R* v. *Howe* [1987] AC p. 417 at p. 433.

[115] See *R* v. *Howe*, id.

[116] See HL Hansard, 18 April 1991, Col.1566.

Last, Lord *Irvine of Lairg* QC, echoed the above opinions when he made the following statement:

> 'A mercy killing is of a different moral order from a sadistic sex-based child murder. Where murder has a much more extended definition so that the mental element is satisfied by an intention to cause serious bodily harm, combined if need be with an awareness of the possibility of death, I would suggest that it is beyond argument that murder embraces such a multitude of diverse sins that the single mandatory life sentence must be inappropriate.'[117]

Finally, what all of the above statements point to is the fact that it is too simplistic to say that offences such as murder, torture and rape, when committed under national law, are equal to similar offences when committed as a crime against humanity or as a war crime, and therefore that the same penalties apply as is the case with the same interest approach. This is because of the fact that, in reality, there are different degrees of each of these offences, which may attract different levels of punishment. Therefore, there still needs to be an additional inquiry into which degree of murder under domestic law corresponds with murder as a crime against humanity, and which matches with murder as a war crime prior to the imposition of penalties.

3.2.2.2.2 Lack of Transparency

Transparency plays an important role in combating concerns about arbitrary disparities in sentencing. It principally obliges judges to give reasons for their choice of sentence. This type of information is crucial if the public is to be sufficiently informed to be able to contribute to meaningful debate on the purpose of sentencing.[118]

Furthermore, to the extent that the same interest approach has encouraged the imposition of global sentences for war crimes and crimes against humanity, it has created a lack of transparency in the imposition of penalties for both categories of international crimes.[119] This opinion can be clarified by comparing the cases of *Furundzija*[120] and *Galic.*[121]

---

[117] See HL Hansard, 6 November 1989, Col.521.

[118] See Justice (2001), *Response to the Halliday Review*, p. 4. Available at <http://www.justice.org.uk/parliamentpress/parliamentarybriefings/> (last visited June 2004).

[119] See Walther, S., *Cumulation of Offences, supra* note 33, Chapter 1, p. 486. Tracing the historical origin of the ICTY's approach of imposing single sentences to the Nuremberg Trials, as demonstrated by the following statement: '...two conclusions can be drawn: ...second, nothing in Rule 101 ("Penalties") forecloses the sentencing option of handing down a *single* sentence. Indeed, this position has been taken in several ICTY decisions, ... where the chambers, in support of their holdings, pointed to prior ICTR decisions, to the practice of the military Tribunals at Nuremberg and Tokyo....'

[120] See *Prosecutor* v. *Furundzija*, Case no. IT-95-17/1, 10 December 1998, (ICTY Trial Chamber).

[121] See *Prosecutor* v. *Galic*, Case no. IT-98-29, 5 December 2003, (ICTY Trial Chamber).

In relation to the *Furundzija* case, the accused was sentenced for torture and outrages upon personal dignity as war crimes, in the following way:

> **'With respect to the accused, ANTO FURUNDZIJA:**
> Count 13: GUILTY of a Violation of the Laws or Customs of War (torture).
> For torture as a Violation of the Laws or Customs of War, the Trial Chamber sentences Anto Furundzija to 10 years' imprisonment.
> Count 14: GUILTY of a Violation of the Laws or Customs of War (outrages upon personal dignity, including rape).
> For outrages upon personal dignity, including rape, as a Violation of the Laws or Customs of War, the Trial Chamber sentences Anto Furundzija to 8 years' imprisonment. The foregoing sentences are to be served concurrently, *inter se*.'[122]

As is evident from the above, each count of war crimes has been considered individually. Thus torture, which was considered to have been the more serious of the two offences, attracted a sentence of 10 years imprisonment; whilst outrages upon personal dignity, which was considered to be the less serious of the two offences, attracted a lower sentence of 8 years imprisonment.[123]

On the other hand, in terms of the *Galic* case, the accused was sentenced for war crimes and crimes against humanity on the basis of the same acts, in the following way:

> **'VI. DISPOSITION**
> 769 FOR THE FOREGOING REASONS, having considered all of the evidence and the arguments of the parties, and having excluded from consideration those incidents which the Prosecution has failed to prove exemplary of the crimes charged in the Indictment, the Trial Chamber, Judge Nieto-Navia dissenting, makes the following disposition in accordance with the Statute and Rules:
> Stanislav Galic is found GUILTY on the following counts, pursuant to Article 7(1) of the Statute of the Tribunal:
> COUNT 1: Violations of the Laws or Customs of War (acts of violence the primary purpose of which is to spread terror among the civilian population, as set forth in Article 51 of Additional Protocol I to the Geneva Conventions of 1949) under Article 3 of the Statute of the Tribunal.

---

[122] See *supra* note 120, Chapter 3, para. 296.

[123] See Walther, S., *Cumulation of Offences*. In: Cassese *et al.* (2002), *supra* note 33, Chapter 1, p. 487. Making the following relevant statement in relation to the sentencing of the defendant in this case: 'It follows, then, that in international law as in national law any situation of multiple convictions gives rise to the possibility that a tribunal or court may *not* find legitimate grounds (based on the concepts of "single set of crimes", "single transaction", or the like) for imposing only one sentence, but may spell out one sentence for each crime of conviction. This was the case, for instance, in *Furundzija*....'.

COUNT 2: Crimes against Humanity (murder) under Article 5(a) of the Statute of the Tribunal.

COUNT 3: Crimes against Humanity (inhumane acts – other than murder) under Article 5(i) of the Statute of the Tribunal.

COUNT 5: Crimes against Humanity (murder) under Article 5(a) of the Statute of the Tribunal.

COUNT 6: Crimes against Humanity (inhumane acts – other than murder) under Article 5(i) of the Statute of the Tribunal.

The finding of guilt on count 1 has the consequence that the following counts are DISMISSED:

COUNT 4: Violations of the Laws or Customs of War (attack on civilians as set forth in Article 51 of Additional Protocol I and Article 13 of Additional Protocol II to the Geneva Conventions of 1949) under Article 3 of the Statute of the Tribunal.

COUNT 7: Violations of the Laws or Customs of War (attack on civilians as set forth in Article 51 of Additional Protocol I and Article 13 of Additional Protocol II to the Geneva Conventions of 1949) under Article 3 of the Statute of the Tribunal.

The Trial Chamber, by Majority, hereby SENTENCES Stanislav Galic to a single sentence of 20 (twenty) years of imprisonment.'[124] [emphasis added]

As is evident from the above, rather than considering each count individually, the Trial Chamber instead selected the term of imprisonment appropriate to punish the offender for the overall criminality and imposed a sentence of that length in relation to each count. The identical sentence imposed in relation to each count, therefore, reflected only the principle of totality and not the gravity of each of the individual crimes.[125]

This one sided approach leads to arbitrary disparities in sentencing and, therefore, a lack of transparency, because it encourages judges to avoid making specific decisions about the harm resulting from the individual acts.[126] In

---

[124] See *supra* note 121, Chapter 3, para. 769.

[125] See *Pearce* v. *R* (1998) 194 CLR p. 624 (the court noted the importance of applying a holistic approach to fixing sentences in cases of cumulative convictions).

[126] See Danner, A.M. (2001), *Constructing a Hierarchy of Crimes in International Criminal Law*; see Walther, S., *Cumulation of Offences, supra* note 33, Chapter 1, p. 487, giving the following justifications for this approach: 'Of particular interest next, is what, if anything, can be said with regard to a potential preference for a single sentence (which may be a principal, joint, or unified sentence) that determines the (enforceable) punishment. In this regard, it has already been noted that some judgments of the international tribunals found multiple offences of convictions but opted to hand down single sentences. In their arguments for support, the chambers pointed to the fact that the offences committed had been the result of, or formed part of, "a single set of crimes"....'. For a criticism of the above statement, see generally Olusanya, O. (2004), *Double Jeopardy Without Parameters: Re-characterization in International Criminal Law.*

addition, this opinion can be explained by focusing on the issue of concurrent and consecutive penalties in cases of cumulative convictions. Thus concurrent sentences in cases of multiple convictions for war crimes and crimes against humanity based on the same act would, for example, mean that the overall sentence of the accused would be X (years of imprisonment for example for murder has a crime against humanity) + Y (years of imprisonment for murder has a war crime) = Z (average of years of imprisonment for murder has a crime against humanity and murder has a war crime).

However, the situation at present is that when murder is committed and sentenced as both a crime against humanity and a war crime, the ICTY merely specifies that Z years of imprisonment is applicable for both murders, without demonstrating how or telling us why this is the case. This in turn makes it difficult to know whether or not, in reality, concurrent and not consecutive sentences have been imposed for both convictions.

The above opinion was also reiterated by Judge *Hunt* and Judge *Mohamed*, in their separate and dissenting opinion in the *Celibici* case, when they argued that whether consecutive or concurrent sentences are imposed does not necessarily mitigate the punitive consequences of cumulative convictions.[127] According to them, merely fixing a sentence for each count and making them concurrent, rather than consecutive, does not make it clear that consideration has been given to the possibility of duplicative penalty when fixing individual sentences.[128]

Finally, it should be observed in relation to the above discussion that, under the Rome Statute of the International Criminal Court, the practice of imposing a single sentence in cases of multiple convictions for war crimes and crimes against humanity will no longer be tolerated.[129] Thus, Article 78(3) of the Rome Statute provides that when a person has been convicted of more than one crime, the Court shall pronounce a sentence for each crime and a joint sentence specifying the total period of imprisonment. This implies that a specific penalty should be attached to each crime and that the Court cannot impose a single term of imprisonment for a variety of crimes.[130]

[127] See Separate and Dissenting opinion of Judge David Hunt and Judge Mohamed, *Prosecutor* v. *Zejnil Delalic et al.*, (*Celibici* case), Case No. IT-96-21-A, Judgement of 20 February 2001, (ICTY Appeals Chamber).

[128] See id.

[129] See Cassese, A.(2003), *International Criminal Law, supra* note 17, Chapter 3, p. 218.

[130] See id. For general literature on the sentencing under the ICC see Pickard, D.B. (1997), *Proposed Sentencing Guidelines for the International Criminal Court,* 20 Loy. L.A. International and Comparative Law Journal, p. 123.

3.2.2.3 The Widespread and Systematic Attacks v. Isolated Acts Approach

The widespread and systematic attacks[131] v. isolated acts approach is based on the characterisation of crimes against humanity as crimes involving large scale premeditated attacks[132] and war crimes or as crimes entailing comparatively small scale isolated attacks. The implication, therefore, is that the former category of international crimes, crimes against humanity, should attract a higher penalty than the latter. Both the justification for this line of reasoning as well as the reasons why it has failed to attract widespread support amongst the judges of the ICTY are examined in greater detail below, in connection with the *Tadic*[133] and *Kupreskic*[134] cases.

3.2.2.3.1 Prosecutor v. *Kupreskic*

The *Kupreskic* case is the first ICTY case to attempt to adopt a co-ordinated approach to sentencing in international criminal law.[135] In other words, this case involved building a system of 'lesser included offences' for international crimes and using this system *inter alia* for the purpose of sentencing.[136]

In addition, the key to the workability of the *Kupreskic* system of 'lesser included offences' for international crimes are the widespread and systematic attacks and isolated acts elements.[137] This approach from the perspective of crimes against humanity and war crimes, involves the following steps:

1. Selecting the underlying offence, *e.g.* murder.
2. Matching the underlying offence *i.e.* murder, with crimes against humanity and its widespread and systematic attacks criterion and with war crimes and its isolated acts criterion.
3. Using the widespread and systematic attacks criterion of murder as a crime against humanity to cancel out the isolated acts criterion of murder as a war crime.
4. Ultimately awarding a higher penalty for murder as a crime against humanity than would have been the case had the finding been one of murder as a war crime.

---

131 See Heine & Vest, *Murder/Wilful Killing, supra* note 50, Chapter 1.

132 See report of the Secretary-General pursuant to Security Council Resolution 808 (S/25704, 3 May 1993, para. 48). Article 3 of the Statute of the International Criminal Tribunal for Rwanda and Article 7 of the Statute of the International Criminal Court also state this element explicitly. The Legal Committee of the United Nations War Crimes Commission also adopted this position (History of the U.N. War Crimes Commission, p. 179).

133 See *Prosecutor* v. *Tadic*, Appeals Chamber, *supra* note 31, Chapter 1.

134 See *Prosecutor* v. *Kupreskic et al., supra* note 5, Chapter 1.

135 See id., para. 668.

136 See id.

137 See for example id., paras. 700-704.

Furthermore, the above enumerated steps beg the following question: what criteria is used to allocate the widespread and systematic attacks element and the isolated acts elements, respectively to crimes against humanity and war crimes? The *Kupreskic* answer to this question is revealed in the following statement:

> 'In general terms, the very nature of the criminal acts over which the International Tribunal has jurisdiction under Article 5, in view of the fact that they must be "directed against any civilian population," ensures that what is to be alleged will not be one particular act but, instead, a course of conduct. Nevertheless, in certain circumstances, a single act has comprised a crime against humanity when it occurred within the necessary context. For example, the act of denouncing a Jewish neighbour to the Nazi authorities – if committed against a background of widespread persecution – has been regarded as amounting to a crime against humanity. An isolated act, however – *i.e.* an atrocity which did not occur within such a context – cannot.'[138]

From the above statement, it is clear that the key to allocating the widespread and systematic elements in the case of crimes against humanity is the historical circumstances in which they were committed; for example, , the fact that they are historically synonymous with Hitler's policy to persecute the Jewish people which was a widespread and systematic event.

On the other hand, in the case of war crimes, it is impossible to determine how the isolated acts element was identified with this category of crimes, since there is no discussion by the Trial Chamber in the *Kupreskic* case of this issue.[139]

Not surprisingly, this approach has been criticised as being too artificial.[140] This criticism is in turn based on two opinions. First, is the fact that the elements used to separate crimes against humanity and war crimes, *i.e.*, the widespread and systematic attacks criterion and the isolated acts criterion, for purposes of sentencing are questionable. This point of view is evident for example in the following statement made by Judge *Li* in the *Erdemovic* case:

---

[138] See id., para. 550; see Frulli, M. (2001), *Are Crimes against Humanity More Serious than War Crimes?*, p. 336, writing: 'The *dolus* required for crimes against humanity includes the knowledge of being part of a widespread or systematic attack against civilians: *i.e.* it is more specific than that characterizing war crimes'. See also Bohlander, M. (2000), *Prosecutor* v. *Dusko Tadic: Waiting to Exhale*, p. 246.

[139] See *Prosecutor* v. *Kupreskic et al., supra* note 5, Chapter 1.

[140] See Separate Opinion of Judge Robinson, *Prosecutor* v. *Tadic, supra* note 26, Chapter 3, writing: 'the requirement of a differentiation in penalty would seem to lead to an artificiality in sentencing, totally removed from the facts of the particular case'.

> 'Of course, crimes against humanity have the characteristics of being committed systematically or on a large scale. However, war crimes can also be committed in such a manner. For instance, prisoners of war may be killed systematically or on a large scale, as they were habitually and atrociously executed by the Nazi regime in the Second World War.'[141]

The above statement basically suggests that the *Kupreskic* approach has no merit. The second opinion is a practical criticism. In other words, since there are no precedents for utilising the widespread and systematic attacks criterion and the isolated acts criterion as a basis for determining penalties for offences under national law, it would be impossible for judges to apply these criteria vis-à-vis international offences such as murder, rape, torture etc. This point of view can be inferred from the following statement by Judge *Robinson* in the *Tadic* case:

> 'For sentencing purposes, the relevant comparison is not between the four categories of crimes on the basis of their classification or nomenclature; rather, the comparison should be between the specific acts that constitute the specific crimes....'[142]

The above opinion suggests that it is more practical to award penalties for crimes against humanity and war crimes offences based on penalties awarded for similar offences under the penal code of the former Yugoslavia than to invent a new penalty index.

3.2.2.3.2 Prosecutor v. *Tadic (Dissenting Opinion of Judge Cassese)*

Judge *Cassese*, in his separate and dissenting opinion in the *Tadic* case, toed the line adopted in the *Kupreskic* above.[143] In other words, he equally based his argument for higher penalties for crimes against humanity vis-à-vis war crimes on the widespread and systematic attacks v. isolated acts approach. This opinion is evident in the following statements made by him:

> 'As was correctly held by Trial Chamber II in *Kupreskic et al.*, whenever the same fact may be regarded as falling under two different provisions of the International Tribunal's Statute, for instance Article 3 (on war crimes) and Article 5 (on crimes against humanity) ... pursuant to the principle of speciality the latter characterisation should prevail. Indeed, the crimes under Article 5 ... may often turn out to be lex specialis vis-à-vis war crimes respectively, because they require the presence of certain legal elements that are not necessary under Article 3....'.[144]

---

[141] See Separate and Dissenting Opinion of Judge Li, *Prosecutor* v. *Erdemovic, supra* note 28, Chapter 1, para. 20.

[142] See Separate Opinion of Judge Robinson, *Prosecutor* v. *Tadic, supra* note 26, Chapter 3.

[143] See Separate and Dissenting Opinion of Judge Cassese, *supra* note 31, Chapter 1.

[144] See id., para. 18.

And:

> 'It follows that the murder at issue forms part of a whole pattern of criminality, and may amount to what the great Dutch international lawyer B.V.A. Röling termed "system criminality" (encompassing large-scale crimes perpetrated to advance the war effort, at the request of, or with the encouragement or toleration of government authorities), as opposed to "individual criminality" (embracing crimes committed by combatants on their own initiative and often for reasons known only to themselves). If the above consideration are accepted, it follows that whenever an offence committed by an accused is deemed to be a "crime against humanity", it must be regarded as inherently of greater gravity, all else being equal (ceteris paribus), than if it is instead characterised as a "war crime". Consequently, it must entail a heavier penalty'.[145]

Judge *Cassese's* justification for higher penalties for crimes against humanity vis-à-vis war crimes is that they involve a policy of planned and premeditated attacks, whilst war crimes entail the isolated acts of combatants. To the extent that this line of reasoning is identical to that of the Trial Chamber in the *Kupreskic* case,[146] it equally attracts the criticisms mentioned in connection with that case.[147]

3.2.2.4 Limitations of the Widespread and Systematic Attacks v. Isolated Acts Approach

3.2.2.4.1 Failure to Ensure Consistency

The notion of consistency as an important element in the imposition of penalties for international crimes,[148] is evident in the following statement of the ICTY in the *Celibici* case:

---

[145] See id., paras. 14-16.

[146] See *supra* Section 3.2.2.3.1.

[147] See id.

[148] For critical literature on consistency in sentencing under the ICTY see University of California-Berkeley International Human Rights Law Clinic & University of Sarajevo Human Rights Center (2000), *Report: Justice, Accountability, and Social Reconstruction: An Interview Study of Bosnian Judges & Prosecutors*, 18 Berkeley Journal of International Law, p. 102; Ivkovic, S.K. (2001), *Justice by the International Criminal Tribunal for the Former Yugoslavia*, 37 Stanford Journal of International Law, p. 255, at p. 323. For literature on consistency in general, see Sunstein, C.R., Kahneman, D., Schkade, D., Ritov, I. (2002), *Predictably Incoherent Judgments*, 54 Stanford Law Review, p. 1153. See also Ashworth, A. (1998), *Four Techniques for Reducing Sentencing Disparity*. In: von Hirsch and Ashworth (eds) *Principled Sentencing: Readings on Theory and Policy*, 2nd ed, Oxford: Hart Publishing, p. 227 p. 236, writing: 'Disparity [in sentencing] is a manifest form of injustice, which may bring a sentencing system into public disrepute.'

> 'Public confidence in the integrity of the administration of criminal justice (whether international or domestic) is a matter of abiding importance to the survival of the institutions that are responsible for that administration. One of the fundamental elements in any rational and fair system of criminal justice is consistency of punishment.'[149]

Furthermore, the term consistency, as used in this section, means parity between crimes. In other words, the view that crime against humanity offences, if indeed they are more serious than war crime offences because of their widespread and systematic elements, should always consistently attract a higher level of penalties.

However, the basic problem with the widespread and systematic attacks v. isolated acts approach is that it cannot guarantee the type of consistency stated above. This opinion is evident in the following statement by Judge *Cassese* in his dissenting opinion in the *Tadic* case:

> 'It follows that, generally speaking, one cannot infer from international criminal provisions on penalties that a criminal offence is regarded as more serious than another. Thus faced with two different offences falling under the same provision (for example, "extermination" of civilians and "persecution [of civilians] on political, racial or religious grounds", both covered by Article 5 of the Statute), one cannot say *a priori* which of them is more serious and must therefore entail a heavier penalty. The same holds true for conduct falling under different criminal provisions, for instance plunder of private property as a war crime and taking civilians as hostages as a grave breach of the Geneva Conventions. This is all the more true given that some categories of crimes which, in theory, might be considered as less serious than other categories, may in practice instead prove inherently much graver: suffice is to mention war crimes such as the bombardment of an undefended town or the killing of hundreds of enemy combatants through the use of prohibited weapons. It goes without saying that these war crimes may in practice turn out to be more inhumane and devastating than some instances of crimes against humanity such as the deportation or imprisonment of civilians....'[150]

The above statement clearly suggests that it is impossible to achieve consistency in sentencing crime against humanity and war crime offences on the basis of the widespread and systematic attacks v. isolated acts approach.[151]

---

[149] See *Prosecutor* v. *Delalic et al., supra* note 19, Chapter 1.

[150] See Dissenting opinion of Judge Cassese, *supra* note 31, Chapter 1.

[151] See Carcano, A. (2002), *Sentencing and the Gravity of the Offence in International Criminal Law*, p. 593. The above statements when read together support the view that the murder category of crimes against humanity, which has a non-discriminatory element, is equivalent to war crimes.

3.2.2.5 Persecution-type v. Murder-type Approach

The persecution-type v. murder-type approach is based on a comparison of the persecution category of crimes against humanity, which has an additional persecutory element with the murder category of crimes against humanity that is said to be equivalent to war crimes and which does not have such an element.[152] The assumption is, therefore, that the former category of crimes against humanity should attract a higher penalty than war crimes.[153] Both the justification for this line of reasoning and the reason why it has failed to attract popular support amongst the judges of the ICTY are examined in greater detail below, in connection with the *Kupreskic*[154] and *Blaskic*[155] cases.

3.2.2.5.1 Prosecutor v. *Kupreskic*

The persecution-type v. murder-type approach is the second sentencing approach to have emerged from the *Kupreskic* case.[156] This approach from the viewpoint of the imposition of penalties for crimes against humanity and war crimes, basically involves the following steps:

1. Selecting the underlying offence, *e.g.*, torture.
2. Matching the underlying offence, *i.e.*, torture, with crimes against humanity and its additional persecutory element criterion and with war crimes, which does not have such an element.
3. Using the additional persecutory element criterion of torture as a crime against humanity to cancel out torture as a war crime.
4. Ultimately awarding a higher penalty for torture as a crime against humanity owing to its additional persecutory element criterion than would have been the case had the finding been one of torture as a war crime.

---

[152] See Schwelb, E. (1946), *Crimes Against Humanity*, British Year Book of International Law, p. 206. Stating that the term crimes against humanity: '...denotes a particular type of war crime, and is a kind of *clausa generalis*, the purpose of which is to make sure that inhumane acts violating general principles of the laws of all civilized nations committed in connexion with war should not go unpunished'. See also Orentlicher, *The Law of Universal Conscience: Genocide and Crimes against Humanity*, p. 18, at <http://www1.ushmm.org/conscience/events/conference_98/orentlicher.pdf> (last visited December 2004). Writing: 'To the extent that crimes against humanity as they were defined in the Nuremberg prosecutions did not overlap with war crimes, the law was addressed principally through the 1948 Convention on the Prevention and Punishment of the Crime of Genocide'. The above statements when read together support the view that the murder category of crimes against humanity, which has a non-discriminatory element, is equivalent to war crimes.

[153] See *infra*.

[154] See *Prosecutor* v. *Kupreskic et al.*, *supra* note 5, Chapter 1.

[155] See *Blaskic*, Trial Chamber, *supra* note 81, Chapter 3.

[156] See *Prosecutor* v. *Kupreskic et al.*, *supra* note 5, Chapter 1.

In addition, in support of the utilisation of the persecution-type v. murder-type approach as a basis for imposing higher penalties for crimes against humanity vis-à-vis war crimes is the following statement made by *Danner*:

> 'While the chapeau provision of war crimes has no particular mens rea, and the mens rea of the chapeau of crimes against humanity requires that the defendant knowingly associated himself with collective atrocity, the mens rea of persecution demands, in addition to the other elements of a crime against humanity, that the defendant have selected his victims based on their affiliation with a religious, political, or racial group. For this reason, persecution should generally be considered more serious, and punished with a longer sentence, than other crimes against humanity or war crimes. With persecution, the link between international crimes and bias crimes moves from the structural to the explicit. As explained earlier, the heavier punishments associated with bias crimes derive from the conviction that these crimes inflict greater harm on a greater number of victims than other kinds of crimes. Increasing the punishment for crimes committed on the basis of the victim's group identity is particularly appropriate for the kinds of crimes litigated before the Tribunals. Many of the worst violations of human rights are committed on discriminatory grounds. The nature of the conflicts that precipitated the crimes heard by the Tribunals, conflicts which pitched Serbs against Croats and Muslims, and Hutus against Tutsis, supports this assertion. Crimes based on discriminatory animus are also more likely to be committed on a wider scale. Discrimination may serve as a prelude to other crimes: Dehumanizing parts of the population of a country through propaganda and other discriminatory actions facilitates the subsequent commission of greater crimes by other groups in that society. In addition, the perpetrator of a bias crime deserves greater punishment because his motivation offends important societal norms. Punishing discriminatory motive is particularly appropriate in an international forum. A commitment to equality constitutes one of the foundational principles of the United Nations. Punishing bias crimes more severely than other crimes expresses the international community's condemnation of such crimes, which have posed great danger to the lives of civilians throughout the twentieth century. International criminal proceedings may, in fact, have a particularly powerful role in the articulation of a universal human dignity. International crimes motivated by group bias challenge and degrade this ideal. For these reasons, defendant R, convicted of persecution as a crime against humanity, should generally receive a longer sentence than either defendant Q, convicted of a murder-type crime against humanity or defendant Z, convicted of a war crime.'[157]

[157] See Danner, A.M. (2001), *Constructing a Hierarchy of Crimes in International Criminal Law.*

The above statement, basically justifies higher penalties for crimes against humanity vis-à-vis war crimes because of the presence of the additional persecutory element criterion.

3.2.2.5.2 Prosecutor v. *Blaskic (Trial Chamber)*

The persecution-type v. murder-type approach is the second sentencing approach to have emerged from this case.[158] This opinion is evident in the following sources: first, is the following paragraph extracted from the judgment of the Trial Chamber:

> 'Here, the Trial Chamber takes note of the ethnic and religious discrimination which the victims suffered. In consequence, the violations are to be analysed as persecution which, in itself, justifies a more severe penalty.'[159]
>
> 'Neither the Statute nor the Rules lays down expressly a scale of sentences applicable to the crimes falling under the jurisdiction of the Tribunal. Article 24(2) of the Statute draws no distinction between crimes when determining the sentence. The Trial Chamber passes only prison sentences, the maximum being life imprisonment pursuant to Sub-rule 101(A) of the Rules.'[160]
>
> 'The Trial Chamber is of the view that the provisions of Rule 101 of the Rules do not preclude the passing of a single sentence for several crimes. In this regard, the Trial Chamber takes note that although until now the ICTY Trial Chambers have rendered Judgements imposing multiple sentences, Trial Chamber I of the ICTR imposed single sentences in the Kambanda and Serushago cases.
>
> Moreover, the Trial Chamber recalls that in the cases brought before the military Tribunals at Nuremberg and Tokyo, a single sentence was passed even for multiple crimes... In light of this overall consistency, the Trial Chamber finds that there is reason to impose a single sentence for all the crimes of which the accused has been found guilty.'[161]

To the extent that the above statement recognizes that persecution as a crime against humanity offences deserve higher penalties than war crime offences, it can be viewed as endorsing the persecution-type v. murder-type approach.

Finally, the second source is the following criticism by the Appeals Chamber, of the Trial Chamber's sentencing approach:

> 'The Trial Judgement's wording does not make this clear, however, and the Appeals Chamber is *left with no option but to conclude that the Trial Chamber may have erred in its application of the law in allowing the Appellants' discriminatory*

[158] See *Blaskic*, Trial Chamber, *supra* note 81, Chapter 3.

[159] See *Blaskic*, id. para. 785.

[160] See id. para. 795.

[161] See id. paras 805-809.

> *intent to be used as an aggravating factor in calculating his sentence for persecutions.* The Trial Chamber should have stated its reasoning more clearly in order to ensure that the legal requirements of sentencing the Appellants were respected.'[162] [emphasis added]

3.2.2.6 Limitations of the Persecution-type v. Murder-type Approach

3.2.2.6.1 Violation of Nullum Crimen Sine Lege Principle

The *nullum crimen sine lege* principle, as recognized under Article 15 of the International Covenant on Civil and Political Rights (ICCPR), provides that:

> 'No one shall be held guilty of any criminal offence on account of any act or omission which did not constitute a criminal offence, under national or international law, at the time when it was committed. Nor shall a heavier penalty be imposed than the one that was applicable at the time when the criminal offence was committed.'[163]

Reliance on the persecution-type v. murder-type approach, in so far as the imposition of penalties for war crimes and crimes against humanity is concerned, may violate the *nullum crimen* principle, since national and international law do not recognize the offence of persecution. This opinion is evident in the following statement made by the ICTY in the *Kupreskic* case:

> 'The Trial Chamber will now discuss previous instances in which a definition of persecution has been suggested: firstly, in the *corpus* of refugee law and secondly, in the deliberations of the International Law Commission. The purpose of this discussion is to determine whether the definition propounded there may be held to reflect customary international law. It has been argued that further elaboration of what is meant by the notion of persecution is provided by international refugee law. In its comments on the Draft Code presented in 1991, the government of the Netherlands stated: "It would be desirable to interpret the term 'persecution' in the same way as the term embodied in the Convention on refugees is interpreted". The concept of persecution is central to the determination of who may claim refugee status under the Convention Relating to the Status of Refugees of 1951, as supplemented by the 1967 Protocol. However, the corpus of refugee law does not, as such, offer a definition of persecution. Nor does human rights law provide such a definition. The European Commission and the Court have on several occasions held that exposing a person to a risk of persecution in his or her country of origin

---

162 *Prosecutor* v. *Blaskic*, Appeals Chamber, *supra* note 33, Chapter 3, para. 695.

163 See Article 15, *supra* note 13, Chapter 1.

> may constitute a violation of Article 3 of the European Convention on Human Rights. However, their decisions give no further guidance as to the definition of persecution. In an attempt to define who may be eligible for refugee status, some national courts have delivered decisions on what acts may constitute persecution. Other cases show that national courts in applying refugee law have given persecution a broad definition, and have held that it includes denial of access to employment or education or more generally have drawn the conclusion that "there is an open ended category of forms of conduct capable of amounting to persecution, to be evaluated in the light of the Convention from case to case". The Trial Chamber finds, however, that these cases cannot provide a basis for individual criminal responsibility. *It would be contrary to the principle of legality to convict someone of persecution based on a definition found in international refugee law or human rights law*."[164] [emphasis added]

Finally, the above statement highlights the disadvantage of the persecution-type v. murder-type approach as a basis for sentencing war crimes and crimes against humanity. It should be recalled in this respect that the principle of legality also stipulates that fair notice must be given to defendants so as to guard against arbitrary judicial action.[165] It follows that where there are no provisions, which define persecution, imposing a higher sentence for persecution as a crime against humanity vis-à-vis war crimes would violate the principle of legality.

3.3 Conclusion

The purpose of this chapter was to identify and examine the main impediments to the imposition of relative penalties for war crimes and crimes against humanity under the ICTY. This was achieved in the context of the same interest approach, the widespread and systematic attacks v. isolated acts approach and the persecution-type v. murder-type approach.

Furthermore, as was demonstrated above, the three schools of thought on the imposition of relative penalties for war crimes and crimes against humanity under the ICTY constitute the main impediments for different reasons. Thus, in respect to the first of the above-mentioned approaches, *i.e.*, the same interest approach, to the extent that this approach is based on the opinion that war crime and crime against humanity offences, should attract the same level of penalties; it in any case constitutes an impediment to the imposition of relative penalties for both categories of international crimes.

In addition, as was explained above, this approach violates the principle of proportionality and the rule of transparency, which are important rules that

[164] See *Prosecutor* v. *Kupreskic et al.*, *supra* note 5, Chapter 1, paras. 586-589.

[165] See for example Bassiouni, M.C., *Crimes against Humanity in International Criminal Law*, Kluwer Law International, p. 124 (2d rev. ed. 1999), describing the purposes of the principle of legality.

have a binding effect upon sentencers. It follows that in terms of how the same interest approach impacts on the principle of proportionality, as it was explained above, that it is too simplistic to say that defendant X committed murder and therefore that murder will attract the same level of penalties whether it is classified as a war crime or as a crime against humanity. This is because additional questions such as the motive for the murder still need to be asked and connected with the substantive law on war crimes and crimes against humanity, *e.g.*, was the murder planned and calculated? Was it committed for material gain? Was it committed under severe pressure? Was it committed as a result of negligence? And so on and so forth.

In addition, all of the above questions challenge the notion that murder, when perpetrated in an international context, is automatically the same whether or not it is committed as a war crime or as a crime against humanity. This in turn means that the same interest approach does not adequately take into consideration the principle of proportionality in the sentencing of defendants for war crimes and crimes against humanity, and therefore it cannot be relied upon as a reliable and credible basis for imposing penalties for both categories of international crimes.

On the other hand, in relation to the impact of the same interest approach on transparency in the imposition of penalties for war crimes and crimes against humanity, it was clarified above that a lack of transparency is symptomatic of this approach. In other words, this approach negates any deeper discussion of the connection between offences underlying war crimes and crimes against humanity and both categories of international crimes. This opinion was illustrated by reference to the practice of imposing global sentences in cases of multiple convictions for war crime and crime against humanity offences, which is synonymous with the same interest approach. It was stated that this practice leads to a lack of transparency because it makes it impossible to verify whether or not concurrent and not consecutive sentences have been imposed in such cases.

From the point of view of transparency, the same interest approach will obviously lead to arbitrariness in sentencing for war crimes and crimes against humanity, since judges can simply pick and choose penalties with little constraint.

The second approach, which was identified and analyzed above and which was in favor of the imposition of relative penalties for war crimes and crimes against humanity, was the widespread and systematic attacks v. isolated acts approach. This approach is based on the assumption that crimes against humanity should attract higher penalties than war crimes, because they involve large scale premeditated attacks and, therefore, have the potential to result in a greater loss of life.

However, as was earlier demonstrated, this approach violates the principle of consistency. This opinion is based on the fact that it is too simplistic to say, for example, that crime against humanity offences are collectively more serious than war crime offences on the basis of the widespread and systematic elements. This is because more complex situations may arise which expose the weakness of this rationale, such as the bombardment of a city resulting in the death of thousands as a war crime vis-à-vis the murder of one person as a crime against humanity. In such a situation, it is difficult to see how crimes against humanity can be punished more severely than war crimes.

Finally, the third approach, which was identified and examined above and which was also in favor of the imposition of relative penalties for war crimes and crimes against humanity, was the persecution-type v. murder-type approach. This approach is based on a comparison of the persecution category of crimes against humanity, which has a persecutory element, with the murder category of crimes against humanity, which is said to be equivalent to war crimes and which does not have such an element. The assumption was that the former category of crimes against humanity should attract a higher penalty than war crimes because of the presence of the additional persecutory element. However, this approach violates the *nullum crimen sine lege* principle. This is because of the fact that, unlike the other offences listed under crimes against humanity, the offence of persecution does not exist in most municipal and international law systems. It follows that owing to this factor, formulating a sentencing policy for war crimes and crimes against humanity on the basis of the persecution-type v. murder-type approach would clearly clash with the *nullum crimen sine lege* principle.

CHAPTER 4

Solution to the Imposition of Relative Penalties for War Crimes and Crimes against Humanity under the ICTY

4.1 Introduction

Three main conclusions can be drawn from the previous chapters, which are of relevance to the present one. First, any sentencing framework for war crimes and crimes against humanity under the ICTY must take account of the following set of factors: proportionality, consistency, retroactive application of the law and transparency. Second, important clues exist on how the issue of sentencing for war crimes and crimes against humanity can be successfully resolved both in the context of the ICTY and globally. And, third, an ideal sentencing framework for war crimes and crimes against humanity is one, which can achieve the following:

1. Establish a credible link between the substantive law on both categories of international crimes and the determination of penalties.
2. Utilize the link mentioned in (1) above, to ensure proportionality in the imposition of penalties for war crimes and crimes against humanity, whilst taking into consideration all other relevant variables apart from the gravity of the offence, which are necessary for the sentencing calculus of both categories of international crimes such as the nature of the offender and the offender's response to the charges; and
3. Guarantee consistency in the following types of problematic situations:
   a) Situations where one defendant, on the basis of the same act, has been cumulatively convicted of and sentenced for both crimes against humanity and violations of the laws and customs of war.
   b) Situations where two different defendants have been convicted of the same offence *albeit* under two different headings *i.e.*, one, defendant A, convicted of murder as a crime against humanity and another defendant B, convicted of wilful killing as a violation of the laws and customs of war.
   c) Situations where two different defendants have committed two different crimes *e.g.* torture as a crime against humanity vis-à-vis murder as a war crime.

The purpose of this chapter is to establish a sentencing framework for war crime and crime against humanity offences under the ICTY, which takes account of all of the above factors.

Furthermore, under the proposed framework, crime against humanity offences will be treated as the more serious category of offences and will consequently attract the more severe sentences. The placement of crimes against humanity above war crimes is primarily due to the combined results of the analysis in chapters 2 and 3, which revealed the following:

- during the World War II trials, typical crime against humanity offences, attracted higher penalties than typical war crime offences; and
- the only credible difference between crimes against humanity and war crimes, is the fact that the former can be committed with a persecutory intent.

Finally, the solution adopted in this chapter essentially builds on the above findings by implementing the following tasks:

- developing the law on discriminatory and non-discriminatory motive offences, and using it to establish a substantive/sentencing framework for war crimes and crimes against humanity;
- utilizing the above substantive/sentencing framework to calculate sentencing ranges for war crime and crime against humanity offences.

4.2 The Discriminatory Motive v. Non-discriminatory Motive Approach

The discriminatory motive v. non-discriminatory motive approach is an approach that draws a line between racists who take advantage of the chaotic atmosphere in armed conflict situations to actualise their ideologies, by committing exceptionally brutal acts[1] and other individuals whose offences were merely a product of their being infected by the violence around them.[2] It

[1] See *Prosecutor* v. *Krstic*, Case No. IT-98-33, 2 August 2001, (ICTY Trial Chamber), para. 711. Stating: 'In determining the appropriate sentence, a distinction is to be made between the individuals who allowed themselves to be drawn into a maelstrom of violence, even reluctantly, and those who initiated or aggravated it and thereby more substantially contributed to the overall harm. Indeed, reluctant participation in the crimes may in some instances be considered as a mitigating circumstance.' See also *Prosecutor* v. *Dragan Nikolic*, Case No. IT-94-2-S, 18 December 2003, (ICTY Trial Chamber), para. 213. The Trial Chamber seemed to have convicted *Nikolic* of persecution as a crime against humanity based on the enormous brutality of the offences attributed to him: 'In conclusion, evaluating the abovementioned circumstances, the Trial Chamber accepts the following factors as especially aggravating: (i) The acts of the Accused were of an enormous brutality and continued over a relatively long period of time. They were not isolated acts. They expressed his systematic sadism. The Accused apparently enjoyed his criminal acts.' See also *Prosecutor* v. *Blaskic*, *supra* note 81, Chapter 3, para. 785. Stating: 'The motive of the crime may also constitute an aggravating circumstance when it is particularly flagrant. Case-law has borne in mind the following motives: ethnic and religious persecution, desire for revenge and sadism. Resultantly, the Trial Chamber considers that it is essential to review the motives of the crimes violating international humanitarian law imputed to the accused. Here, the Trial Chamber takes note of the ethnic and religious discrimination which the victims suffered. In consequence, the violations are to be analysed as persecution which, in itself, justifies a more severe penalty.'

[2] See for example *Prosecutor* v. *Delalic et al.*, *supra* note 16, Chapter. 1, para. 1285. The Trial Chamber seemed to have convicted one of the defendants, *Landzo*, of war crimes instead of persecution as a crime against humanity based on the finding that he was infected by the violence around him: 'This armed conflict created an environment clearly not of Mr. Landzo's own choosing. His home town of Konjic was shelled over a continued period of time in 1992, resulting in an atmosphere of constant fear of injury or death for himself and his family, and it was also under a blockade such that living conditions became very difficult. Many displaced persons were arriving in the town, having been expelled from their own

is this distinction, which underlies the argument in this chapter that crimes against humanity offences, *e.g.*, murder, rape and torture when committed on the basis of a discriminatory motive, should attract higher sentences than identical offences when committed as war crimes.[3]

However, before delving into the workings of the discriminatory motive v. non-discriminatory motive approach, it is important at this stage to draw attention to both the international customary law precedent for this approach and to the empirical evidence on the qualitative differences between offences committed with a discriminatory motive and those committed without such a motive. This is because of the fact that both factors give this approach credibility and legitimacy.

It follows that in relation to the international customary law precedent for the discriminatory motive v. non-discriminatory motive approach, the first port of call is the following statement made by *Blackstone:*[4]

> 'it is but reasonable that among crimes of different natures those should be most severely punished, which are the most destructive of the public safety and happiness.'[5]

---

homes in other parts of Bosnia and Herzegovina, and the stories of their mistreatment, and that of the Bosnian Muslim population in general, at the hands of the Bosnian Serbs and Croats, were undoubtedly circulating. Additionally, among the casualties of the conflict were persons close to Mr. Landzo. Given that the detainees in the Celebici prison-camp were Bosnian Serbs who had been arrested upon the execution of military operations by Bosnian government forces to break up pockets of resistance against the lawful authorities in the municipality, along with Mr. Landzo's immature and impressionable state of mind, it is not surprising that he might identify these detainees with the enemy that had inflicted this suffering and hardship upon himself, his family and his fellow members of the population of Bosnia and Herzegovina.'

3 Note that both Nikolic and Landzo were more or less of the same military rank, but that Nikolic was sentenced to 27 years imprisonment for his persecution as a crime against humanity convictions, See *infra* end note 1; whilst Landzo was sentenced to 15 years imprisonment for his war crimes convictions, see *infra* end note 2, See also *Prosecutor* v. *Todorovic,* Case No. IT-95-9/1, 31 July 2001, (ICTY Trial Chamber), para. 32; *Prosecutor* v. *Banovic,* Case No. IT-02-65/1, 28 October 2003, (ICTY Trial Chamber), para. 41.

4 See opinion of Chief Justice Rehnquist in *Wisconsin* v. *Todd Mitchel,* 61 United States Law Week 4575.

5 See id. at p. 4578, quoting Blackstone.

The above statement was utilised by Chief Justice *Rehnquist* in the U.S. case of *Wisconsin* v. *Todd Mitchel*,[6] as a basis for justifying penalty-enhancement for crimes committed with a discriminatory motive.[7]

Similarly, a system of penalty-enhancement for crimes committed on the basis of a discriminatory motive is recognized under U.S. Federal laws, as evidenced by subsection 3A1.1 of the United States Sentencing Commission Guidelines Manual (2003), which states:

> '**§3A1.1 Hate Crime Motivation or Vulnerable Victim**
> (a) If the finder of fact at trial or, in the case of a plea of guilty or nolo contendere, the court at sentencing determines beyond a reasonable doubt that the defendant intentionally selected any victim or any property as the object of the offense of conviction because of the actual or perceived race, color, religion, national origin, ethnicity, gender, disability, or sexual orientation of any person, increase by 3 levels.
> (b) (1) If the defendant knew or should have known that a victim of the offense was a vulnerable victim, increase by 2 levels.
>
> (2) If (A) subdivision (1) applies; and (B) the offense involved a large number of vulnerable victims, increase the offense level determined under subdivision (1) by 2 additional levels.
> (c) Special Instruction
> (1) Subsection (a) shall not apply if an adjustment from §2H1.1(b) (1) applies.'[8]

Furthermore, evidence of a system of penalty-enhancement for crimes committed on the basis of a discriminatory motive is also noticeable in other criminal law jurisdictions. One example is the United Kingdom, where the Crime and Disorder Act (1998)[9] imposes higher penalties for offences committed with a discriminatory motive. One way of illustrating how the Act works is with the aid of the offence of assault. Under this provision, the offence of assault is

---

6 The facts of the case are as follows. The accused was one of a group of young black men. After discussing a scene from the movie 'Mississippi Burning', which showed a white man beating a young black man, the group subsequently attacked a white boy. The accused was convicted of aggravated battery, but, because he was found to have selected the victim because of the victim's race, the penalty was increased pursuant to the Wisconsin hate crime statute to four years in jail (the maximum otherwise would have been two years). See id.

7 See id.

8 See United States Sentencing Commission, Guidelines Manual, § 3A1.1. Available at <http://www.ussc.gov/2003guid/2003guid.pdf >(last visited January 2004).

9 See Crime and Disorder Act (1998). Available at <http://www.hmso.gov.uk/acts/acts1998/19980037.htm> (last visited January 2004).

divided into basic assault and racially aggravated assault;[10] the latter, owing to its perceived greater individual and societal harm, is punished more severely than the former.[11]

Other countries, which recognize penalty enhancements for crimes committed on the basis of a discriminatory motive, include Portugal[12] and Norway.[13] In the case of Portugal, Section 132 of the Criminal Code of Portugal provides that:

---

10 See id. at Subsection 29(1) (c). 'Racially Aggravated Assault' is prohibited under subsection 29(1)(c) of the Crime and Disorder Act 1998 and carries a potential maximum sentence of 2 years imprisonment whilst 'ordinary' common assault carries a potential maximum sentence of only 6 months imprisonment.

11 See commentary of Home Office Racial Equality Unit Guide. Available at <http://www.homeoffice.gov.uk/docs/racagoff.html> (last visited January 2004). See also *R* v. *Saunders* [2000] 1 Criminal Appeal Reports 458. In this case the Court of Appeal suggested a sentencing structure for the racially aggravated offence based on a notional sentence for the 'basic' offence: '. . . it will often be helpful if the sentencing judge first considers, though he or she need not express it, the appropriate sentence for the offence in the absence of racial aggravation and then adds a further term for the racial element, so that the total sentence reflects the overall criminality. Even if the basic offence would not cross the custody threshold so as to merit imprisonment, the element of racial aggravation may well result in the custody threshold being passed. At what level in the sentencing scale a case falls . . . will depend on all the circumstances of the particular case.' *Saunders* was a case of racially aggravated actual bodily harm, for which the maximum penalty was increased by section 29 of the 1998 Act from 5 years for the basic offence to 7 years for the aggravated version. This led the Court of Appeal to suggest that, in such a case, it was possible to *add a maximum of two years* to what would have been the appropriate sentence if the offence had not been racially aggravated. See *R* v. *Morrison* [2000] Criminal Law Review 605. The applicant had been convicted, and sentenced concurrently, on three counts. These included one count of racially aggravated criminal damage, for which the sentence at first instance was three years' imprisonment, and one of burglary which had been treated as racially aggravated under section 82 of the 1998 Act. On that count the trial judge had said that normally a four and a half year sentence would have been imposed, and had added two years to take account of the racial aggravation. The applicant sought leave to appeal against sentence on the grounds that the total of six and a half years was 'manifestly excessive', and that the addition for racial aggravation had been too great. In refusing leave, the Court of Appeal said that the maximum enhancement for racial aggravation would be two years in a case where the statutory maximum had been increased from 5 to 7 years for a racially aggravated offence, but refused to accept defence counsel's submission that two years should be regarded as the *maximum* addition for racial aggravation in other types of cases: 'The court should certainly take account of the fact that a period of two years has been added by Parliament to the maximum for offences such as wounding, but the appropriate amount to add for racial aggravation in other cases will depend on all the circumstances of the case.'

12 See Section 132 of the Criminal Code of Portugal; see also Stockholm Race Hate Crimes Grotius Seminar, 11th – 15th of February 2001, Appendix 1. Available at <http://www.mpa.gov.uk/committees/mpa/2001/010308/16.htm> (last visited January 2004).

13 See Stockholm Seminar, id.

'...the severity of the punishment shall be increased if the motivation is the killing of a person on grounds of race, colour, national or ethnic origin or faith...the offender shall be sentenced to imprisonment from 12 to 25 years.'[14]

Whilst in the case of Norway, the Norwegian Penal Code was amended to ensure that the Courts should 'take into account racial motivation in setting higher sentences of imprisonment for crimes of coercion, (s222), threats (s227); offences against a person's life, body and health (s228-232) and vandalism (s292).'[15]

There is also evidence of the recognition of penalty enhancements for crimes committed on the basis of a discriminatory motive at the regional level. For instance, Article 8 of the European Union Proposal for a Council Framework Decision on Combating Racism and Xenophobia, stipulates the following:

'Article 8 – Racist and xenophobic motivation

Member States shall ensure that racist and xenophobic motivation may be regarded as aggravating circumstances in the determination of the penalty for offences other than those referred to in Articles 4 and 5.'[16]

In relation to the empirical evidence on the qualitative differences between offences committed with a discriminatory motive and those committed without such a motive, a number of findings suggest that offences committed with a discriminatory motive are more brutal than those committed without such a motive. For instance, research conducted by *Herek et al.*,[17] and *McDevitt, et*

---

[14] See id. For Canada see *R* v. *Ingram and Grimsdale* (1977), 35 Canadian Criminal Cases (2d) 376 (Ontario Court of Appeal). Dublin J.A., in this case, held on appeal that the trial judge erred in failing to hold that racial motivation for the attack was an aggravating factor to be taken into account at the sentencing stage, id., p. 377; See also *R* v. *Lelas* (1990), 41 Ontario Appeal Cases 73. Houlden J.A. argued that an offence that is directed against a particular racial or religious group is more heinous, as it attacks the every fabric of our society, id., p. 77; See *R* v. *Simms* (1990), 66 Canadian Criminal Cases (3d) 599 (Alberta Court of Appeal). The majority of the court held that the racially inspired assault required strong deterrent sentences and therefore increased the sentence, id., pp. 507-508.

[15] See id.

[16] See Article 8 European Union Proposal for a Council Framework Decision on Combating Racism and Xenophobia. Available at <http://europa.eu.int/smartapi/cgi/sga_doc?smartapi!celexplus!prod!DocNumber&lg=en&type_doc=COMfinal&an_doc=2001&nu_doc=664> (last visited January 2004).

[17] See Herek, Cogan and Gillis (2002), *Victim Experiences in Hate Crimes Based on Sexual Orientation*, Journal of Social Issues, 58(2), pp. 319-339; see Perry, B. (2003), *Where Do We Go from Here? Researching Hate Crime.* Paper presented at the first NCSRHC and Solon International Hate Crimes Conference in Nottingham, February 2003. Extracted from <http://www.flashmousepublishing.com/Where%20Do%20We%20Go%20From%20Here.%20Researching%20Hate%20Crime.pdf> (last visited January 2004).

al.,[18] indicate that 'the emotional, psychological, and behavioural impact of hate crimes are beginning to establish a solid pattern of more severe impact on bias crime victims, as compared to non-bias victims.'[19] In addition, in terms of the nature of physical harm on the victim, *Levin and McDevitt* [20] have proven that 'crimes committed with a discriminatory motive are often characterized by extreme brutality.'[21]

Furthermore, another source of the qualitative difference between offences committed with a discriminatory motive and those committed without such a motive, is *Perry*[22] who made the following relevant statement:

> 'Violent personal crimes motivated by bias are more likely to involve extraordinary levels of violence- multiple stabbings, or multiple strikes with a hammer or tire iron, for example, often by multiple perpetrators. It is as if the offender seeks to erase or obliterate the victim's identity.'[23]

Finally, it is noteworthy to mention the fact that, under the ICTY, there is some support for the contention that persecution as a crime against humanity, owing to its requisite discriminatory intent, is more serious than war crimes.[24] What is however problematic is how to streamline the perceived differences in gravity between both categories of international crimes into the context of international criminal law. The next sections therefore focus on this problem in greater detail. This is achieved by adopting the following steps:

1. Re-visiting existing penalties for war crime and persecution as a crime against humanity offences under the ICTY.
2. Identifying factors affecting the institutionalisation of relative penalties for persecution as a crime against humanity vis-à-vis war crimes under the ICTY.
3. Utilizing the results of the analysis in Step (2) to establish a sentencing tariff for crimes against humanity and war crimes.
4. Extending the discriminatory motive v. non-discriminatory motive approach to war crimes and crimes against humanity under domestic law.

---

18 See McDevitt *et al.* (2001), *Consequences for Victims: A Comparison of Bias- and Non-Bias Motivated Assaults*, American Behavioral Scientist, 4584, pp. 679-713; See Perry, id.

19 See McDevitt *et al.* id. See *supra* note 17, Chapter 4, Herek, Cogan and Gillis.

20 See Levin and McDevitt (1993), *Hate Crimes: The Rising Tide of Bigotry and Bloodshed*, New York NY: Plenum.

21 See id.

22 See Perry, B. (2003), *Where Do We Go from Here? Researching Hate Crime*, *supra* note 17, Chapter 4.

23 See id.

24 See for example *Prosecutor* v. *Todorovic*, *supra* note 3, Chapter 4; *Prosecutor* v. *Blaskic*, *supra* note 81, Chapter 3; *Prosecutor* v. *Banovic*, *supra* note 3, Chapter 4.

4.2.1 Step 1: Revisiting Existing Penalties for Persecution as a Crime against Humanity Offences and War Crimes Offences under the ICTY

This subsection involves a comparative analysis of penalties for multiple offences[25] and, where possible, single offences, convicted as persecution as a crime against humanity and as war crimes. The aim is to uncover impediments to the institutionalisation of relative penalties for persecution as a crime against humanity vis-à-vis war crimes, in the context of the ICTY. In addition, this objective will be achieved with the aid of two charts constructed in line with the following criteria:

a) Cases involving single convictions for multiple offences under persecution as a crime against humanity.
b) Cases involving cumulative convictions for persecution as a crime against humanity and war crimes based on the same set of acts, but where the aggravating effect of the former conviction was recognized as *lex specialis* to the latter. In such instances, the overall penalty will be attributed to the persecution as a crime against humanity conviction.
c) Cases involving single convictions for multiple war crimes offences.
d) Cases involving all rank and file war criminals.

[25] See Antonio Cassese, *International Criminal Law, supra* note 17, Chapter 3, p. 217. Discussing the ICTY's approach to awarding penalties, by stating: 'Of course, when a court satisfies itself that the accused is guilty on several heads for the same conduct, it should impose a sentence that reflects the whole of the culpable conduct. It would seem that the principles governing this matter were appropriately set out by the ICTY Appeals Chamber in *Delalic* and *others* (Appeal)....'.

(A) Chart on Penalties for Persecution as a Crime against Humanity offences

Accused	Rank	Murder	Rape	Tor-ture	Assault	Imprison-ment	Depor-tation	Property-Damage	Sen-tence
Kolundzija[26]	CG				1				3 years
Dosen[27]	CG			1	1	1			5 years
Zaric [28]	MM			1	1	1			6 years
Tadic[29]	MM						1		8 years
Banovic	CG	1			1				8 years[30]
Todorovic	HP		1		1	1	1		10 years
Sikirica	CC	1	1	1	1	1			15 years
Simic	HC			1	1	1	1		17 years
Obrenovic	MM	1		1				1	17 years
D. Nikolic	LM	1	1	1	1		1	1	23 years
M. Nikolic	MM	1		1		1			27 years

26 The accused in this case is assumed to have been wrongly convicted of persecution as a crime against humanity. See *infra* subsection 4.2.2.1.2.2.

27 The accused in this case is assumed to have been wrongly convicted of persecution as a crime against humanity. See *infra* subsection 4.2.2.1.2.1.

28 The accused in this case is assumed to have been wrongly convicted of persecution as a crime against humanity. See *infra* subsection 4.2.2.1.2.3.

29 The accused in this case is assumed to have been wrongly convicted of persecution as a crime against humanity. See id.

30 See Separate and Dissenting opinion of Judge Robinson, *supra* note 3, Chapter 4 (disagreeing with the penalty imposed on the defendant by stating: 'In all the circumstances of this case, including the aggravating and mitigating factors set out in this Judgement, I hold that the criminality of the Accused, involving as it does, five murders resulting from his participation in the beating of five persons, and the beating of twenty-seven others, warrants a longer term of imprisonment than eight years.')

(B) Chart on Penalties for War Crime Offences

Accused	Rank	Murder	Rape	Torture	Assault	Imprisonment	Deportation	Property Damage	Sentence
Erdemovic	LM	1							5 years
Furundzija	MM		1	1					9 years
Mucic	CC	1		1	1				9 years
Landzo	CG	1				1			15 years
Delic[31]	CG	1	1	1	1	1			18 years

Key

LM	Low Level Military Officer
CG	Camp Guard
MM	Medium Level Military Officer
HC	High Level Civilian
HP	High Level Police Officer
CC	Camp Commander

A perusal of the above charts reveals the following:

1. There is no clear pattern of higher penalties for persecution as a crime against humanity offences vis-à-vis war crimes offences. This assessment is based on the following evidence:
   a. The sentencing range of persecution as a crime against humanity offences is higher than that of war crimes offences, *i.e.* 3-27 years imprisonment vis-à-vis 5-18 years imprisonment; but the base level of the former is unusually lower than that of war crime offences, *i.e.* 3 years imprisonment vis-à-vis 5 years imprisonment.
   b. Normally for a pattern of higher penalties to emerge, there should be greater consistency between the base levels and the sentencing ranges of the two categories of international crimes. This opinion is, for example, evidenced by a comparison of murder and assault under the U.S. Sentencing Commission Guidelines Manual (2003).[32] Under this provision, murder for first time offenders has a base level of 43 and a sentencing range of life imprisonment. Assault has a base level of 28 and a sentencing range of 78-97 months imprisonment.[33]
2. The lack of a clear pattern of higher penalties for persecution as a crime against humanity offences vis-à-vis war crimes offences has less to do with the perception that persecution as a crime against humanity offences are of equal gravity to war crime offences and more to do with the following factors:

---

31 The accused in this case is assumed to have been wrongly convicted of persecution as a crime against humanity. See *infra* subsection 4.2.2.2.1.

32 See *supra* note 8, Chapter 4.

33 See id.

a. the determination of guilt by association; and
b. mistake of law;

The basis for the second conclusion is explained in greater detail below.

4.2.2 Step 2: Identification of Factors affecting the Institutionalisation of Relative Penalties for Persecution as a Crime against Humanity vis-à-vis War Crimes

4.2.2.1 The Determination of Guilt by Association

The determination of guilt by association is a practise, which is widely condemned under national law. This opinion is, for example, evidenced by the judgment of the United States Supreme Court in the case of *NAACP* v. *Claiborne Hardware Co.*[34] The Supreme Court established in that case that the government must prove specific intent to further the unlawful objectives of an organization that has both lawful and unlawful ends because mere guilt by association is 'alien to the traditions of a free society and the First Amendment itself'.[35] In addition, under the Fifth Amendment's Due Process Clause, guilt cannot be imposed unless it 'is personal'.[36]

In the context of the institutionalisation of relative penalties for persecution as a crime against humanity vis-à-vis war crimes, the determination of guilt by association has the effect of confusing cases involving persecution as a crime against humanity with those involving war crimes and *vice versa*, thereby creating a false picture of equanimity between the two categories of international crimes.

Furthermore, the problem is that some defendants are not convicted on the basis of the requisite intent to substantiate their charges but rather on the basis of the unlawful objectives of the ethnic group to which they belong. In other words, if you are a Serbian war criminal, the chances are that you are guilty of persecution as a crime against humanity instead of war crimes. Or if you are a Muslim war criminal, because you are a member of a persecuted ethnic group, it makes no sense to convict you under persecution as a crime against humanity, and therefore your conviction should instead be for war crimes. This point of view is illustrated at this preliminary stage, with the aid of empirical data on the following categories of cases:

1. Cases where defendants are convicted on the basis of their personal acts for persecution as a crime against humanity.

---

34 See *NAACP* v. *Claiborne Hardware Co.*, 458 United States Reports p. 886, p. 932 (1982).

35 See id.

36 See *Scales* v. *United States*, 367 United States Reports 203, pp. 224-26 (1961).

2. Cases where defendants are assumed to have been convicted on the basis of guilt by association for persecution as a crime against humanity.
3. Cases where defendants are convicted of war crimes.

(A) Defendants Convicted on the Basis of their Personal Acts for Persecution as a Crime against Humanity

Defendant	VS	GA	RM	CP	CA	SR	HF	RC	BA
Obrenovic	1	1	1	1	1	1			
Todorovic		1	1	1			0		
M. Nikolic	0	0	0	0	1				
D. Nikolic		1	1	1				1	
Banovic	1				1				
Sikirica		1							
Simic	0	0		1					

(B) Defendants Assumed to Have Been Convicted on the Basis of Guilt by Association for Persecution as a Crime against Humanity

Defendant	VS	GA	RM	CP	CA	SR	HF	RC	BA
Dosen		1							1
Kolundzija		1			1				1
Tadic	1	1			1				1
Zaric	1	1			1				1

Key

VS	Voluntary Surrender
GA	Guilty Plea and Acceptance of Responsibility
RM	Remorse
CP	Cooperation with the Prosecutor
CA	Character of the Accused
SR	Step towards Rehabilitation
BA	Significant Benevolent acts towards the Victims
HF	Health Factors
RC	Reconciliation

(C) Defendants Convicted of War Crimes

Accused	Murder	Rape	Torture	Assault	Imprisonment	Deportation	Property Damage	Mental Element
Erdemovic	1							Duress
Furundzija		1	1					Intention to forcibly obtain information
Mucic	1		1	1				Negligence
Landzo	1				1			Revenge
Delic	1	1	1	1	1			Revenge

The above charts reveal a number of relevant points, which can be utilised for the purpose of the current analysis. They are as follows:

1. Cases where defendants are convicted on the basis of their personal acts for persecution as a crime against humanity consistently show no evidence of benevolent actions towards their victims. The fact that the defendants complied with all other steps is irrelevant to the negation of the requisite intent for persecution as a crime against humanity, since they occurred after the fact.
2. Cases where defendants are convicted on the basis of guilt by association for persecution as a crime against humanity consistently show evidence of significant benevolent actions towards their victims. This in turn should be sufficient to negate the requisite intent for persecution as a crime against humanity.
3. Cases where defendants are convicted of war crimes consistently show evidence of mental elements, which negate the requisite intent for persecution as a crime against humanity, but substantiate that for war crimes. However, one exception to the rule is the *Delic* case as will be explained below.

Finally, since the characterisation of cases in the second category above is based on an assumption, the forthcoming subsections will utilise the *ratio* of cases in the third category, *i.e.* cases on mental elements which negate the requisite intent for persecution as a crime against humanity, as a basis for substantiating the claims made in relation to the former category of cases.

4.2.2.1.1 Defendants Convicted of War Crimes

The following subsections examine three cases where the ICTY correctly held that the defendants committed war crimes. These cases are: *Furundzija,*[37] *Mucic*[38] *and Lanzo.*[39] The aim is to identify the *ratio decidendi* of each case and

[37] See *Prosecutor* v. *Furundzija, supra* note 120, Chapter 3.

[38] See *Prosecutor* v. *Delalic et al., supra* note 16, Chapter 1.

[39] See id.

to utilise this *ratio* in the context of cases where the defendants were convicted of persecution as a crime against humanity offences on the basis of guilt by association.

4.2.2.1.1.1 Prosecutor v. *Furundzija*

This case involves the rape and torture of a Muslim woman by the accused *Furundzija*, who is a Serb.[40] It followed that in relation to his role in the aforementioned atrocities, the accused was convicted of war crimes.[41] The key statement, which indicates the basis for his conviction, is the following:

> '...it is alleged that the accused continued to interrogate her about her children, her alleged visits to the Moslem part of Vitez and why certain Croats had helped her when she was Moslem. The witness testified that the accused also issued threats against her children. She spoke of a direct relationship between his dissatisfaction with her answers and the assaults inflicted upon her by Accused B. She stated: "it was one at the same time the interrogation and the ill-treatment and the abuse".'[42]

As is evident from the above, the fact that there was a direct relationship between the victim's failure to provide satisfactory answers to the accused whilst she was being questioned and the ill-treatment and abuse that she was subjected to negated the requisite mental element for establishing discriminatory motive.[43] It is therefore this factor, which was instrumental in the accused conviction for war crimes.

4.2.2.1.1.2 Mucic (Prosecutor v. *Delalic)*

The facts of this case revolve around atrocities committed against Serbian detainees in an infamous prison camp known as the Celebici prison camp.[44] In relation to his role in these atrocities, the accused was convicted of war crimes.[45] The key statement, which indicates the basis for his conviction, is the following:

---

40 See *supra* note 120, Chapter 3.

41 See id.

42 See id., para. 82.

43 See Ambos and Wirth, *The Current law of Crimes Against Humanity, An Analysis of UNTAET Regulation 15/2000*, p. 67, distinguishing between the different motives for torture by stating: 'As to the content of the purpose requirement, *Kunarac* held: 'The following purposes have become part of customary international law: (a) obtaining information or a confession (b) punishing, intimidating or coercing the victim or a third person, (c) discriminating, on any ground, against the victim or a third person.' One can deduce from this statement that *Furundzija's* war crime convictions are based on (a) and (b) above.

44 See *supra* note 16, Chapter 1.

45 See id.

'The criminal liability of Mr. Mucic has arisen entirely from his failure to exercise his superior authority for the beneficial purpose of the detainees in the Celebici prison-camp. In the instant case, Mr. Mucic, by means of deliberate neglect of his duty to supervise his subordinates, thereby enabling them to mistreat the detainees in the Celebici prison-camp, has been imputed with knowledge of their crimes. Mr. Mucic was consciously creating alibis for possible criminal acts of subordinates. It would constitute a travesty of justice, and an abuse of the concept of command authority, to allow the calculated dereliction of an essential duty to operate as a factor in mitigation of criminal responsibility. In this particular case, the reason for staying away from the prison-camp at nights without making provision for discipline during these periods, which was to save himself from the excesses of the guards and soldiers, is rather an aggravating factor.'[46]

As is evident from the above, the accused war crime convictions were based on the fact that he neglected his duty to supervise his subordinates, thereby enabling them to mistreat detainees.[47] It is, therefore, this factor that was instrumental in the accused conviction for war crimes.[48]

4.2.2.1.1.3 Landzo (Prosecutor v. *Delalic)*

The case deals with atrocities committed against Serbian detainees in an infamous prison camp known as the Celebici prison camp.[49] In relation to his role in these atrocities, the accused was convicted of war crimes.[50] The key statement, which indicates the basis for his conviction, is the following:

'This armed conflict created an environment clearly not of Mr. Landzo's own choosing. His home town of Konjic was shelled over a continued period of time in 1992, resulting in an atmosphere of constant fear of injury or death for himself and his family, and it was also under a blockade such that living conditions became very difficult. Many displaced persons were arriving in the town, having been expelled from their own homes in other parts of Bosnia and Herzegovina, and the stories of their mistreatment, and that of the Bosnian Muslim population in general, at the hands of the Bosnian Serbs and Croats, were undoubtedly circulating. Additionally, among the casualties of the conflict were persons close to Mr. Landzo. Given that the detainees in the Celebici prison-camp were Bosnian

46 See id., paras. 1248-1250.

47 See Sarooshi, D., *Command Responsibility and the Blaskic Case, supra* note 67, Chapter 3, identifying negligence as a *mens rea* for war crimes.

48 See Saul, B. (2000), *The International Crime of Genocide in Australian Law.* Id., ruling out the possibility of negligence as a basis for proving discriminatory intent in connection with genocide which is similar to persecution as a crime against humanity.

49 See *supra* note 16, Chapter 1.

50 See id.

> Serbs who had been arrested upon the execution of military operations by Bosnian government forces to break up pockets of resistance against the lawful authorities in the municipality, along with Mr. Landzo's immature and impressionable state of mind, it is not surprising that he might identify these detainees with the enemy that had inflicted this suffering and hardship upon himself, his family and his fellow members of the population of Bosnia and Herzegovina.'[51]

As is evident from the above statement, the accused war crime convictions were based on the fact that he wanted to avenge atrocities committed against people close to him by Serbs.[52] It is, therefore, this factor, which was instrumental to the accused conviction for war crimes. Finally, the following statement made by *Bing Bing Jia*,[53] adds weight to the above point of view:

> 'How could ordinary souls have such an ambitious intention, so to speak, when they inflicted savage sufferings upon a presumed enemy, combatant or not, during a war? In fact, every one of them might think what they were doing was a means of reprisal against wrongs their side had received, unless it was proved that they had the common intent of hatred towards a certain ethnic group...However, this hatred if proven may, it is admitted, provide a significant indicator to the distinct purpose of discrimination which is always behind the commission of crimes against humanity.'[54]

Bing Bing Jia, in the above statement, basically differentiates between revenge and ethnic hatred.

4.2.2.1.2 Defendants Convicted on the Basis of Guilt by Association for Persecution as a Crime against Humanity

The forthcoming subsections examine five cases where the ICTY is assumed to have convicted defendants of persecution as a crime against humanity offences on the basis of guilt by association. These cases are: *Dosen*,[55] *Kolundzija*,[56] *Simic*,[57] *Tadic*[58] and *Zaric*.[59]

---

[51] See id., para. 1285.

[52] See *Prosecutor* v. *Blaskic, supra* note 81, Chapter 3, para. 785 and note 1708, pointing out that the desire for revenge was instrumental in the selection of war crime convictions in the *Celibici* case.

[53] See Bing Bing Jia, N., *The Differing Concepts of War Crimes and Crimes against Humanity in International Criminal Law.*

[54] See id. p. 253.

[55] See *Prosecutor* v. *Sikirica et al.*, Case No. IT-95-8, 13 November 2001, (ICTY Trial Chamber).

[56] See id.

[57] See *Prosecutor* v. *Blagoje Simic et al.*, Case No. It-95-9, 17 October 2003, (ICTY Trial Chamber).

[58] See id.

[59] See id.

4.2.2.1.2.1 Dosen (Prosecutor v. *Sikirica et al.)*

This case involves atrocities committed against Croatian and Muslim detainees in a prison camp, known as the Keraterm camp, by the accused *Dosen,* who is a Serb.[60] The accused was convicted of beatings and harassments under persecution as a crime against humanity and sentenced to 5 years imprisonment.[61]

In order to fully appreciate the wrongfulness of the Trial Chamber's holding, certain factors have to be taken into account. First, is the following statement made by the Trial Chamber, which will be assumed here as a significant factor in the defendant's persecution as a crime against humanity convictions:

> 'Practically every case prosecuted before the International Tribunal has involved ethnic cleansing, in which particular groups have been specifically targeted for various kinds of abuse and mistreatment, including murder and detention...the Chamber sees no essential difference between this case and the other trials for ethnic cleansing in the Prijedor municipality.'[62]

The above statement constitutes proof of guilt by association. This is because of the fact that it was not directed at the case at hand but, rather, at the policy of ethnic cleansing implemented by the Serbs against Muslims and Croats. In addition, although the above statement was made in relation to another defendant in the case,[63] it is nevertheless important since it suggests that a similar approach may have been applied to *Dosen,* who was one of the joint defendants in this case.[64]

Furthermore, in support of the above opinion is the evidence relating to the charges against the defendant. In relation to the defendant's conviction for beatings as a form of persecution as a crime against humanity, the relevant statement is the following:

> 'As noted, there was also evidence that beatings occurred on Dosen's shift although he himself was not present. For instance, Witness B said that one night he and many others were beaten during Dosen's shift, as was Drago Tokmadzic (a Croat) who died as a result of his beating. Witness D said that he was so badly beaten that night during Dosen's shift that he called out: "Kajin, they are killing me." Dosen came over and told the guards to stop beating the witness and the

60 See *supra* note 55, Chapter 4.

61 See id.

62 See *Prosecutor* v. *Sikirica et al.* Judgement on Defence Motion to Acquit, 3 September 2001.

63 This statement was made in relation to another defendant in the same case, *Sikirica.*

64 One major factor in suggesting that guilt by association was a major factor in *Dosen's* trial is the fact that it was the same set of Judges who made the statement on guilt by association, during the motion for acquittal, that ended up convicting and sentencing the accused. Compare note 55, Chapter 4 with note 62, Chapter 4.

beating stopped. Jusuf Arifagic said that beatings were less frequent on Dosen's shift: "if he was physically present there and had control over it, then there wasn't as much beating and mistreatment. However ... if his shift was on and he was not present, it would start immediately".

Finally, there was some evidence that Dosen intervened or prevented beatings. Witness H said that on one occasion, the arrival of Dosen saved his life while he himself was under attack from Cupo Banovic. Hajrudin Zubovic said that on his arrival at Keraterm he was in a column of detainees who were being interrogated and mistreated by Cupo Banovic and that on Sikirica's intervention, Dosen stopped him twice, telling him to let the prisoners be: on the second occasion Banovic obeyed him and moved away. Witness G described an occasion when Zigic lined up two rows of inmates, beat them, and made them fight each other, until Dosen arrived and told Zigic to stop.'[65]

A key point in the above statement, which clearly demonstrates that the Trial Chamber was wrong in convicting the accused for beatings as a form of persecution as a crime against humanity, is the fact that the accused, *Dosen*, clearly tried to stop the beatings of detainees in his camp.[66]

Second, in relation to the conviction for harassment as a form of persecution as a crime against humanity, the following is the relevant statement:

'Damir Dosen admits that many detainees were beaten during their detention in the Keraterm camp and that the beatings caused both serious physical and mental harm to the victims and mental harm to those who witnessed such events. This contributed in large part to the atmosphere of terror in Keraterm. These acts were perpetrated by some of the guards and sometimes by army personnel and others who entered the camp without authority and who would beat and mistreat detainees on a regular and frequent basis.'[67]

---

[65] See *supra* note 55, Chapter 4, paras. 158-159.

[66] See, for example, the Mucic trial, *supra* note 16, Chapter 1, para. 1247, evidencing the fact that Mucic's positive interventions in the mistreatment of detainees by guards was critical to his conviction for war crimes instead of persecution as a crime against humanity. See also Carcano, A., *Sentencing and the Gravity of the Offence in International Criminal Law*, at p. 608. Writing in connection with the psychology of a perpetrator of a crime against humanity that: '..., an individual in committing a crime against humanity, reveals total disregard for the consequences to the victims of his actions. This disregard becomes evident when one considers that if an individual objects to a given attack against civilians, he should simply refrain from it and not join in. The existence of an overall criminal plan or a definite course of conduct should act as a brake to the commission of certain deeds rather than as an authorisation. In the case of crimes against humanity, the perpetrator is reckless to the consequences that may derive from his actions and this reveals a special wickedness.'

[67] See *supra* note 55, Chapter 4, para. 160.

As is evident from the above, the defendant was neither involved in the harassments nor did he authorise it. This factor is equally important because it adds weight to the fact that he did not commit the offences attributed to him with a discriminatory motive.

4.2.2.1.2.2 Kolundzjia (Prosecutor v. *Sikirica et al.)*

This case revolves around atrocities committed against Croatian and Muslim detainees in a prison camp, known as the Keraterm camp, by the accused *Kolundzija*, who is a Serb.[68] The accused was convicted of persecution as a crime against humanity for failing to take positive action against the mistreatment of Muslim detainees.[69]

In order to fully appreciate the wrongfulness of the Trial Chamber's holding, certain factors have to be taken into account. First, is the fact that this trial was actually part of a joint trial involving *Dosen, i.e.* the defendant in section 4.2.2.1.2.1 above. With this in mind, the statement on guilt by association, which appeared to have influenced *Dosen's* conviction of persecution as a crime against humanity, may therefore be considered as having a bearing on the assessment of the convictions in the present case.

Furthermore, another way of exonerating the accused is by examining the evidence against him. The relevant statements here are the following:

> 'The Prosecution concedes that almost all the witnesses testified that Kolundzija did not personally mistreat or condone the mistreatment of detainees and, indeed , frequently prevented guards on his shift from doing so, and that he also attempted to prevent some visitors from mistreating or killing the detainees under his care during his shift.
>
> The Chamber has heard ample evidence of Dragan Kolundzija's efforts to ease the harsh conditions in the Keraterm camp for many of the detainees. It considers that, on the basis of the testimony as to his benevolent attitude towards the detainees, Dragan Kolundzija should receive a significant reduction in his sentence.'[70]

The above statements highlight the inconsistent approach of the ICTY to the attribution of criminal responsibility for persecution as a crime against humanity and war crimes. In other words, how can people like *Kolundzija*, who took positive action to alleviate the suffering of Muslim and Croatian detainees, possess the requisite intent for persecution as a crime against humanity when people like *Landzo*[71] and *Furundzija*,[72] who attacked their victims with impunity, were convicted of war crimes?

---

68 See id.

69 See id.

70 See id., paras. 204 and 230.

71 See *supra* subsection 4.2.2.1.1.3.

72 See *supra* subsection 4.2.2.1.1.1.

4.2.2.1.2.3 Zaric (Prosecutor v. *Blagoje Simic et al.)*

This case pertains to atrocities committed against Croats and Muslims in a town known as Bosanski Samac, by the accused *Zaric,* who is a Serb.[73] The accused was convicted of crimes against humanity for persecutions for aiding and abetting cruel and inhumane treatment including beatings, torture and confinement under inhumane conditions.[74]

In terms of assessing the guilt of the accused for persecution as a crime against humanity, two factors have to be taken into account: The first is statements made by the Trial Chamber in the course of its deliberations in the case, whilst the second is the allegations against the accused. In relation to the first factor, the relevant statement is the following:

> 'The Trial Chamber accepts the evidence that Blagoje Simic, through his activities with the Crisis Staff, helped to improve the daily life conditions of some inhabitants of Bosanski Samac, regardless of their ethnicity. This, however, does not detract from the fact that he was actively participating in the persecution of Bosnian Muslims and Croats at the same time. Blagoje Simic chose to be associated with members of the military, the police, and Serbian paramilitaries. In particular, he chose to continue to be involved in activities along with paramilitaries, and members of the police, who were known for their violent and brutal behaviour. In particular, despite having had strong disagreements with Stevan Todorovic, and generally disapproving of his behaviour...All these elements lead the Trial Chamber to consider Blagoje Simic as one of the principal participants in the campaign of persecution which befell non-Serbs in the Municipality of Bosanski Samac.'[75]

The above statement constitutes proof of guilt by association. This is because of the fact that it considered the accused's association with persons involved in violent and brutal behaviour as the essential factor in his persecution as a crime against humanity conviction. In addition, although the above statement was made in relation to another defendant in the case,[76] who was coincidentally guilty of the crimes attributed to him owing to his high level position in the town, it is nevertheless important since it suggests that a similar approach may have been applied to *Zaric,* who was one of the joint defendants in this case.

Furthermore, another one way of exonerating the accused is by examining the evidence against him. The relevant statement here is the following:

---

[73] See *supra* note 57, Chapter 4.

[74] See id., para. 1123.

[75] See id., paras. 1079-1081.

[76] This statement was made in relation to another defendant in the same case, *Simic.*

> 'There is some evidence before the Chamber that Simo Zaric attempted to change the course of events. Although this conduct had been taken into consideration in the determination of Simo Zaric's criminal liability, the Trial Chamber feels that some of these acts at the time also ought to be taken into account in mitigation : (1) that in April 1992, Simo Zaric advocated the release of Sulejman Tihic, Witness N, and of Muslim members of the 4th Detachment who had been arrested and were detained at the SUP and TO; (2) that Simo Zaric initiated and organised the transfer of a group of detainees from the Brcko barracks, which some of the detainees testified saved their lives; (3) that Simo Zaric, as soon as he heard about the Crkvina massacre, took steps to report the matter to higher authorities within the Municipality and in Serbia; (4) that Simo Zaric conducted his interrogations humanely in that no beatings accompanied them, and proper records of interviews were made ; (5) that Simo Zaric authored the "Thirteen Signatories" Report which documented some of the problems happening at the time, in an attempt to improve the situation.'[77]

The above statement clearly shows that the accused did not posses any discriminatory intent.[78] Finally, Judge *Per-Johan Lindholm*, in his Separate and Partly Dissenting Opinion in the same case, also expressed a similar point of view when he stated:

> 'No evidence has been adduced by the Prosecution as to whether the perpetrators of the persecutions felt any reassuring and encouraging effect from Simo Zaric's presence in the detention facilities or his participation in the interrogations. The appalling conditions in the SUP had been set up and orchestrated by the Chief of Police, Stevan Todorovic and his henchmen, the paramilitaries, brought in by him among others from Serbia and consisting of a group of ruthless thugs like "Lugar", "Crni", and "Debeli" and others of the same kind which by Stevan Todorovic were given free access to the different places of detention, day and night, in order to be able to beat up and torture, even kill, the detainees whenever they found themselves in the mood to do so. I fail to see how these people and their co-perpetrators could have been encouraged and morally supported to a substantial degree by the interrogations and presence of Simo Zaric, who on more than one occasion publicly denounced the mistreatment of detainees.

77 See *supra* note 57, Chapter 4, para. 1109.

78 See *Kupreskic* case, *supra* note 5, Chapter 1, para. 634, identifying the requisite elements for establishing persecution by stating: 'When examining some of the examples of persecution..., one can discern a common element: those acts were all aimed at singling out and attacking certain individuals on discriminatory grounds, by depriving them of the political , social, or economic rights enjoyed by members of the wider society. The deprivation of these rights can be said to have as its aim the removal of those persons from the society in which they live alongside the perpetrators, or eventually even from humanity itself.'

> Therefore, I arrive at the conclusion that the presence of Simo Zaric and the conduct of interrogations at the SUP did not in any way affect the prevalent terror regime in the SUP or in the other detention facilities. It continued after his presence in the same manner as before. In the eyes of the paramilitaries, who were the worst torturers, Simo Zaric did not have any air of authority, which perhaps is best depicted by the way he was treated by some of them.
>
> For these reasons, I find that the Prosecution has failed to prove its case against Simo Zaric beyond reasonable doubt, and that therefore Simo Zaric should have been found not guilty in respect of Count 1.'[79]

The above statement basically rules out the possibility that *Zaric* was a collaborator in the persecutions committed against Muslims and Croat detainees.

4.2.2.1.2.4 Tadic (Prosecutor v. *Blagoje Simic et al.)*

This case deals with atrocities committed against Croats and Muslims in a town known as Bosanski Samac by the accused *Tadic,* who is a Serb.[80] The accused was convicted of deportation as a form of persecution as a crime against humanity.[81]

In terms of assessing the guilt of the accused for persecution as a crime against humanity, two factors have to be taken into account: The first is the fact that this trial is actually part of a joint trial involving *Zaric, i.e.* the defendant in section 4.2.2.1.2.3 above. With this in mind, the statement on guilt by association, which appeared to have influenced *Zaric's* conviction of persecution as a crime against humanity, may therefore be considered as having a bearing on the assessment of the convictions in the present case.

Furthermore, the other relevant factor exonerating the accused is the strength of the evidence against him. The relevant statements here are the following:

> 'The Trial Chamber accepts the evidence showing that Miroslav Tadic helped some Bosnian Muslims during the war. Further, although Miroslav Tadic is found to have substantially contributed to exchanges found to constitute deportation, his motives were to help "the other side to find their relatives so that the other side would do the same for the Serbs".'[82]

---

79 See id., Separate and Partly Dissenting Opinion of Judge Per-Johan Lindholm, 17 October 2003, paras. 33-35.

80 See id.

81 See id., para. 1119.

82 See id., para. 1096.

And,

> 'For all these reasons, I am convinced that Miroslav Tadic sincerely believed that the exchanges were the only means to get the non-Serb civilians out of their miserable and – in many cases – terrifying living conditions, and that he helped them to a better life. As Miroslav Tadic stated at the closure of the case: "I thought I was doing something humane, helping people in distress." His participation in their deportation helped them to exercise their right to freedom to a greater degree than during their detention and avoided the constant danger to the life and limb of the non-Serb prisoners in the detention facilities in Bosanski Samac. Furthermore, it has not been made out on the evidence that any other adequate means was available to Miroslav Tadic to free the non-Serb civilians from the situation they were in. I am convinced beyond all doubts that Miroslav Tadic should be found not guilty in respect of Count 1 and Count 2.'[83]

The above statements, particularly the second one made by Judge *Per-Johan Lindholm* in his Separate and Partly Dissenting Opinion in the same case, clearly show that both the words and the actions of the accused failed to establish any concrete evidence of discriminatory motive.[84]

4.2.2.2 "Mistake of Law"

The term "mistake of law" as used here means wrong decisions attributable to bad judgment. In the context of the institutionalisation of relative penalties for persecution as a crime against humanity vis-à-vis war crimes, "mistake of law" has the effect of juxtaposing cases involving persecution as a crime against humanity with those involving war crimes and *vice versa*. This in turn creates a false picture of equanimity between the two categories of international crimes. Finally, the forthcoming subsection will be used to illustrate this opinion.

4.2.2.2.1 Delic (Prosecutor v. *Delalic)*

This case involves atrocities committed against Serbian detainees in an infamous prison camp known as the Celebici prison camp.[85] In relation to his role in these atrocities, the accused was convicted of war crimes.[86]

---

[83] See id., Separate and Partly Dissenting Opinion of Judge Per-Johan Lindholm, 17 October 2003, paras. 27-28.

[84] See *Prosecutor* v. *Kayishema and Ruzindana*, Case no. ICTR-95-1-T May 21, 1999, (ICTR Trial Chamber), para. 93 (stating: 'The Chamber finds that the intent (discriminatory intent) can be inferred from either words or deeds and may be determined by a pattern of purposeful action.')

[85] See *supra* note 16, Chapter 1.

[86] See id.

In order to fully appreciate the wrongfulness of the Trial Chamber's holding, it is necessary to re-examine the allegations made in respect of the accused war crimes convictions. The relevant statement is:

> 'The motive for the commission of these breaches of humanitarian law is also a relevant aggravating factor to be taken into account in the sentencing of Hazim Delic. The evidence indicates that, as well as having a general sadistic motivation, Hazim Delic was driven by feelings of revenge against people of Serb ethnicity. Before raping Ms. Antic, he stated that "the Chetniks were guilty for every thing that was going on. He [Delic] started to curse my Chetnik mother". Nedeljko Draganic, stated that Mr. Delic "walked into the [sic] Hanger Number 6 on one occasion and he told us that we are all detained because we were Serbs". Mirko Dordic testified that, on one occasion, Mr. Delic took detainees outside into the sunshine. The guards switched on spiritual Muslim songs while the detainees had to shout certain slogans in response to Mr. Delic's, and others, prompting, such as "Hazim is the greatest" or "Sieg Heil". Risto Vukalo stated that Mr. Delic took the detainees out in front of Hanger 6, and ordered them to say slogans of a religious nature which were distasteful to them.'[87]

What is immediately striking about the above statement is the similarities, which it shares with the facts of the *Jelisic* case.[88] This opinion can be explained by a comparison of the factual allegations in both cases. The relevant statement in the *Jelisic* case is therefore the following:

> 'Often, Goran Jelisic insulted the Muslims by calling them "balijas" or "Turks". Of one detainee whom he had just hit, Goran Jelisic allegedly said that he must be have been made to dirty his hands with a "balija" before then executing him.
>
> It also appears from the testimony that Goran Jelisic allegedly humiliated the Muslims by forcing them to sing Serbian songs. At the police station, he supposedly made them line up facing the Serbian flag and sing. The Trial Chamber concludes that in this case the discriminatory intent has been proved.'[89]

As is evident from the above statements, *Delic* was found to have forced Serbian detainees to sing Muslim songs during the commission of his atrocities. This action is similar to that of *Jelisic's*, who forced Muslim detainees to sing Serbian songs during the commission of his atrocities. In addition, one should also bear in mind the fact that the above statement, made in connection with the *Jelisic* case, was instrumental in the finding that *Jelisic* committed his offences with a discriminatory intention.[90]

---

87 See id. para. 1269.

88 See *Prosecutor* v. *Jelisic*, Case no. IT-95-10, 14 December 1999, (ICTY Trial Chamber).

89 See id., paras. 75-77.

90 See id.

Perhaps the strongest evidence against *Delic's* war crime convictions is that his actions were used as a basis for convicting another defendant, *Nikolic,*[91] of persecution as a crime against humanity. This opinion is evident in the following statement extracted from the *Nikolic* case:

> 'Such behaviour recalls that commented upon by the Trial Chamber in "Celebici" with which this Trial Chamber fully agrees:
>
> [...] The most disturbing, serious and thus, an aggravating aspect of these acts, is that [Mr. ...] apparently enjoyed using this device upon his helpless victims. [...] There is little this Trial Chamber can add by way of comment to this attitude, as its depravity speaks for itself.
>
> [...]
>
> The manner in which these crimes were committed are indicative of a sadistic individual who, at times, displayed a total disregard for the sanctity of human life and dignity. This is only amplified by the fact that [Mr. ...] was the deputy commander of the prison-camp. His victims were captive and at his mercy, he abused his position of power and trust [...] [T]hese circumstances are considered significant aggravating factors in the sentencing of [Mr. ...].'[92]

Finally, in light of the above, it is surprising that, despite the similarities between *Delic's* actions and those of *Jelisic* and *Nikolic,* the former defendant was convicted of war crimes, whilst the latter were convicted of persecution as a crime against humanity.

4.2.3 Step 3: Utilizing the Results of the Analysis in Step (2) to Establish a Sentencing Tariff for Crimes against Humanity and War Crimes

This subsection utilizes the results of the above analysis to revise the penalty charts in subsection 4.2.1 on persecution as a crime against humanity and war crimes. The aim is to prove that where there is greater consistency in judicial decisions on cases involving persecution as a crime against humanity and war crimes, it will be much easier to institutionalise relative penalties for persecution as a crime against humanity offences vis-à-vis war crime offences under the ICTY.

---

91 See *supra* note 1, Chapter 4.

92 See id., para. 193.

(A) Revised Chart on Penalties for Persecution as a Crime against Humanity Offences

Accused	Rank	Murder	Rape	Tor-ture	Assault	Impris-onment	Depor-tation	Property Damage	Sentence
Banovic	CG	1			1				8 years[93]
Todorovic	HP		1		1	1	1		10 years
Sikirica	CC	1	1	1	1	1			15 years
Simic	HC			1	1	1	1		17 years
Obrenovic	MM	1		1				1	17 years
Delic	CG	1	1	1	1	1			18 years
D. Nikolic	LM	1	1	1	1		1	1	23 years
M. Nikolic	MM	1		1		1			27 years

(B) Revised Chart on Penalties for War Crime Offences

Accused	Rank	Murder	Rape	Torture	Assault	Impris-onment	Deporta-tion	Property Damage	Sen-tence
Kolundzija	CG				1				3 years
Erdemovic	LM	1							5 years
Dosen	CG			1	1	1			5 years
Zaric	MM			1	1	1			6 years
Tadic	MM						1		8 years
Furundzija	MM		1	1					9 years
Mucic	CC	1		1	1				9 years
Landzo	CG	1				1			15 years

Key

LM	Low Level Military Officer
CG	Camp Guard
MM	Medium Level Military Officer
HC	High Level Civilian
HP	High Level Police Officer
CC	Camp Commander

93 See Separate and Dissenting Opinion of Judge Robinson, *supra* note 3, Chapter 4. Disagreeing with the penalty imposed on the defendant by stating: 'In all the circumstances of this case, including the aggravating and mitigating factors set out in this Judgement, I hold that the criminality of the Accused, involving as it does, five murders resulting from his participation in the beating of five persons, and the beating of twenty-seven others, warrants a longer term of imprisonment than eight years.'

The following relevant inferences can be drawn from the above revised charts:

1. Persecution as a crime against humanity offences has a higher base level than war crime offences, *i.e.* 8 years of imprisonment vis-à-vis 3 years of imprisonment.
2. Persecution as a crime against humanity offences has a higher sentencing range than war crimes offences, *i.e.* 8-27 years of imprisonment vis-à-vis 3-15 years of imprisonment.
3. The best way of making sense out of the different range of sentences above is by comparing the individual circumstances of the above defendants and the gravity of the offences that they committed. In other words, persons guilty of war crimes offences will always be less culpable than those guilty of persecution as a crime against humanity offences. This is because of the fact that the former category of offenders are more likely to have committed their actions out of duress, negligence, immature feelings of revenge, etc. which are considered as mitigating factors, whilst the latter are more likely to have committed their actions out of sheer brutality, sadism etc. which are considered as aggravating factors. This distinction leads to the following conclusions:
   a. War crimes offences will always attract lower penalties than identical offences committed as persecution as a crime against humanity, because they are intrinsically less serious than the latter category of international crimes.
   b. Persons guilty of persecution as a crime against humanity are more likely to commit a wider range of multiple offences than those guilty of war crimes and, therefore, are more likely to be punished more severely.

4.2.4 Step 4: Extending the Discriminatory Motive v. Non-discriminatory Motive Approach to War Crimes and Crimes against Humanity under Domestic Law

Having established a sentencing tariff for war crimes and crimes against humanity under the ICTY, based on a discriminatory motive v. non discriminatory motive approach, the next sections will now try to achieve the same result vis-à-vis domestic law.

4.2.4.1 The United Kingdom

The previous chapter demonstrated how reliance on the same interest approach under UK law led to the imposition of identical penalties for war crimes and crimes against humanity, in violation of the principles of proportionality and transparency.

This section explains how the discriminatory motive v. non-discriminatory motive approach provides a more legally acceptable and effective solution for punishing crimes against humanity and war crimes under UK law. Since the sentencing ranges for persecution as a crime against humanity and war crimes developed above are unique to the ICTY, one way of developing sentencing ranges for both categories of international crimes, in the context of the UK, is *via* the Crime and Disorder Act.[94] This is because of the fact that Section 82 of the Act provides that where there is evidence of a racist element in the commission of a crime then the sentencer should consider this as an aggravating factor meriting an increased sentence.[95] In terms of penalties for persecution as a crime against humanity vis-à-vis war crimes under UK law, the implication of section 82 is therefore that it would mean that persecution as a crime against humanity, because of its additional discriminatory element, would attract a higher penalty vis-à-vis war crimes, which would be considered as equivalent to a basic offence under UK law.

In addition, another important aspect of the Act, which facilitates its use as a framework for penalizing persecution as a crime against humanity and war crimes, is the wide interpretation of the term 'racist element'. Thus racist element could encompass offences motivated by any form of discrimination against the victim's ethnic or national origin, sex, religious beliefs, political views or sexual preference.[96] This means that most of the grounds for persecution as a crime against humanity as recognized under the International Criminal Court Act, which recognizes *verbatim* the provisions of the Rome Statute, can be criminalized under the Act.

Furthermore, although the UK Crime and Disorder Act does not apply to murder, this however does not affect the possibility of imposing higher sentences for murder when committed as persecution as a crime against humanity vis-à-vis when committed as a war crime under UK law. This is because of the fact that the basic considerations governing the sentencing tariff of the ICTY would apply. In other words, persons guilty of war crimes offences will always be less culpable than those guilty of persecution as a crime against humanity offences. This is because the former category of offenders are more likely to have committed their actions out of duress, negligence, immature feelings of revenge, etc. which are considered as mitigating factors, whilst the latter are more likely to have committed their actions out of sheer brutality, sadism etc. which are considered as aggravating factors.

Finally, the Crime and Disorder Act is also useful from a procedural point of view. This is because of the fact that the Act creates a system of lesser included offences and alternative verdicts, which establishes which offences need to be separately charged in the indictment and which offences are automatically considered as lesser alternatives for crimes committed with a racist element

---

94 See Crime and Disorder Act (1998), *supra* note 9, Chapter 4.

95 See Section 82, id.

96 See Crime and Disorder Act, id.

vis-à-vis those committed without such an element.[97] In terms of cases involving multiple convictions for persecution as a crime against humanity and war crimes based on the same act, this would mean that the former would be *lex specialis* to the latter and, therefore, that only the former would be retained.

4.2.4.2 Canada

The previous chapter explained how reliance on the same interest approach under Canadian law led to the imposition of identical penalties for war crimes and crimes against humanity in violation of the principles of proportionality and transparency. This section explains how the discriminatory motive v. non discriminatory motive approach provides a more legally acceptable and effective solution for punishing crimes against humanity and war crimes under Canadian law. One way of developing sentencing ranges for both categories of international crimes, in the context of Canada, is *via* its case law. This is because of the decision in *R.* v. *Miloszewski et al.*[98]

Furthermore, the relevant facts of *R.* v. *Miloszewski et al*, are the following. Five young men were sentenced for their involvement in the brutal beating to death of the elderly caretaker of a local Sikh temple. All five accused were found to have been neo-Nazi skinheads at the time of the offence and to have been motivated in their manslaughter by bias, prejudice or hate based on the deceased's race, national or ethnic origin, colour or religion.[99] In the decision, Judge *Stewart* analysed the cases in which hate had been considered as an aggravating factor in sentencing and came to the following conclusion that section 718.2(1)(a)(i) of the Canadian Criminal Code:

> '...is more than simply a reaffirmation of the existing sentencing principles. It is a direction to sentencing judges to give substantial weight to this aggravating factor as the section now reflects the will of Canadians expressed by Parliament.'[100]

In addition, a second case, which is relevant in this respect, is *R* v. *L.E.N. and Synderek*. This is because the British Columbia Court of Appeal, in that case, endorsed the comments of Judge *Stewart* in *Miloszewski* and consequently dismissed the appeals from the sentence.[101]

Finally, in light of the precedent set in *R.* v. *Miloszewski et al.*, persecution as a crime against humanity because of its additional discriminatory element would attract a higher penalty vis-à-vis war crimes, which would be considered as equivalent to a basic offence under Canadian law.

---

97 See id.

98 See *R.* v. *Miloszewski et al.*, [1999] B.C.J. No. 2710.

99 See id.

100 See id. pp. 135-141.

101 See *R* v. *L.E.N. and Synderek*, [2001] B.C.J. No. 2765 (QL).

4.2.4.3 Australia

The previous chapter demonstrated how the recognition of the same interest approach, under Australian law, resulted in the imposition of identical penalties for war crimes and crimes against humanity in violation of the principles of proportionality and transparency.

This section explains how the discriminatory motive v. non-discriminatory motive approach provides a more legally acceptable and effective solution for punishing crimes against humanity and war crimes under Australian law. One way of developing sentencing ranges for both categories of international crimes, in the context of Australia, is by adopting the recommendation of the Australian Law Reform Commission.[102] It called for the creation of a crime of racist violence based on the law governing the Jervis Bay Territory, a Commonwealth territory located in the southeast of New South Wales and the only mainland jurisdiction for which the Commonwealth makes criminal law, as a model.[103]

Furthermore, the Australian Law Reform Commission recommendation, stipulates the following:

> **'PART VII BA--OFFENCES RELATING TO RACIST ACTIVITIES**
> *Interpretation*
> 85KZC. In this Part, "identifiable group" means a section of the public distinguished by colour, race, religion or national or ethnic origin.
> Racist offences involving violence
> 85ZKD. (1) If:
> (a) a person commits or threatens to do an act of violence that, if it had been committed in the Jervis Bay Territory, would be an offence specified in the Schedule against a law in force in that Territory; and
> (b) the person intended the act or the threat to cause, or ought reasonably to have foreseen that the act or threat would cause, members of an identifiable group to fear for their physical safety because they are members of the group; and
> (c) the act or threat is likely to cause members of the group to fear for their physical safety because they are members of the group; the person is guilty of an offence punishable on conviction by a penalty not exceeding one and one-half times the penalty prescribed as the maximum penalty for the act under the law concerned.
> (2) An offence ... under subsection (1) is not an indictable offence unless, because of that subsection, the act is punishable by imprisonment for a period of more than 12 months.'[104]

[102] See The Law Reform Commission (1992), *Multiculturalism and the Law*, Sydney, Australia, Report No. 57.

[103] See id. pp. 156-157.

[104] The draft legislation for the proposed offence is included in Appendix A of the Report, id. p. 283.

Finally, in terms of penalties for persecution as a crime against humanity vis-à-vis war crimes, the proposed definition contains two interesting features. First, it includes most of the identifiable grounds of persecution as a crime against humanity, *i.e.* colour, race, religion or national or ethnic origin. And second, the maximum penalty proposed for these crimes is set out as a general rule: one and one-half times the usual penalty. This would mean that persecution as a crime against humanity, because of its additional discriminatory element, would attract a higher penalty vis-à-vis war crimes, which would be considered as equivalent to a basic or usual offence.

4.2.4.4 Finland

The previous chapter demonstrated how the recognition of the same interest approach, under Finnish law, led to the imposition of identical penalties for war crimes and crimes against humanity in violation of the principles of proportionality and transparency.

This section explains how the discriminatory motive v. non-discriminatory motive approach provides a more legally acceptable and effective solution for punishing crimes against humanity and war crimes under Finnish law. One way of developing sentencing ranges for both categories of international crimes, in the context of Finland, is by focusing on Section 6 of the Finnish Penal Code which defines and penalizes genocide in the following way:

> '1. A person who for the purpose of entirely or partially destroying a race, a national, ethnic or religious group or another comparable group... shall be sentenced for at least four years or for life.'[105]

In addition, *Nuutila* made the following relevant statement in relation to the above provisions:

> '... the definition of *genocide* is broader in the Finnish Penal Code than in the Rome Treaty. The Rome Treaty protects "in whole or in part, a national, ethnical, racial or religious group, as such"; the Finnish Penal Code covers also "other comparable groups". The national protection is mean to cover also, *e.g.* immigrants, minority language groups and other relatively stable folk groups. The definition can be problematic from the point of view of the principle of legality....'[106]

Furthermore, it is submitted that the above statement by *Nuutila,* which was made in relation to section 6, is contrary to international customary law. In other words, what section 6 is actually prosecuting is persecution as a crime

---

[105] See Finnish Penal Code, *supra* note 89, Chapter 3.

[106] See Nuutila, A.M. (2003), *Implementing the Rome Statute: A Pragmatic Approach from a Small Jurisdiction, supra* note 86, Chapter 3, p. 100.

against humanity and not genocide. This opinion is evident in the following clarification by the ICTY in the *Jelisic* case:

> 'Apart from its discriminatory character, the underlying crime is also characterised by the fact that it is part of a wider plan to *destroy*, in whole or in part, the group *as such*. As indicated by the ILC, "the intention must be to destroy the group "as such", meaning as a separate and distinct entity, and not merely some individuals because of their membership in a particular group". By killing an individual member of the targeted group, the perpetrator does not thereby only manifest his hatred of the group to which his victim belongs but also knowingly commits this act as part of a wider-ranging intention to destroy the national, ethnical, racial or religious group of which the victim is a member. The Tribunal for Rwanda notes that "[t]he perpetration of the act charged therefore extends beyond its actual commission, for example, the murder of a particular individual, for the realisation of an ulterior motive, which is to destroy, in whole or in part, the group of which the individual is just one element". Genocide therefore differs from the crime of persecution in which the perpetrator chooses his victims because they belong to a specific community but does not necessarily seek to destroy the community as such.'[107]

As is evident from the above, the crime of genocide, unlike persecution, is limited to the protection of victims belonging to a national, ethnical, racial or religious group and excludes members of political groups. The rationale behind this limitation is that the former category of groups are regarded as stable groups objectively defined and to which individuals belong regardless of their own desires.

In light of the above clarification, it is difficult to see how immigrants and minority language groups, as stated by *Nuutila,* could constitute genocide groups. This is because of the fact that it is possible for an immigrant to perhaps one day acquire Finnish citizenship and therefore no longer remain an immigrant. It is also possible for minority language groups to give up their language and adopt that of the majority. In contrast, it is not possible, for example, for a black person to change his race and become white.

Finally, the implications of the above discussion are therefore the following. First, it suggests that acts constituting persecution as a crime against humanity will be prosecuted under the heading of genocide in the Finnish Penal Code. And, second, were such a situation to arise, it would lead to relatively higher penalties for persecution as a crime against humanity vis-à-vis war crimes under Finnish Law. This is because of the fact that Section 1 of the Finnish penal code imposes a comparatively lower sentencing range of four months to six years, for war crimes.[108]

---

107 See *Prosecutor* v. *Jelisic, supra* note 88, Chapter 4, para. 79.

108 See Finnish Penal Code, *supra* note 89, Chapter 3.

4.2.4.5 Other Countries

The findings in relation to the countries examined above serve as a model for penalizing war crimes and crimes against humanity under New Zealand's and Holland's domestic laws.[109]

4.3 Conclusion

The purpose of this chapter was to propose an alternative solution to the imposition of penalties for war crimes and crimes against humanity under the ICTY. This process involved an endorsement of the discriminatory motive v. non-discriminatory motive approach.

Furthermore, the basis for supporting the discriminatory motive v. non-discriminatory motive approach over current approaches is the fact that it utilizes the most realistic method of comparing crime against humanity offences, particularly the persecution type vis-à-vis war crime offences. In other words, where A is convicted of the murders of B, C, and D in the course of an armed conflict, the decision to convict A under persecution as a crime against humanity or under war crimes will ultimately be dependent on factors such as duress, negligence, immature feelings of revenge, sheer brutality in the commission of the offence, sadism etc.

It follows, for example, that a finding of some form of compulsion, which may not necessarily amount to duress or negligence at the time of the commission of the murders, will automatically lead to war crimes convictions (since these factors negate the requisite intent for persecution as a crime against humanity) and a relatively low sentence. In contrast, a finding that the murders were committed out of sheer brutality or sadism will automatically lead to a conviction of persecution as a crime against humanity and a relatively high

[109] In the case of New Zealand, it recognizes the crime of inciting to racial disharmony under both Section 25 of its Race Relations Act 1971 and Part VI of the Human Rights Act 1993. The former provision for instance states that every person commits an offence: 'who with intent to excite hostility or ill-will against, or bring into contempt or ridicule, any group of persons in New Zealand on the ground of the colour, race, or ethnic or national origins of that group of persons, publishes or distributes written matter or broadcasts words which are threatening, abusive, or insulting or uses in any public place, etc., words which are threatening, abusive, or insulting, being matter or words likely to excite hostility or ill-will against, or bring into contempt or ridicule, any such group of persons in New Zealand on the ground of the colour, race or ethnic origins of that group of persons.' However, there is no specific crime of hate-motivated violence in New Zealand. It has generally seemed satisfactory for such crime to be dealt with under the offences listed in the Crimes Act 1961 according to the specific injury or damage committed.

sentence, since these factors are indicative of the requisite intent for persecution as a crime against humanity.

Finally, from a comparative perspective, the advantage of the discriminatory motive v. non-discriminatory motive approach, over current approaches, is the fact that it utilizes the intrinsic nature of an act as a basis for determining its classification, *i.e.* as a war crime or as persecution as a crime against humanity, as opposed to the other way round, *i.e.* using the classification of an act to determine its gravity. It is this factor that ultimately justifies the imposition of higher penalties for persecution as a crime against humanity offences vis-à-vis similar offences when committed as war crimes.

CHAPTER 5

Conclusion

This book deals with the imposition of penalties for war crimes and crimes against humanity under the International Criminal Tribunal for the former Yugoslavia. Currently, this process is akin to a lottery system because penalties are picked randomly rather than methodologically. The present situation is, therefore, markedly different than that of domestic law. This is because of the fact that, under domestic law, judges are obliged to give reasons for the sentences that they impose. Thus, in a situation where a person is cumulatively sentenced for murder and theft on the basis of the same transaction, it is normal for a judge to award different penalties for both offences and to explain why each penalty has been imposed. This process involves an identification of the different interests protected by both offences and an explanation of why one offence should attract a higher penalty than the other. Theft is usually considered as a less serious offence than murder, because the right of property is not, generally speaking, regarded by society as important as the right to life. Murder will, therefore, attract a higher penalty than theft, because the right violated by murder, is considered to be of greater importance.

However, in the case of war crimes and crimes against humanity under the ICTY, there is a problem. There is no knowledge of how the sentencing process works. How does one distinguish, for the purpose of imposing punishment of different degrees of severity, war crime offences from similar offences when committed as a crime against humanity? After all, it appears to make no difference to the victim whether offences such as murder, torture, or imprisonment are committed as war crimes or as crimes against humanity. Instead, what is more important is that the victim was murdered, tortured or imprisoned. On the other hand, even if it is somehow possible to distinguish between war crime and crime against humanity offences, how does one reconcile this distinction with other variables, which are relevant to the sentencing calculus for both categories of international crimes, such as the rank of the offender and the offender's response to the charges?

Owing to the above difficulties, the sentencing of defendants for war crimes and crimes against humanity under the ICTY has become a game of Russian roulette. This is because the penalty a particular defendant receives is entirely dependent on a particular judge, who may or may not be in favour of higher penalties for crimes against humanity vis-à-vis war crimes. A pro-higher penalties for crimes against humanity vis-à-vis war crimes judge will be more likely to impose a higher overall sentence in a situation where a defendant is convicted of war crimes and crimes against humanity on the basis of the same act. On the other hand, an anti-higher penalties for crimes against humanity vis-à-vis war crimes judge will be less likely to impose a higher overall sentence in the type of situation described above.

In addition, the above scenario can be illustrated with the aid of the *Erdemovic* case. In that case, the accused was charged with war crimes and crimes against humanity but was convicted initially only of crimes against humanity and sentenced to ten years' imprisonment for his role in relation to a series of executions. His conviction for crimes against humanity was based on the view that they are a more serious category of international crimes than war crimes, and therefore they should attract a higher sentence than war crimes. However, on appeal, as a result of the contrary opinion that both categories of international crimes are of similar levels of gravity and, therefore, that they deserve the same penalties, his conviction was changed to that of war crimes and his sentence was commuted to five years imprisonment.[1]

A second way of illustrating how the sentencing of defendants for war crimes and crimes against humanity, under the ICTY, has become a game of Russian roulette is by comparing the opinions of Judge *Cassese* and Judge *Robinson* in the *Tadic* case, on the issue of relative penalties for both categories of international crimes. Thus, Judge *Cassese*, who is a supporter of higher penalties for crime against humanity offences vis-à-vis war crime offences, made the following relevant statement:

> 'For, if classified as a crime against humanity, the murder possesses an objectively greater magnitude and reveals in the perpetrator a subjective frame of mind which may imperil fundamental values of the international community to a greater extent than in the case where that offence should instead be labeled as a war crime. The international community and the judicial bodies responsible for ensuring international criminal justice therefore have a strong societal interest in imposing a heavier penalty upon the author of such a crime against humanity, thereby also deterring similar crimes.'[2]

As is evident from the above, Judge *Cassese* considers crimes against humanity to protect a distinct and more fundamental societal interest than war crimes. He also believes that these factors constitute a basis for imposing higher penalties for the former vis-à-vis the latter.

In contrast, Judge *Robinson*, who is a supporter of equal penalties for crime against humanity and war crime offences, stated the following:

> 'It is well-established that the purpose of creating the new offence of crimes against humanity in 1945 was not to establish a crime of a graver nature than the existing war crimes, but simply to fill a gap in the law as to culpability for crimes committed by a combatant against its own nationals. Thus, Bassiouni writes "[t]he essential difference between acts deemed war crimes and those deemed 'crimes against humanity' is that the former are acts committed in time of war against nationals of another state, while the latter are acts committed against nationals of the same state as that of the perpetrators. Thus, the Charter took a step forward

1 See *supra* note 3.2.2.1.1.

2 See *Tadic*, Separate and Dissenting Opinion of Judge Cassese, *supra* note 31, Chapter 1, p. 15.

in the form of a jurisdictional extension when it provided that the victims of the same types of conduct that constitute war crimes were protected without the requirement that they be of a different nationality than that of the perpetrators." This is, no doubt, a correct analysis because the acts proscribed by Article 6(c) of the Charter as crimes against humanity are substantially the same acts proscribed by Article 6(b) as war crimes...For sentencing purposes, the relevant comparison is not between the four categories of crimes on the basis of their classification or nomenclature; rather, the comparison should be between the specific acts that constitute the specific crimes; to adapt the illustration given by Judge Li relating to his second reason why crimes against humanity are not necessarily more serious than war crimes, it could not be argued that any of the crimes against humanity for which the appellant has been convicted (*e.g.* the murder of five men in Jaskici under Count 31), is more serious than a war crime under Article 3(c) of the Statute in which an undefended town is bombarded, resulting in the death of a million civilians. In sum, therefore, where both crimes are constituted by the same acts, as in the instant case, there should be no differentiation in penalty.'[3]

The above statement by Judge *Robinson* leads to a different conclusion. In other words, he believes that crimes against humanity and war crimes serve the same interests and, therefore, that they should attract the same level of penalties.

Furthermore, apart from the issue of the relative gravity of war crimes and crimes against humanity offences, the additional issue of how other variables that are relevant to the sentencing calculus for both categories of international crimes, such as the rank of the offender and the offender's response to the charges, further complicates the sentencing process. There are two main concerns. The first is that a rigid list of sentences, that is, one that employs a system of mandatory sentences whereby war crime and crime against humanity offences would each have a level beyond which penalties for them cannot fall, could result in as much injustice as that having no regard to comparative sentencing. The second concern is in relation to the practical difficulties of establishing a sentencing framework that is sufficiently flexible or sensitive to incorporate all of the relevant variables for war crime and crimes against humanity offences.

Owing to the above concerns, ICTY judges have resorted to imposing penalties for war crimes and crimes against humanity on a case-by-case basis. The penalization of both categories of international crimes is caught between a rock and a hard place, because injustice seems to be the overall result, regardless of which option is selected.

It was precisely what seemed to be the intractability of the issue of sentencing for war crimes and crimes against humanity under the ICTY, which provided the impetus for this book. The assumption therefore was that in

---

3 See *Tadic*, Separate Opinion of Judge Robinson, *supra* note 26, Chapter 3.

spite of current concerns, it is nevertheless possible to devise a system of fixed penalties for war crimes and crimes against humanity, which can be utilised as a basis for distinguishing between both categories of international crimes in terms of gravity and which is sufficiently flexible to accommodate the full ambit of relevant sentencing variables, thereby treating like cases alike and different cases differently.

Furthermore, the main results of the analysis in this book have been that, first, this book has demonstrated that it was the World War II Tribunals' overly relaxed attitude to the imposition of penalties for war crimes and crimes against humanity, which is ultimately responsible for the misperception that both categories of international crimes are of equal levels of gravity and, therefore, deserve the same penalties. Thus, the Nuremberg sentencing laws, which constituted the only yardstick for the ICTY, effectively sowed the seeds for present day problems associated with the imposition of penalties for war crimes and crimes against humanity. The second significant result of the analysis in this book was the establishment of a sentencing tariff for war crimes and crimes against humanity. The tariff essentially utilises domestic law on bias and non-bias motivated offences as a substantive/sentencing framework for both categories of international crimes.

Apart from the above explanation of the main questions and results of the examination in this book, it is equally essential to give a brief overview of the different chapters so as to build a comprehensive picture of what has been achieved.

After an introductory chapter, Chapter 2 focused on the historical impediments to the imposition of penalties for war crimes and crimes against humanity under the ICTY. The primary aim of that chapter was to trace the source of the current problems associated with this process. The assumption was that because the case law of the World War II Tribunals constitutes the legal wellspring for the imposition of penalties for war crimes and crimes against humanity under the ICTY, the source of the ICTY's current difficulties, therefore, lies with it.

Furthermore, this approach, as evidenced by the results obtained in that chapter, results in the following conclusions:

1. That war crimes and crimes against humanity clearly protected different interests which could have been relied upon as a basis for imposing relative penalties for them, in 1945; and
2. That it was the lackadaisical attitude of the World War II Tribunals towards the task of translating the different interests protected by both categories of international crimes into their sentencing frameworks, that is responsible for the current misperception that crimes against humanity and war crimes are of equal levels of gravity.

In addition, the above results lead to two significant conclusions on the history of the imposition of penalties for both categories of international crimes: The first is the fact that, in contrast to what is presently assumed by those against higher sentences for crimes against humanity vis-à-vis war crimes based on their history, their history clearly demonstrates that they protected different interests and that these interests were reflected in terms of penalties.

The views of scholars, such as *Bing Bing Jia* on this issue, are untenable. In this respect is the following conclusion made by *Bing Bing Jia* vis-à-vis the treatment of war crimes and crimes against humanity by World War II Tribunals:

> 'This short survey of cases shows that the military tribunals sitting at Nuremberg did not adopt a consistent line of reasoning with regard to the difference between war crimes and crimes against humanity, but that they did not seem to consider that crimes against humanity should be punished more severely than war crimes. For them it was the nature and consequence of the underlying offence and the existence *vel non* of mitigating circumstances that determined the penalties imposed. The various crimes contained in the London Charter and Control Council Law no. 10 provided necessary jurisdictional grounds for the tribunals, and a detailed prescription of elements of the crimes was not required. The joint charge of war crimes and crimes against humanity was frequently considered by the military tribunals in respect of one and the same act, and the majority of the decisions normally ended by imposing a joint penalty.'[4]

The problem with the author's conclusion is that it takes the jurisprudence of the World War II Tribunals at face value. In other words, a revisiting of a cross section of World War II cases in Chapter 2, demonstrated that the fact that the World War II Tribunals cumulatively convicted individuals for war crimes and crimes against humanity in relation to the same set of acts and did not appear to distinguish between them in terms of penalties, did not necessarily mean that they served the same interest or attracted the same levels of penalty. Rather what it meant was that the Tribunals were lax in their matching of the facts of each count to war crimes and crimes against humanity. Thus the characterization of persecution against the Jewish people and other groups as war crimes had no legal basis. In fact, such a characterization, although it did not, could have led to the ridiculous situation where atrocities against the Jewish people could have been legalized if they met with the war crime principles of necessity and proportionality. Equally, the branding of atrocities against military personnel as crimes against humanity made no sense because the provisions of the statutes of World War II Tribunals on crimes against humanity clearly limited this category of crimes to civilian victims. Had a stricter approach been employed,

4 See Bing Bing Jia, N., *The Differing Concepts of War Crimes and Crimes against Humanity in International Criminal Law*, p. 263.

crimes against humanity would have clearly attracted higher penalties than war crimes in 1945.

The second conclusion that can be drawn from Chapter 2 is that, contrary to what is presently believed by those who are in favour of higher sentences for crimes against humanity vis-à-vis war crimes based on a rejection of their past, the history of crimes against humanity, actually lends more weight to the view that they should attract higher penalties than war crimes than their evolution since the trials of World War II, which to say the least, has been confusing.[5]

It is, therefore, difficult to support the views of scholars such as *Danner* who argue that crime against humanity offences should attract higher penalties than war crime offences, because they have evolved to protect a different societal interest today from the one that they protected in 1945.[6] In expressing such an opinion, she equally appears to have taken the jurisprudence of World War II Tribunals at face value.

Furthermore, resolving this issue once and for all is the following clarification. War crimes were created to limit the inflicting of suffering caused by the warring factions. Thus, culpability for war crimes was based on such issues as whether or not a particular act met the requirements of military necessity and proportionality. In contrast, under crimes against humanity, attacks against the Jewish people and members of other groups targeted for extermination were prohibited in all circumstances. This approach made sense, otherwise it would be ridiculous to say that persecution as a crime against humanity or genocide can be determined on the basis of the principles of military necessity and proportionality. In fact, this was equally the view of the Tribunal in the *Einsatzgruppen* case, as evidenced by the following statement:

> 'Thus, taking into consideration all that has been said in this particular phase of the defense, the Tribunal concludes that the argument that the Jews in themselves constituted an aggressive menace to Germany, a menace which called for their liquidation in self-defense, is untenable as being opposed to all facts, all logic and all law.'[7]

Finally, the main contributions of Chapter 2 are the following:

- The development of a thorough understanding of the historical roots of sentencing for war crimes and crimes against humanity; and
- The clarification of major aspects of the legal history of the prosecution and sentencing of both categories of international crimes.

---

5 This opinion relies on the fact that there are eleven international texts today defining crimes against humanity, which differ as to their definition of that crime and its legal elements. See generally Olusanya, O. (2004), *Double Jeopardy Without Parameters: Re-characterization in International Criminal Law.*

6 See See Danner, A.M. (2001), *Constructing a Hierarchy of Crimes in International Criminal Law.*

7 See Trials of War Criminals, Vol. IV, p. 470.

Chapter 3 forms the core of this book since it dealt with the imposition of relative penalties for war crimes and crimes against humanity under ICTY. The purpose of that chapter was to identify and examine the main impediments to this process. This was achieved in the context of the following sentencing approaches: the same interest approach, the widespread and systematic attacks v. isolated acts approach and the persecution-type v. murder-type approach.

Furthermore, as was demonstrated above, the three schools of thought on the imposition of relative penalties for war crimes and crimes against humanity, under the ICTY, constitute the main impediments for different reasons. Thus, in respect to the first of the above-mentioned approach, *i.e.* the same interest approach, to the extent that this approach is based on the opinion that war crime and crime against humanity offences should attract the same level of penalties, it in any case constitutes an impediment to the imposition of relative penalties for both categories of international crimes.

In addition, as was explained in that chapter, this approach violates the principle of proportionality and the rule of transparency, which are important rules that have a binding effect upon sentencers. In terms of how the same interest approach impacts on the principle of proportionality, it was explained that it is too simplistic to say that defendant X committed murder and, therefore, that murder will attract the same level of penalties whether it is classified as a war crime or as a crime against humanity. This is because of the fact that, even under domestic law, murder rarely always attracts the same level of penalties. This opinion can be demonstrated with aid of the following six different scenarios involving the commission of the offence of murder, which have been derived from the 'Report of the Royal Commission on Capital Punishment 1949 – 1953':

> 'Case 1. A man struck his brother in the groin with a knife after an altercation about payment for drinks. They had been drinking but were not drunk, and had previously been close friends. The offender made frantic efforts to obtain help for the victim, who nonetheless died.
>
> Case 2. A man killed his fiancée because she persisted in going out with another man on the two evenings each week when she did not go out with him. He was a man of good character and was said to be of even temper and quiet disposition.
>
> Case 3. A man killed his sweetheart who was pregnant by him but whom he had not enough money to marry. He was worried on this account and also because he thought he had infected her with syphilis. He said that he had contemplated suicide; that on the night of the crime he had told her that they could not marry but could not bring himself to tell her the reason; and that when she began to cry he lost all control of himself. He could not explain the crime.
>
> Case 4. A woman gassed her son, aged 30, a hopeless imbecile, who had to be attended to like a baby. She had been told that she must enter a hospital immediately to undergo an operation. She at first said that she could not have the operation because there was no one to look after her son, but it was made clear

to her that she could not live for more than six months unless the operation was performed.

Case 5. A Chinese pursued for four years the man who had killed his father in Hong Kong, and finally confronted him in a Chinese hostel in England and killed him after a desperate struggle. The offender said that he had committed the crime from motives of filial piety. By Chinese doctrine a son was bound to avenge his father's death.

Case 6. A man killed his wife with an axe. She was an epileptic who also suffered from disseminated sclerosis, and in the last few months her mental state had degenerated into insanity. In a statement to the police he said he had killed her to end her suffering and had then tried to commit suicide but could not bring himself to do so. The crime was evidently due to mental strain.'[8]

What all of the above cases demonstrate is that murder is an offence of vastly differing degrees of culpability ranging from brutal, cynical and repeated offences to the almost venial, if objectively immoral, mercy killing of a beloved partner.

The fact that the same interest approach fails to recognize the possibility that offences such as murder, torture or assault have differing degrees of culpability and that each degree of culpability may correspond to a different category of international crime, *i.e.* war crimes or crimes against humanity, is essentially what undermines its credibility.

On the other hand, in relation to the impact of the same interest approach on transparency vis-à-vis the imposition of penalties for war crimes and crimes against humanity, it was clarified above that a lack of transparency is symptomatic of this approach. In other words, this approach negates any deeper discussion of the connection between offences underlying war crimes and crimes against humanity and both categories of international crimes. This opinion was illustrated by reference to the practice of imposing global sentences in cases of multiple convictions for war crime and crime against humanity offences, which is synonymous with the same interest approach. It was stated that this practice leads to a lack of transparency, because it makes it impossible to verify whether or not concurrent and not consecutive sentences have been imposed in such cases.

From the point of view of transparency, the same interest approach will obviously lead to arbitrariness in sentencing for war crimes and crimes against humanity, since judges can simply pick and choose penalties with little constraint.

The second approach which was identified and analyzed above, and which was in favor of the imposition of relative penalties for war crimes and crimes against humanity, was the widespread and systematic attacks v. isolated acts

---

8 See Cmnd 8932, App. 4, p. 320.

approach. This approach, as was earlier explained, is based on the assumption that crimes against humanity should attract higher penalties than war crimes, because they involve large scale premeditated attacks and, therefore, have the potential to result in a greater loss of life.

However, as was earlier demonstrated, this approach violates the principle of consistency. This opinion is based on the fact that it is too simplistic to say, for example, that crime against humanity offences are collectively more serious than war crime offences on the basis of the widespread and systematic elements. This is because more complex situations may arise, which expose the weakness of this rationale, such as the bombardment of a city resulting in the death of thousands as a war crime vis-à-vis the murder of one person as a crime against humanity. In such a situation, it is difficult to see how crimes against humanity can be punished more severely than war crimes.

The third approach, which was identified and examined above and which was also in favor of the imposition of relative penalties for war crimes and crimes against humanity, was the persecution-type v. murder-type approach. This approach is based on a comparison of the persecution category of crimes against humanity, which has a persecutory element, with the murder category of crimes against humanity, which is said to be equivalent to war crimes and which does not have such an element. The assumption was that the former category of crimes against humanity should attract a higher penalty than war crimes, because of the presence of the additional persecutory element. However, as was earlier demonstrated, this approach violates the *nullum crimen sine lege* principle. This is because of the fact that, unlike the other offences listed under crimes against humanity, the offence of persecution does not exist in most municipal and international law systems.

Owing to this factor, formulating a sentencing policy for war crimes and crimes against humanity on the basis of the persecution-type v. murder-type approach would clearly clash with the *nullum crimen sine lege* principle.

Finally, Chapter 3 highlighted the following valuable points:

1. The current difficulties experienced by the ICTY, in relation to the imposition of penalties for war crimes and crimes against humanity, are a reflection of the failure to establish a credible substantive/sentencing framework; and
2. Ultimately the solution to the imposition of penalties for both categories of international crimes lies in the establishment of a credible substantive/sentencing framework.

A sentencing tariff for war crimes and crimes against humanity under the ICTY was proposed under Chapter 4, the third and final main chapter of this book. Also proposed was sentencing tariffs for both categories of crimes vis-à-vis a number of countries that are signatory to the Rome Statute of the International Criminal Court. In the case of the ICTY, the proposed tariff was designed to accommodate the full ambit of relevant sentencing variables, and as a result, it was able to take into consideration not only the gravity of the offence but also other relevant variables such as the rank of the offender and the offender's response to the charges.

Furthermore, the proposed tariff involved the following steps:

- step 1: establishing a substantive framework for war crimes and crimes against humanity based on a discriminatory motive v. non- discriminatory motive approach;
- step 2: re-visiting existing penalties for war crime and persecution as a crime against humanity offences under the ICTY, in light of the discriminatory motive v. non- discriminatory motive approach;
- step 3: identifying factors affecting the institutionalisation of relative penalties for persecution as a crime against humanity vis-à-vis war crimes under the ICTY;
- step 4: utilizing the results of the analysis in step (3) to establish a sentencing tariff for crimes against humanity and war crimes;
- step 5: Extending the discriminatory motive v. non-discriminatory motive approach to war crimes and crimes against humanity under domestic law.

In addition, the following critical distinctions were made:

a) In situations where one defendant, on the basis of the same act, has been cumulatively convicted of and sentenced for both persecution as a crime against humanity and war crimes, the crime against humanity conviction would be classified as *lex specialis* to the war crime conviction, on the basis of its additional discriminatory element requirement. This would in turn ensure that only the sentence for the former is imposed and that that sentence, as will be explained in steps (b) and (c) below, would be higher than would have been the case had the defendant been sentenced for war crimes.

b) In situations where two different defendants have been convicted of the same offence, albeit under two different headings *e.g.*, one defendant A, convicted of murder as persecution as a crime against humanity and another defendant B, convicted of wilful killing as a violation of the laws and customs of war. Defendant A's sentence would be higher than that of defendant's B. This is because of the fact that defendant A is more likely to have committed his murder out of sheer brutality, sadism, etc. which are considered as aggravating factors, whilst defendant B is more likely to have committed his murder out of duress, negligence, immature feelings of revenge, etc. which are considered as mitigating factors.

c) In situations where two different defendants have committed two different crimes, *e.g.* torture as a crime against humanity vis-à-vis murder as a war crime. The rationale expressed in (b) above, would apply here. In other words, murder as a war crime, when committed out of duress or out of negligence, is still likely to be less severe than torture as a crime against humanity when committed out of sheer brutality or sadism.

Last, the following set of ideas was advanced:

- the solution to imposing relative penalties for war crimes and crimes against humanity ultimately lies in their history;
- the full transplantation of criminal law rules to the field of international criminal law, in the form of the over reliance on the underlying offences of war crimes and crimes against humanity, such as murder etc., rather than on the actual international crimes themselves, is unwise, but that, nevertheless, there remains secondary aspects of criminal law which may be of primary value to international criminal law in so far as the issue of sentencing is concerned, *i.e.* motive.[9]

Finally, apart from establishing a sentencing tariff for war crimes and crimes against humanity, the underlying objective was to stimulate a re-thinking of the substantive law on both categories of international crimes. In other words, there needs to be a clear and coherent approach particularly in relation to the treatment of crimes against humanity today. This opinion is based on the fact that currently under the ICTY, crimes against humanity are in almost all cases convicted and sentenced alongside war crimes, whilst in the case of its counterpart, the ICTR, they are in almost all cases convicted and sentenced alongside genocide. Both approaches obviously undermine the legal independence of crimes against humanity thereby creating the false impression that there role is to act as some kind of proxy for war crimes and genocide. However, the adoption of the Rome Statute of the International Criminal Court indicates that the subjugation of crimes against humanity will no longer be tolerated. This opinion is based on a reading of Article 78(3) of the Rome Statute of the International Criminal Court, which provides that when a person has been convicted of more than one crime, the Court shall pronounce a sentence for each crime and a joint sentence specifying the total period of imprisonment. This, therefore, leads to the conclusion that both the clarification of the substantive law on war crimes and crimes against humanity and the establishment of a sentencing tariff for both categories of international crimes are no longer a choice but a necessity, and, therefore, that the results of the analysis herein will in the long run be of value to other international criminal law enforcement institutions.

9 See generally Olusanya, O. (2004), *Double Jeopardy Without Parameters: Re-characterization in International Criminal Law, supra* note 9, Chapter 1.

Bibliography

Books

BASSIOUNI, M.C. (1992)
Crimes against Humanity in International Criminal Law, Dordrecht: Martinus Nijhoff.

BASSIOUNI, M.C. (1999)
Crimes against Humanity in International Criminal Law, Kluwer Law International 2nd edition.

CASSESE, A., GAETA, P., & JONES, J.W.R.D. (EDS.) (2002)
The Rome Statute of the International Criminal Court, Vol. 1, New York: Oxford University Press.

CASSESE, A. (2003)
International Criminal Law, New York: Oxford University Press.

FISCHER, H., KRESS, C., & LÜDER, R. (EDS.) (2001)
International and National Prosecution of Crimes under International Law: Current Developments, Berlin: Berlin Verlag Arno Spitz.

FLETCHER, G.P. (1978)
Rethinking Criminal Law, Boston: Little, Brown.

HIRSCH, A. VON (1976)
Doing Justice: The Choice of Punishments: Report of the Committee for the Study of Incarceration, New York: Hill and Wang.

LEVIN, J. & MCDEVITT, J. (1993)
Hate Crimes: The Rising Tide of Bigotry and Bloodshed, New York NY: Plenum.

MORRIS, V., & SCHARF, M.P. (1995)
An Insiders Guide to the International Criminal Tribunal for the Former Yugoslavia, Vols. I and II, New York: Transnational Publishers.

NEUNER, M. (ED.) (2003)
National Legislation Incorporating International Crimes: Approaches of Civil and Common Law Countries. Berlin: Berliner Wissenschafts Verlag.

OLUSANYA, O. (2004)
Double Jeopardy Without Parameters: Re-characterization in International Criminal Law. Antwerp; Oxford: Intersentia.

PAUST, J.J., BASSIOUNI, M.C., WILLIAMS, S.A., SCHARF, M., GURULE, J., ZAGARIS, B. (1996)
International Criminal Law. 8th ed., Carolina Academic Press.

PICTET, J. (1985)
Development and Principles of International Humanitarian Law, Dordrecht/Geneva: Martinus Nijhoff and Henry Dunant Institute.

ROGERS, A.P.V. (1996)
Law on the Battlefield, Manchester; New York: Manchester University Press.

ROBERTSON, A.H. (1972)
Human Rights in the World, Manchester: Manchester University Press.
SANDOZ, Y., SWINARSKI, C., & ZIMMERMAN, B. (EDS.) (1987)
Commentary on the Additional Protocols of 8 June 1977 to the Geneva Conventions of 12 August 1949, Geneva: Martinus Nijhoff Publishers.
WENGLER, W. (1964)
Völkerecht, Berlin / Göttingen / Heidelberg: Springer Verlag.
ZIMRING, E. & HAWKINS, G. (1973)
Deterrence: The Legal Threat in Crime Control, Chicago: University of Chicago Press.

Chapters, Articles and Monographs

ALDRICH, G.H. (1991)
Prospects for United States Ratification of Additional Protocol I to the 1949 Geneva Conventions, 85 American Journal of International Law, at p. 13.
AMBOS, K. & WIRTH, S. (2002)
The Current Law of Crimes against Humanity, An Analysis of UNTAET Regulation 15/2000, 13 Criminal Law Forum, No. 1, 2002, p. 47.
AMBOS, K. & WIRTH, S. (2000)
Sentencing, Cumulative Charging, Genocide and Crimes against Humanity. In Klip, A. and Sluiter, G.(eds.) (2000), *Annotated Leading Cases of International Criminal Tribunals*, Volume II The International Criminal Tribunal for Rwanda 1994 -1999, Antwerp: Intersentia, chapter 11.
ASHWORTH, A. (1995)
Sentencing and Criminal Justice. Principles of Criminal Law, 2nd ed., Oxford, p. 331.
ASHWORTH, A. (1998)
Four Techniques for Reducing Sentencing Disparity. In: von Hirsch and Ashworth (eds) *Principled Sentencing: Readings on Theory and Policy*. 2nd ed, Oxford: Hart Publishing, p. 227, p. 236.
AUKERMAN, M.J. (2002)
Extraordinary Evil, Ordinary Crime: A Framework for Understanding Transitional Justice, 15 Harvard Human Rights Journal, p. 39, at pp. 54, pp. 77–78.
BALKIN, R. (1997)
International Law and Domestic Law. In Blay, S. Piotrowicz, R. and Tsamenyi, M. (eds.). *Public International Law: An Australian Perspective*. Oxford: Oxford University Press, pp. 119–45.

BASSIOUNI, M.C. (1994)
The Commission of Experts Established Pursuant to Security Council Resolution 780: Investigating Violations of International Humanitarian Law in the Former Yugoslavia, 5 Criminal Law Forum, p. 279, pp. 322–23.
BASSIOUNI, M.C. (1999)
The Sources and Content of International Criminal Law: A Theoretical Framework. In: Bassiouni, M.C. (ed.). *International Criminal Law,* 2nd ed., Vol. 1, Kluwer Law International.
BASSIOUNI, M.C.
The Journey to a Permanent International Criminal Court. In: *International Criminal Court: Compilation of United Nations Documents and Draft ICC Statute Before the Diplomatic Conference.* Available at <http://www.npwj.net/cdrom/intro/intro.pdf > (last visited June 2004).
BEVERS, H., ROORDING, J., & SWAAK-GOLMAN, O. (2003)
The Dutch International Crimes Act (Bill). In: Neuner, M. (ed.) (2003), *National Legislation Incorporating International Crimes: Approaches of Civil and Common Law Countries.* Berlin: Berliner Wissenschafts Verlag, p. 179.
BING BING JIA, N. (1999)
The Differing Concepts of War Crimes and Crimes against Humanity in International Criminal Law. In: Goodwin-Gill, G. and Talmon, S., (eds.), *The Reality of International Law,* Oxford: Clarendon Press, p. 269.
BOHLANDER, M. (2000)
Prosecutor v. Dusko Tadic: Waiting to Exhale, 11 Criminal Law Forum, p. 246.
BRUIN, G. DE (1993)
Yugoslavia: War Crimes Tribunal Inaugurated in The Hague, Inter Press Service, 17 Nov. 1993, available at 1993 WL 2532943.
CARCANO, A. (2002)
Sentencing and the Gravity of the Offence in International Criminal Law, 51 International and Comparative Law Quarterly, p. 590.
COTIC, D. (1996)
Introduction to the Prosecution of International Crimes. In: Clark, R.S., and Sann, M., (eds.), *The Prosecution of International Crimes: A Critical Study of the International Tribunal for the Former Yugoslavia,* London: Transaction Publishers, 1996, p. 3, pp. 8-9.
DANNER, A.M. (2001)
Constructing a Hierarchy of Crimes in International Criminal Law, 87 Virginia Law Review p. 415. Extracted from <http://www.psci.unt.edu/~meernik/danner.htm> (last visited July 2004).

DEGUZMAN, M.M.
The Road from Rome: The Developing Law of Crimes against Humanity. Extracted from <http://www.soc.umn.edu/~boyle/22.2deguzman.html> (last visited May 2004).

DOHERTY, K.L. & MCCORMACK, T.L.H. (1999)
Complementarity as a Catalyst for Comprehensive Domestic Penal Legislation, 5 University of California, Davis Journal of International Law and Policy, p. 147, at pp. 156–161.

DOLINKO, D. (1999)
The Future of Punishment, 46 University of California, Los Angeles, School of Law Review, p. 1719, p. 1720.

FENRICK, W.J. (1997)
Attacking the Enemy Civilian as a Punishable Offense, 7 Duke Journal of Comparative & International Law, p. 539.

FENRICK, W.J. (1999)
Should Crimes Against Humanity Replace War Crimes? 37 Columbia Journal of Transnational Law, p. 767, p. 777.

FERENCZ, B. (1999)
Getting Aggressive about Preventing Aggression, The Brown Journal of World Affairs. Extracted from < http://www.iccnow.org/html/ferencz199907.html> (last visited June 2004).

FERENCZ, B. (2003)
From Nuremberg to Rome: A Personal Account. In: Lattimer, M. & Sands, P. (2003), *Justice for Crimes against Humanity*, Hart Publishing. Extracted from <http://www.benferencz.org/remarks2.htm> (last visited July 2004).

FOX, R.G. (1994)
The Meaning of Proportionality in Sentencing, 19 Melbourne University Law Review, p. 489.

FRULLI, M. (2001)
Are Crimes against Humanity More Serious than War Crimes? 12 European Journal of International Law, Issue 2, pp. 329–350.

GAETA, P. (1999)
The Defence of Superior Orders: The Statute of the International Criminal Court versus Customary International Law, 10 European Journal of International Law, p. 172.

GARDAM, J.G. (1993)
Proportionality and Force in International Law, 87 American Journal of International Law, p. 391.

GARDAM, J.G. (1988)
Canadian Law, War Crimes and Crimes against Humanity, British Year Book of International Law, pp. 217–235.

GILBERT, J.A. (2003)
Legislation and Ratification: The UK's Approach to the Implementation

of the Rome Statute. In: Neuner, M. (ed.) (2003), *National Legislation Incorporating International Crimes: Approaches of Civil and Common Law Countries.* Berlin: Berliner Wissenschafts Verlag, pp. 57-58.

GREEN, L.C. (1988)
Canadian Law, War Crimes and Crimes against Humanity, British Year Book of International Law pp. 217-235

HANNIKAINEN, L. (1992)
Implementation of International Humanitarian Law in Finnish Law. In Hannikainen, L., Hanski, R., and Rosas, A. (1992), *Implementing Humanitarian Law Applicable in Armed Conflict: The Case of Finland,* Dordrecht: Martinus Nijhoff Publishers, at p. 120.

HAY, J. (2003)
Implementing the Rome Statute: A Pragmatic Approach from a Small Jurisdiction, In: Neuner, M. (ed.) (2003), *National Legislation Incorporating International Crimes: Approaches of Civil and Common Law Countries.* Berlin: Berliner Wissenschafts Verlag, pp. 13-33

HEINE, G. & VEST, H.
Murder/Wilful Killing. In: Kirk McDonald, G. & Swaak-Goldman, O., (eds.) (2000), *Substantive and Procedural Aspects of International Criminal Law,* The Hague: Kluwer Law International, pp. 175, 194.

HEREK, G.M., COGAN, J.C., & GILLIS, J.R. (2002)
Victim Experiences in Hate Crimes based on Sexual Orientation, 58(2) Journal of Social Issues, pp. 319-339.

IVKOVIC, S.K. (2001)
Justice by the International Criminal Tribunal for the Former Yugoslavia, 37 Stanford Journal of International Law, p. 255, at p. 323.

KAFALA, T (2001)
What is a war crime? Available at <http://news.bbc.co.uk/2/hi/europe/1420133.stm> (last Visited April 2003).

KELK, C. ET AL.
Sentencing Practice, Policy, and Discretion. In Fennell, P. et al. (eds.) (1995), *Criminal Justice in Europe,* Oxford: New York: Clarendon Press; Oxford University Press, p. 319, p. 323.

KING, F.P. & LA ROSA, A.M. (1998)
Jurisprudence of the International Criminal Tribunal for the Former Yugoslavia – Current Survey, European Journal of International Law Vol. 9, No. 4.

KITTO, F. (1992)
Why Write Judgments, 66 Australian Law Journal, p. 787.

KRESS, C. (1998)
Penalties, Enforcement and Cooperation in the International Criminal Courts Statute (Parts VII, IX, X), 6/4 European Journal of Crime, Criminal Law and Criminal Justice, pp. 442-46.

LIPPMAN, M. (1991)
Nuremberg and American Justice, 5 Notre Dame Journal of Law Ethics and Public Policy, p. 951.
LIPPMAN, M. (1991)
Nuremberg: Forty Five Years Later, 7 Connecticut Journal of International Law, p. 1.
LIPPMAN, M. (1992)
The Other Nuremberg: American Prosecutions of Nazi War Criminals in Occupied Germany, 3 Indiana International and Comparative Law Review, p. 1.
LIPPMAN, M. (1993)
The Nazi Doctors Trial And The International Prohibition On Medical Involvement In Torture, 15 Loyola of Los Angeles International and Comparative Law Journal, p. 395.
LIPPMAN, M. (1997)
Crimes Against Humanity, 17 Boston College Third World Law Journal, p. 181.
MCCORMACK, T.L.H. (2003)
Australia's Legislation for the Implementation of the Rome Statute. In: Neuner, M. (ed.) (2003), *National Legislation Incorporating International Crimes: Approaches of Civil and Common Law Countries.* Berlin: Berliner Wissenschafts Verlag, p. 66.
MCDEVITT, J. ET AL. (2001)
Consequences for Victims: A Comparison of Bias- and Non-Bias Motivated Assaults, American Behavioral Scientist, 4584, pp. 679-713.
MEERNIK, J. & KING, K. (2003)
The Sentencing Determinants of the International Criminal Tribunal for the Former Yugoslavia: An Empirical and Doctrinal Analysis, 16 Leiden Journal of International Law, pp. 717-750.
MERON, T. (1993)
The Case for War Crimes Trials in Yugoslavia, 72 Foreign Affairs, p. 122.
MERON, T. (1994)
War Crimes in Yugoslavia and the Development of International Law, 88 American Journal of International Law, p. 78.
NUOTIO, K. (1999)
Transforming International Law and Obligations into Finnish Criminal Legislation – Dragon's Eggs and Criminal Law Irritants, Vol. X Finnish Yearbook of International Law.
NUUTILA, A.M. (2003)
Implementing the Rome Statute: A pragmatic Approach from a Small Jurisdiction. In: Neuner, M. (ed.) (2003), *National Legislation Incorporating International Crimes: Approaches of Civil and Common Law Countries.* Berlin: Berliner Wissenschafts Verlag.

O'BRIEN, J.C. (1993)
The International Tribunal for Violations of International Humanitarian Law in the Former Yugoslavia, 87 American Journal of International Law, p. 639.

OLUSANYA, O. (2004)
Do Crimes against Humanity Deserve a Higher Sentence than War Crimes?, 4 International Criminal Law Review, pp. 430-473.

ORENTLICHER, D.F. (1991)
Settling Accounts: The Duty to Prosecute Human Rights Violations of a Prior Regime, 100 Yale Law Journal, p. 2594.

ORENTLICHER, D.F. (1998)
The Law of Universal Conscience: Genocide and Crimes against Humanity, at <http://www1.ushmm.org/conscience/events/conference_98/orentlicher.pdf> (last visited December 2004).

PICKARD, D.B. (1997)
Proposed Sentencing Guidelines for the International Criminal Court, 20 Loyola of Los Angeles International & Comparative Law Journal, p. 123.

RABY (1968)
Bombardment of Land Targets, p. 67, cited in Rosenblad, E. (1979), *International Humanitarian Law of Armed Conflict,* Geneva: Henri Dunant Institute, p. 141.

ROBINSON, D. (2003)
Implementing International Crimes in National Law: The Canadian Approach. In: Neuner, M. (ed.) (2003), *National Legislation Incorporating International Crimes: Approaches of Civil and Common Law Countries.* Berlin: Berliner Wissenschafts Verlag, pp. 45-54.

SAROOSHI, D.
Command Responsibility and the Blaskic Case. In: Evans, M.D. (ed.) (2001), *Decisions of International Tribunals,* International and Comparative Law Quarterly, p. 456.

SAUL, B. (2000)
The International Crime of Genocide in Australian Law, 22 Sydney Law Review, p. 567.

SCHABAS, W.A. (1997)
Sentencing by International Tribunals: A Human Rights Approach, 7 Duke Journal of Comparative and International Law, p. 461, at p. 514.

SCHABAS, W.A. (2003)
Canadian Implementing Legislation for the Rome Statute: Jurisdiction and Defences. In: Neuner, M. (ed.) (2003), *National Legislation Incorporating International Crimes: Approaches of Civil and Common Law Countries.* Berlin: Berliner Wissenschafts Verlag, pp. 35-43.

SCHARF M.P. (2000)
The Tools for Enforcing International Criminal Justice in the New Millennium: Lessons from the Yugoslavia Tribunal, 49 DePaul Law Review, p. 925.

SCHWELB, E. (1946)
Crimes Against Humanity, British Year Book of International Law, p. 206.

SHARP, W.G. (1999)
The International Criminal Tribunal for the Former Yugoslavia: Defining Offenses, 23 Maryland Journal of International Law and Trade, p. 15, at pp. 20-26.

SPIGELMAN, J.J. (2000)
Seen to be Done: The Principle of Open Justice: Part 1, 74 Australian Law Journal, p. 290, especially at pp. 294 and 295.

SUNSTEIN, C.R., KAHNEMAN, D., SCHKADE, D., RITOV, I. (2002)
Predictably Incoherent Judgments, 54 Stanford Law Review, p. 1153.

SZASZ, P.C. (1993)
The Proposed War Crimes Tribunal for Yugoslavia, 25 New York University Journal of International Law and Politics, p. 405.

SZUREK & RONA
Débats', L'Article 31, § 1 c, Du Statut de la Cour Pénale Internationale, Revue Belge de Droit International, 2000/2, p. 478.

TAYLOR, T. (1949)
The Nuremberg War Crimes Trials, International Conciliation No. 450, p. 321.

TOMUSCHAT, C. (1994)
International Criminal Prosecution: The Precedent of Nuremberg Confirmed, 5 Criminal Law Forum, Nos. 2-3, p. 240.

TRÄSKMAN, P.O. (1989)
Finland: National Report: Part II: Legal Problems Emerging from the Implementation of International Crimes in Domestic Criminal Law, 60 Revue International de Droit Pénal.

UNIVERSITY OF CALIFORNIA-BERKELEY INTERNATIONAL HUMAN RIGHTS LAW CLINIC & UNIVERSITY OF SARAJEVO HUMAN RIGHTS CENTER(2000)
Report: Justice, Accountability, and Social Reconstruction: An Interview Study of Bosnian Judges & Prosecutors, 18 Berkeley Journal of International Law, p. 102.

WALD, P.M. (2001)
The International Criminal Tribunal for the former Yugoslavia Comes of Age: Some Observations on Day-To-Day Dilemmas of an International Court, 5 Washington University Journal of Law and Policy, p. 89.

WEDGWOOD, R. (2000)
Augusto Pinochet and International Law, 46 McGill Law Journal, p. 252.

WEXLER, L.S. (1994)
The Interpretation of the Nuremberg Principles by the French Court of Cassation: From Touvier to Barbie and back again, 32 Colombia Journal of Transnational Law, p. 289, pp. 307–08.

Unpublished Papers, Conference, United Nations Documents and Seminar Presentations

Agreement for the Prosecution and Punishment of the Major War Criminals of the European Axis, 8 Aug. 1945, Annex, 59 Stat. 1544, 82 U.N.T.S. 279.
Covenant on Civil and Political Rights, Adopted and opened for signature, ratification and accession by General Assembly resolution 2200A (XXI) of 16 December 1966, entry into force 23 March 1976.
Geneva Convention (I) for the Amelioration of the Condition of the Wounded and Sick in Armed Forces in the Field (Geneva I), adopted 12 Aug. 1949, 6 U.S.T. 3114, 75 U.N.T.S 31, (entered into force 21 Oct. 1950) (entered into force for U.S. 2 Feb. 1956).
Geneva Convention (III) Relative to the Treatment of Prisoners of War (Geneva III), adopted 12 Aug. 1949, 6 U.S.T. 3316, 75 U.N.T.S. 135 (entered into force 21 Oct. 1950) (entered into force for U.S. 2 Feb. 1956).
HL Hansard, 18 April 1991, Col.1566.
HL Hansard, 6 November 1989, Col.521.
Interim Report of the Commission of Experts Established Pursuant to Security Council Resolution 780 (1992), U.N. SCOR, Annex I, p. 49, U.N. Doc. S/25274 (1993).
Law-Reports of Trials of War Criminals, The United Nations War Crimes Commission, Volume XII, London, HMSO, 1949, para. 46.
Perry, B. (2003). *Where Do We Go From Here? Researching Hate Crime.* Paper presented at the first NCSRHC and Solon International Hate Crimes Conference in Nottingham, February 2003.
Protocol Additional to the Geneva Conventions of 12 August 1949, and Relating to the Protection of Victims of International Armed Conflicts, Dec. 12, 1977, 1125 U.N.T.S. 3, 16 I.L.M. 1391 (1977).
Report of the 8th UN Congress on the Prevention of Crime and Treatment of Offenders, UN Doc. A/Conf.144/28, rev.1 (91.IV.2), Res. 1(a), 5(c), 1990.
Rome Statute of the International Criminal Court, Opened for Signature 17 July 1998, U.N. Diplomatic Conf. of Plenipotentiaries on the Establishment of an Int'l Crim. Ct., U.N. Doc. A/CONF.183/9 (1998).

SC Res. 827 (May 25, 1993).
S.C. Res. 1315 (2000), 14 August 2000.
Statute of the International Criminal Tribunal for the Prosecution of Persons Responsible for Genocide and Other Serious Violations of International Humanitarian Law Committed in the Territory of Rwanda and Rwandan Citizens Responsible for Genocide and Other Such Violations Committed in the Territory of Neighbouring States Between 1 January 1994 and 31 December 1994, S.C. Res. 955, U.N. SCOR, 49th Sess., 3453d mtg., Annex, U.N. Doc. S/RES/955 (1994), *reprinted in* 33 I.L.M. 1598, 1602 (1994).
The Law Reform Commission (1992). Multiculturalism and the Law. Sydney, Australia, Report No. 57.
Trials of War Criminals before the Nuremberg Military Tribunals under Control Council Law No. 10, IV (Washington, DC, 1949), II, 773, 797.
Universal Declaration of Human Rights, adopted and proclaimed by General Assembly Resolution 217 A (III) of December 1948.

Internet (www) Reference

Bill C-19, 2nd Sess., 36th Parl., pp. 48-49 Elizabeth II, 1999-2000, assented to 29 June 2000 (obtainable from: < http://www.parl.gc.ca/>) (last visited June 2004).
Canada Introduces New Act to Implement International Criminal Court. Available at <http://www.icc.gc.ca> (last visited on June 2004).
Commentary of Home Office Racial Equality Unit Guide. Available at <http://www.homeoffice.gov.uk/docs/racagoff.html> (last visited January 2004).
European Union Proposal for a Council Framework Decision on Combating Racism and Xenophobia. Available at <http://europa.eu.int/smartapi/cgi/sga_doc?smartapi!celexplus!prod!DocNumber&lg=en&type_doc=COMfinal&an_doc=2001&nu_doc=664> (last visited January 2004).
International Criminal Court Act 2002, available at <http//scaleplus.law.gov.au/html/comact/11/6513/pdf/0412002.pdf> (last visited July 2004).
International Criminal Court (Consequential Amendments) Act 2002, available at <http://scaleplus.law.gov.au/html/comact/11/6514/pdf/0422002.pdf> (last visited July 2004).
Justice (2001). *Response to the Halliday Review.* p. 4. Available at <http://www.justice.org.uk/parliamentpress/parliamentarybriefings/> (last visited June 2004).
Stockholm Race Hate Crimes Grotius Seminar, 11th–15th of February

2001, Appendix 1. Available at <http://www.mpa.gov.uk/committees/mpa/2001/010308/16.htm> (last visited January 2004).

UK Crime and Disorder Act (1998). Available at <http://www.hmso.gov.uk/acts/acts1998/19980037.htm> (last visited January 2004).

US v. Wilhelm List, et al. (Hostage Case) Trials of War Criminals, available at <http://real-ale.wcl.american.edu/etp/MilitaryTribunals/NMT/HostageCase.html> (last visited June 2004).

United States Sentencing Commission, Guidelines Manual, § 3A1.1. Available at <http://www.ussc.gov/2003guid/2003guid.pdf > (last visited January 2004).

Table of Cases

Index